PERSIAN OR PERSIANS
UNKNOWN

By

Ian Jarvis

Paperback ISBN 978-1-80424-790-7
ePub ISBN 978-1-80424-791-4
PDF ISBN 978-1-80424-792-1

Published by MX Publishing
335 Princess Park Manor, Royal Drive,
London, N11 3GX
www.mxpublishing.co.uk

Cover design by Awan

Chapter 1

Egypt: The Land of Pyramids and Pharaohs.
Printed large across the tourist poster, the description of this country couldn't have been much clearer, yet there was a noticeable lack of pyramids here in Luxor. Those iconic stone structures seemed to have been a northern thing, like flat caps and whippets in the north of England, and no one had spotted a Pharaoh around here for quite some time. A red-haired girl relaxed outside a street café, gazing at the colourful wall poster and vaguely wondering about the Egyptian rules of false advertising.

Sitting in jeans and a black T shirt, the young woman smoked a cigarette and sipped wine as the evening crowds bustled past, the beggars and salesmen never crossing the rope cordon to disturb the café clientele. Tourism provided this nation with the bulk of its income and, during her short time here in Luxor, she'd found that most Egyptians were eager to please their foreign visitors.

Aromas of incense and roasting meat filled the hot night air and, like all Egyptian cities, a background hubbub of noise was ever-present both day and night. Vehicles congested the road, the incessant honking of their horns beginning whenever the traffic slowed, as if these warning devices were connected to the brakes. Mixed in with the cars and buses, an endless procession of horse-drawn carriages clip-clopped past the street café, the grinning coachmen all eager to give overpriced lifts to the tourists. Their hopeful cries of "caleche, caleche" could be heard above the sounds of haggling outside nearby shops.

Aware of someone beside her table, the girl looked up to find an elderly Egyptian lady quietly studying her. Snowy-haired, wrinkled and stooped, she wore a blue cotton blouse and skirt and carried a dark leather handbag over her shoulder.

"Can I help you?" she asked, half-expecting some trinket to

1

be produced from the bag for a *bargain price*.

"Hello, Cyra." The old woman read the laminated pass dangling on the lanyard around the girl's neck. "It took a while, but I've finally managed to track you down."

Cyra stared warily for a moment, stiffening as realisation suddenly dawned. "Kymina? Is that *you?*" She rose to her feet, glaring at the newcomer before taking deep breaths to calm her anger. "Yes, of *course* it's you. After the explosion in Iraq, I knew you'd be searching for me and you had to show up sooner or later."

"You left something of a... *trail.*" Kymina smiled faintly. "Despite everything, it's really good to be with you again."

"You could have *been with me* whenever you wanted," hissed Cyra. Looking the old woman up and down, she managed to contain her fury. "I have to say, your scabbard is unimpressive, but oh, so typical of you."

"*Scabbard.*" Kymina grimaced. "It's been so long since I heard that derogatory term. I always hated it." She noticed that the empty chair beside Cyra had a red baseball cap hanging from the backrest.

"No, there's no one sitting there; not anymore," said Cyra, anticipating her question and smiling sarcastically as she sat. "Perhaps you'd care to join me?"

"I mean it, you know?" Settling herself beside the girl, Kymina placed her bag by her foot, away from opportunist thieves. "It really *does* feel good to be together again."

"Oh, I'm sure." Cyra drew on her cigarette and held it aloft. "Have you tried these? Someone introduced me to cigarettes recently and I find they help in calming and managing my anger. Believe me, I have a *huge* amount of anger."

"Yes, I would imagine so," said Kymina. "I *have* tried cigarettes, but I was never keen on tobacco. I see you're smoking the Egyptian untipped brand."

"Very bad for my health, I'm guessing? Well, we always had different tastes, didn't we?" Cyra tossed her red hair. "So here we are. The two of us are finally back together, but where are the reunion embraces? Where are the tears of joy?" She paused for several seconds. "And, more to the point, where are the *apologies*?"

"It would take more than a hug to make things right between us." Kymina smiled tightly. "And I can't apologise for something that I don't regret. You've had the time to think this through, and you must know that you were wrong? You *must* understand why I needed to do what I did?"

"*Time to think?*" Cyra laughed loudly, but there was no amusement in the harsh rasping sound. "You dare to talk to me about *time*? Yes, I certainly had plenty of *that*, didn't I? Can you imagine how angrier and angrier I grew in captivity?" She snatched her glass to gulp down the wine, her hand shaking furiously. "You turned your back on me and left me alone, festering in that prison."

Kymina shook her head sadly. "I tried to reason with you, but you refused to listen. You couldn't be allowed to go through with it, but do you honestly believe I found any satisfaction in what I did?" Taking a deep breath, she leant close. "I have to know, Cyra, what are you doing in Luxor?"

"I'm working on a movie." Smirking, the girl puffed on her cigarette. "I'm with a film company named…"

"*Candlemass Productions*," said Kymina, gesturing to her lanyard pass. "And you're called Lisa MacNeil. Yes, I'm aware of all that. I tracked you down to the film set at the Luxor temple and someone told me you'd be here."

Cyra nodded. "I'm what's known as the Script Supervisor."

"So…" Kymina sighed, "why are you *really* here?"

"Surely you must know?" Cyra drew on her cigarette. "I joined the production crew as cover when I first arrived from Iraq. I came here to seek out Koura's tomb."

"Oh, no, Cyra." The old lady closed her eyes. "You actually intend to continue from where you left off? You're telling me that, after all this time, *nothing* has changed?" She shook her head. "I couldn't let you have the amulet *then* and you must know that I can't allow it now?"

"Don't be stupid," snapped Cyra. "I was always stronger than you."

Kymina shrugged. "I stopped you before."

"You did, but as you say, that was *before*." Cyra stubbed her cigarette in the table ashtray. "As it turns out, I was wasting my time. Old museum documents led me to Karnak where Koura was secretly buried, but the temple is now a ruin. His tomb was discovered and emptied by an archaeologist over a century ago. The amulet, as I'm sure you already know, has been in England for many years."

"That's right," confirmed Kymina. "It's changed hands between private collectors several times. I've been watching its progress and whereabouts and I've…"

The old woman's words faltered, her eyes being drawn to a movement on her left. A large snail, its dark brown shell two inches in diameter, was climbing the leg of the table. The creature's head turned slowly, eye-stalks twisting. Bizarrely, it seemed to be staring intently at Kymina.

"Oh, *please*," she whispered, looking again at the red baseball cap that dangled from her chair backrest. "Please don't tell me *this* is something to do with you?"

"Ah, my little friend has reappeared." Plucking the snail from the leg with a sucking plop, Cyra gazed at it. "I'm surprised you didn't tread on him. He was there on the floor beside your chair when you arrived and he's finally crawled up into view. Honestly, they're so tediously slow, aren't they?"

Turning, she spotted a gap in the pavement crowds and tossed the snail into the road. A passing van immediately transformed it into a mollusc pancake and the girl closed her eyes, tilting back her head to deeply inhale the night air.

"That felt good," she whispered, breathing in again. "*So* good. Unfortunately, it's a sensation that you'll never know."

"Oh, Cyra," gasped Kymina, shuddering. "I'd almost forgotten how much this sickened me."

"Hello there." Cyra smiled at three young people who were strolling by the café, a brawny man and two girls. "We were just speaking of the film production and here are some of the crew."

"Lisa." One of the girls rushed to Cyra's table and hugged her. "Caught in the act, eh, Babes? Drinking vino before work, I see? Who's a naughty bitch?"

"Yeah, that's me." Cyra laughed and held up her empty glass. "I was relaxing before they start on the night shoot. A couple of wines is always the best way, isn't it?"

"Ah, Lisa, my favourite ginger," said the man. "They're still setting up at the temple and they'll be ready in about an hour."

"Oh, I'll be back before then," said Cyra. "By the way, this is my new friend, Kymina." She squeezed the old woman's shoulder with sham affection. "She's a lovely lady. We just got chatting, and now I feel like I've known her my entire life. Kymina, I'd like you to meet our brilliant make-up artist, Hayley." She gestured to the other two. "This suntanned hunk is Steve, our principal stuntman, and here's Toni, our film editor."

Kymina ran her eye over them. Hayley was superficially gorgeous, with lengthy blonde hair, expensive branded clothes and her features frozen in a phony smile. Steve resembled a Californian surfer, with his chocolate skin, white grin and tattoos. A set of overly-developed muscles strained his black T shirt, but Kymina guessed there was very little development between his ears. The old lady was more concerned, however, with Toni. Petite and attractive, with short black hair and elfin features, the misery and despair that radiated from this young girl was almost tangible.

"Kymina?" repeated Hayley. "Mmh, what a lovely name, Babes. Egyptian, I'm guessing?"

"Thank you," she said. "But no, my name is Persian."

"Toni?" Cyra also noticed the film editor's expression. "Hey, what's wrong? Are you okay?"

"Yeah, I'm fine," muttered Toni, smiling weakly and rubbing her puffy eyes. "It's nothing."

"She's *not* fine," said Hayley, hugging the girl. "In fact, Toni's *far* from fine, aren't you, Babes? Her fiancé left her again and it's for good this time. He's flown back to London to be with his ex."

"Thanks for reminding me," muttered Toni, tears welling. "He was nothing special, of course – only the love of my life."

"Ah, don't give me that shit, Babes," laughed Hayley. "He was a real twat and he never deserved you." She turned back to Cyra. "Like you, we had a few hours to kill before the night shoot, so Stevie and I brought her into town to cheer her up."

Kymina gazed again at the editor. She guessed it would take more than a drink with these two to make *this* girl feel better.

"Yeah, come on," said Steve, throwing a beefy arm around Toni. "There's plenty more fish in the sea. Big, good-looking fish like *me*, for instance."

"Hey, you're mine, Babes, and don't you forget it." Hayley playfully punched the stuntman in his midriff. "Wow, you should feel these muscles, Lisa. I nearly broke my knuckles on that six-pack."

"Yes." Cyra nodded thoughtfully. "Come to think of it, that *is* a rather excellent body, isn't it?"

"Thanks," said Steve, grinning at Cyra and turning to leave with his friends. "Sixty minutes, Ginger. Don't be late on set, or I might have to put you over my knee and give you a spanking."

"I don't understand," said Kymina, watching as Hayley punched him again and the trio vanished into the passing crowds.

"You joined this film crew as Lisa for cover? If you found the Karnak tomb to be empty, then why are you still here working with them?"

"I didn't choose them at random," said Cyra. "*Candlemass Productions* is a British company and the majority of filming on this movie will take place in England."

Kymina nodded. "Ah, I see."

"They finish work on the Egyptian locations tomorrow and then head home for the main shoot. I'll be travelling with them. Someone bought Koura's amulet at an auction two years ago and I've discovered who."

"Listen to me, please." The old lady reached across the table to take her hand. "We loved each other once. You don't have to…"

"No, you listen to *me*." Jerking her arm free, Cyra stood up. "Follow me; there's something I need to show you." The young woman led the way around the café cordon and through the people on the pavement to the road.

"Please…" said Kymina, clutching her bag and assuming she was about to cross the busy street. "This insane idea of using the amulet to…"

Cyra twisted to glare at her. "Aren't you curious?" she asked, icily. "Surely you must have wondered why I didn't fly into a frenzy and attack you when you showed up here? Wondered how I was able to contain my fury – all that burning fury that intensified every day during my imprisonment? Well, my dear, as you mentioned a few minutes ago, I've had the time to think about this, and that time has taught me patience. I've never known patience before and it's enabled me to hold back my rage. Rather than tear you apart in a blind temper, I'll wait until I possess the amulet and then, and only then, will you see how *truly* angry you made me."

"Cyra?" The old woman noticed her expression change and suddenly guessed her intention. "No, wait…"

"I'm tired of waiting." Unnoticed in the hustle and bustle,

Cyra's foot shot in front of Kymina's shin and she nudged her in the back, toppling her off the kerb and into the path of an approaching bus. "Oh, my God," she shouted, above the screech of brakes. "What happened? For God's sake, someone please help this poor lady."

The bus skidded to a halt, shocked cries and screams erupting as people saw the tangle of broken limbs beneath the wheels. An American tourist gagged as he spotted a smashed water melon, then realised that he was looking at the grisly remains of a human head. Picking up Kymina's fallen bag, Cyra backed away through the gathering crowd and quickly returned to the café table to open it.

"A *Dugdana*," she snarled, taking out a small red bottle, around five inches in height. "Yes, I expected *this*, but what the hell did you hope to do with it? I don't know what you were planning, but it is most definitely *not* going to happen again."

She lay the bottle on the ground, snatched the heavy ashtray from the table and brought the edge down hard, exploding it into glittering red fragments.

"So you were hoping to stop me, were you?" Cyra looked around, smirking. "Well, good luck with that, Kymina… wherever the hell you are."

* * * *

Chapter 2

Yorkshire was created by King Richard II.

The young monarch visited York many times and, in 1396, he presented this small city in the north of England with a royal charter, making the surrounding land a county. Four years later, in a peculiar show of gratitude, the Yorkshire folk starved their king to death in the dungeons of Pontefract Castle. The vast county stretches west from the North Sea coastline to encompass the Dales, the Wolds and the sweeping North York moors. To make things more manageable, the area was eventually divided into the smaller counties of South, West and North Yorkshire with the city of York controlling the latter.

John Watson had lived in York his entire life – all twenty years of it. Described by many as *Britain's most beautiful city*, York stands on the river confluence of the Foss and the larger Ouse, its centre enclosed by medieval walls and filled with a wealth of Tudor, Elizabethan, Georgian, Edwardian and Victorian buildings. Watson's boss constantly pointed out the "breathtaking architecture" and spoke about York's "splendid history," hoping his young assistant would develop an interest and sense of pride in such things. Watson was indeed proud of his home – he just *wasn't*, as he often explained, *bothered about all the crappy old buildings and the boring historical shit.*

An attractive black youth, Watson worked at Bernie Quist's private detective agency, although his boss insisted upon being referred to as a *Consultant Detective*. Six-feet tall, Quist stood two inches above his assistant and appeared to be in his late forties. He wore a calf-length leather trenchcoat, the black folds flapping about him like a theatrical vampire cloak. According to Watson, Quist's aristocratic voice was *also* theatrical, the sort of eloquent English voice that belonged in a stage recital of Shakespeare.

The countless tourist attractions of York include several museums. The *Jorvik Viking Museum* and the *Castle Museum* are two of the most popular, but with more than 600,000 visitors every year, the *National Railway Museum* on Leeman Road beats it hands down. Finishing checking the social media on his phone, Watson gazed up at the steam trains as he walked with Quist through a huge exhibition area named, appropriately enough, the *Great Hall*. Before 1975, when the museum opened, this had been one of the railway's working engine sheds where the rolling stock was maintained and repaired.

The youth nodded to himself. *This place was truly enormous, but he guessed space was something of a necessity if you needed to house over one-hundred locomotives along with dozens of assorted carriages and other displays.*

It was a late Sunday afternoon in March, and Watson turned up the collar on his cherry-red denim jacket before stuffing his hands deep into the pockets.

"Feeling a little cool, are we?" asked Quist.

"Hey, I'm always *cool*." Watson grinned. "You should know that by now, Guv. No, I'm feeling bloody cold." He noticed a group of men walking between two of the engines and glanced at his watch. "Doesn't this place close at five?"

"Yes, fifteen minutes ago," said Quist, in his clipped English accent. "Which is why we entered through those rear loading doors. The people you see here all work for our client."

"Mmh, Calista Dawson." Watson gave a low whistle. "A bit of a posh name, eh? I was out of the office when she called on you. You say she owns an electrical company?"

Quist nodded. "They're installing new technology here throughout the night. Mrs. Dawson is supposedly visiting to inspect the progress, but she's actually here to meet with us." He sniffed the air and smiled. "Ah, can you smell that – the evocative scent of engine oil that constantly infuses the atmosphere here? It conjures up that golden British age of the steam railways."

"Well, as we both know, Guv..." The young man smiled too. "Your sense of smell is *slightly* keener than mine."

"True," conceded Quist. "Have you been here before? I'm aware that you view museums and their educational benefits in the same way that a vampire views garlic, so I don't suppose..."

"Well, you'd be wrong," said Watson. "As a matter of fact, I've visited here a few times with one of my old girlfriends. Laura was obsessed with all this steam train shit."

The youth had to admit, this particular museum *was* impressive. Many men, especially the older generation, grew misty-eyed in the presence of these vintage locomotives, and Laura was the same. She'd bring him here to gasp at the exhibits, before finding concealed spots to indulge in bouts of "danger sex," the pair rushing to finish before they were discovered. The frolics at her apartment had been equally *odd*, with Laura bending over her train set and insisting upon Watson wearing a station master's cap, blowing a whistle and waving a green flag. Their short relationship ended abruptly when she met an *actual* engine driver on a vintage steam railway. Not even the lead singer of a boyband could have competed with *that*.

"Ah, here it is," murmured Quist, approaching the locomotive that stood in the very centre of the hall. Apple green in colour, it sported a pair of large smoke deflectors on either side of its front smokebox and the nameplate above the huge wheels read: *Flying Scotsman*. "This has to be the world's most famous steam engine."

"Yeah," agreed Watson. "I've actually heard of *this* one."

"I should hope so," said Quist. "It's a true icon, isn't it? In 1934, the *Scotsman* was the first locomotive to reach 100 miles per hour. We normally only see these beautiful Goliaths with a station platform obscuring the lower half and it's amazing how colossal they are on full view like this. Good Lord, just look at the size of it."

"Hey, Guv..." Watson winked. "If only I had a pound for

every time I've heard *that* from a girl."

The detective rolled his eyes. "I wonder if it would be possible for you to rein in the juvenile humour when we speak with our client?"

"Don't worry," he grinned. "I know when to watch my P's and Q's."

Walking around the front of the *Flying Scotsman* and passing the *Duchess of Hamilton* steam engine, Quist gestured to another locomotive that stood ahead of them. Vivid blue in colour and elegant Art-Deco in appearance, the boiler and mechanics were obscured by a casing of aerodynamic streamlining.

"And here's the celebrated *Mallard*," said Quist. "The fastest steam engine in the world. Believe it or not, in 1938 she reached a staggering 126 miles per hour."

"Believe it or not?" Watson shrugged. "My mate Omar tops that every time he drives along the A64 in his BMW."

Steps and a metal gantry formed a public viewing area by the side of the *Mallard* engine cab, where a smart middle-aged woman stood speaking to three of the electricians. She turned as Quist neared and left the trio to meet him, her complexion noticeably reddening.

"Oh, here we go," muttered Watson, seeing her blush.

"Mrs. Dawson," said Quist. "It's good to see you again, albeit under these circumstances. This is my assistant, Watson. You can speak freely in front of him."

The youth smiled. "Or even *behind* me, if you like."

The woman glanced at his bright red jacket and yellow trainers before turning her attention back to Quist. "Please call me Calista," she said, quickly tidying her hair and leading the pair along the side of the locomotive and out of earshot of her workmen. "Thanks for meeting away from my home. Calling on me at work like this gives us privacy."

"Apart from all the CCTV," joked Watson, nodding to the

many video units positioned on columns about the *Great Hall.*

"We're re-routing the electrics," said Calista, taking the quip seriously. She walked around a heap of tarpaulins covered in coils of wire and tools. "I have eight of my people here, so it won't take long, but the cameras are switched off for the next three days. It's probably best if you kept that to yourselves."

"Yeah," agreed Watson. "We wouldn't want any scrap dealers stealing the *Flying Scotsman,* would we? So I hear your company is installing new technology?"

"That's right," said Calista, running her eyes over Quist and unconsciously licking her lips. "We're fitting all the exhibits with Wi-Fi. You'll load a simple app when you arrive at the museum and, once you're close enough to each router, your phone will pick up the signal and explain what you're looking at. We've just completed this one."

"The exhibits already have information boards," said Quist, gesturing to the one by the *Mallard.* "Don't they provide that same service?"

"This is the twenty-first century," laughed Watson. "People would rather interact with their mobiles than read boards."

The youth noticed how Calista's gaze remained fixed upon his boss as she opened her overcoat, smoothed down her sweater and, once again, moistened her lips with her tongue. From the unconscious preening, she clearly found him extremely attractive and Watson knew the bizarre reason *why.*

Bernard Quist was quite good-looking, with wavy dark hair, tawny eyes and a large nose. Some people might have described the nose as *aquiline,* but Watson preferred the word *massive* and secretly compared it to an Olympic ski jump. Women weren't sexually drawn to him because of his looks, however. It was all down to the curious pheromones that he constantly exuded.

"So what's with the stupid name?" asked the youth.

"I'm sorry?" said Quist, taken aback. *His assistant wasn't the most tactful of young men and there was always a possibility that he could be referring to their client's name, Calista.*

"If you've completed the Wi-Fi information, then maybe you can explain why it's called the *Mallard*." Watson scratched his curly black hair. "If I had to pick a bird's name, I'd go for the *Swift*, or the *Peregrine Falcon*. I definitely *wouldn't* name the world's fastest train after a duck. It's not even green like a mallard. It's bright blue."

"Perhaps we could get to the matter in hand?" suggested the woman.

"Absolutely," said Quist, frowning at his assistant. "As instructed, we've been watching your husband. You suspected that a young woman named Bethany Price was involved with him, but she's currently holidaying in Ibiza, which means that, so far, we're unable to substantiate this alleged affair…"

"*Alleged*?" hissed Calista. "Believe me, he's definitely seeing that cheap little slut."

Reaching into his trenchcoat, Quist produced a folder of A4 photos. The wide inside pocket was ideal for larger documents such as this. Watson always referred to it as *the Guv's shoplifting pouch.*

"You also mentioned how your husband has er, *wandering hands*," said Quist. "As you can see from the photos, his hands were indeed wandering quite a bit at this Leeds lap dancing club. His behaviour resulted in a slapped face, some nasty threats from the security and a ban from the establishment."

"Yes." Calista grimaced. "This is what happens when you marry someone fourteen years younger."

Quist declined to comment. "The other photos show him indulging in similar behaviour at two massage parlours and, um…" He cleared his throat. "And the *Collingham Donkey Sanctuary*."

Watson bit his tongue hard to prevent a smirk.

"I see," she said, icily. "Yes, I've tolerated his weird dalliances for long enough, and Bethany Price is the final straw. I want the proof for my divorce solicitor and accountant. He won't be seeing a penny from the house or my company."

"We'll continue with this," said Quist. "You can keep those photographs for your legal representative and I'll contact you again as soon as I have the relevant evidence concerning Miss Price."

"Thank you," she said, looking him up and down sexily. "Now what about the other matter that we discussed? The problem at the golf course…"

"I intend to deal with that this very evening." The detective nodded. "We'll drive over there as soon as we leave here, and I'll rectify the situation as promised."

"I'm really curious," said Calista. "How will you do it?"

"This is definitely a case of the less you know, the better." Quist smiled thinly. "I have my methods, but please trust me, you'll have no further trouble."

* * * *

Chapter 3

Watson sprawled in Quist's Ford Mondeo, eating a chocolate bar and looking out at the evening streets as his boss cruised through Heworth. Although the youth loved his home city of York, he had to concede that he didn't reside in the nicest neighbourhood, certainly not as nice as *this* suburb.

Watson lived with his mum on the Grimpen council estate, an area to the west of Acomb which York had tactfully omitted from the tourist guidebooks. Some maps even depicted the place with the archaic warning: *Here Be Dragons*. It was a neglected community of unemployment, prefab concrete, overgrown gardens and feral pitbulls, although none of these things had ever bothered the streetwise Watson. The estate had appeared after World War II and many believed that, if ever there were *another* war with nighttime bombing raids, it might be a good idea to leave the blackout curtains open in Grimpen.

Thanks to multi-millionaire developers being allowed to build too many similar housing estates and retail parks on nearby water meadows, the urban riverside areas of York now flood after heavy rain. Such flooding never occurred in past centuries, but then again, in past centuries, the Black Death wiped out hundreds of thousands of Yorkshire people, so Watson looked upon it as a case of *swingers and roundabouts*. In his opinion, having a soggy carpet was far preferable to vomiting up your lungs and being tossed into a communal plague pit.

Finishing his snack, the young man turned to Quist. "So what exactly is this *extra* job you're doing for Calista?" he asked. "More to the point, how long will it take? You promised me I could go watch the filming."

"You sound like a spoilt child." The detective laughed. "*Oh, Daddy, you promised we could go to the seaside for ice cream.*"

"They'll only be at Walmgate for the next two hours." Watson held up his phone to show a movie fan website. "According to this, they started filming there at twilight. It's amazing to think they were shooting at Egyptian locations until a couple of days ago and now they're here in York."

""Yes, *amazing*," drawled Quist, indifferently. "Don't worry about the time. We'll be at the golf club shortly and it shouldn't take me long."

"To do what?"

"Just wait and you'll see." Quist gave a lopsided smile, the peculiar smile he always pulled when feeling awkward. "Then I won't need to bother with explanations."

Heworth is an upmarket suburb to the north east of York city centre, celebrated these days for being the birthplace and childhood home of the actress Dame Judi Dench. Large Victorian houses and newer detached and semi-detached dwellings line the tree-lined streets. Quist negotiated a small roundabout in the blue Mondeo and turned north off Heworth Green onto the more rural Malton Road. Spreading out to the left of the car, a dark golf course could be seen through the gaps in the bushes. Founded in 1912, the eleven-hole club describes itself as a "city centre course," but although it lies just one mile from York Minster, this rolling patch of greenery and mature trees feels surprisingly rustic.

"This is going to be really cool for me," confessed Watson, swiftly checking through the social media on his phone. "I can't believe I'm going to see Kitten in the flesh. I've always had a thing for her."

"*Kitten*?" repeated Quist, frowning.

"Yeah, the film star, Kitten Maye."

"I take it she's never been nominated for Academy Awards?" The detective shook his head. "Presumably, Kitten is a stage name, but she sounds like someone who *performs* in the adult film industry."

"Yeah, yeah," Watson smirked.

His boss knew all about name changes. Bernard Quist had originally been called Richard Quist, but he'd changed this and, for good reason, had changed it again and again at intervals over the years, always keeping it similar – Quinn, Quayle and Quiller.

"Hey, speaking of girls," said Watson, "I noticed how old Calista was eyeing you up back there at the museum."

"Yes, I'm afraid the attraction was unmistakeable," sighed Quist. "Her Italian stiletto shoes were totally inappropriate for a work inspection and had obviously been selected because she was about to see me. Her scent too. She wore no perfume on our first meeting at the office, but for tonight's second meeting she'd decided upon an expensive *Chanel* fragrance which…"

"Never mind all the *little* clues," snorted Watson. "How about the main clue? She was bloody well *drooling* over you. I've always said, I wish I could bottle whatever it is that you give off."

"That would be difficult," said Quist. "Unfortunately, it's a cross I have to bear."

"Yeah, we'd all hate to bear *that* cross." The youth laughed. "Having girls wanting sex with us the entire time. Hey, speaking of which, I've got a hot date later with Linzi. Aaron Bea is gigging tonight at the *Duck and Diogenes*, my local pub, and Linzi plays in his band."

"Aaron Bea?" His boss glanced at him. "As in R and B, rhythm and blues? Mmh, that's rather clever."

Watson nodded. "Unfortunately, Linzi *isn't* too clever, but she *is* tastier than Taylor Swift in a bath of custard. She might be a bit dim, but she plays brilliant guitar, her arse is so firm, you could bounce a tennis ball off it, *and* she's got no gag reflex."

"Good Lord!" sighed Quist. "And to think, some people dare to suggest that romance is dead. It's almost as if I'm listening to a passage from *Jane Austen*. As a matter of fact, I have an appointment with a lady *myself* after I've dropped you off to watch your film shoot. As I said, this little diversion won't take too long."

"Yeah, well you might want to stick around for a while when you find out the title of the movie."

"Oh?" Quist frowned curiously. "Which is?"

"Nah, it'll be a surprise. Just like *you* won't tell me what we're doing on the golf course." Watson smirked. "So you're seeing a *lady*, eh? That'll be your lady cop, Katie Bradstreet? I imagine you'll be taking her clubbing? Plenty of deafening music, leaping around on the dance floor and throwing back shots?"

"Well…" Quist shuddered. "Either that or a quiet drink in the *Red Lion* with a little stimulating conversation."

"Oh, yeah," laughed Watson. "You really know how to entertain the girls, Guv."

The detective turned off the main Malton Road and onto the more secluded Muncastergate. The greens of the Heworth golf course lay on either side of this lane and the clubhouse, with its bar and restaurant buildings, appeared up ahead on their left. Instead of using the club car park, Quist pulled up beside a wooden gate in the hedge on his right.

"This is it," he said, killing the engine and climbing out of the car. He lit a cigarette, the flame illuminating his lean features, and took a couple of puffs before gesturing to the clubhouse. "Calista Dawson is the assistant secretary here, and the problem that we need to rectify is somewhere over this way. Come along."

Most of the fairways lay on the southern side of the lane, but Quist headed through the latch gate and onto the northern side of the course that stretched between here and the distant street lights of Elmfield Avenue.

"So again," said Watson, following him and squinting into the freezing blackness. "What the hell are we supposed to be doing here?"

"Apparently, the golf course has a resident family of foxes."

Quist drew on his cigarette and looked around to ensure they were alone and unobserved on the fairway. "It seems these animals are digging on the greens, presumably for worms and suchlike to eat."

Watson walked beside him, tugging up his jacket collar against the cold and spotting several white flashes at ground level in the darkness ahead. He realised they were the tails of rabbits scattering away in panic on sensing his boss.

"*Worms*?" He shrugged. "I thought foxes raided henhouses for chickens?"

Quist smiled. "The hen houses you're thinking of vanished, for the most part, after the pastoral days of *Beatrix Potter*. Modern chickens are mostly raised in intensive battery farms and even the *free-range* birds are kept in secure pens. No, foxes are opportunistic feeders and they'll eat pretty much anything."

"Okay," murmured Watson. "But aren't urban foxes a bad thing? Don't they snatch babies from prams and shit?"

The detective shook his head. "People have been coerced into believing that, but these creatures actually provide an admirable service. The only reason they're in our towns is because of all the edible rubbish we discard. The rubbish attracts vermin, and rats and mice are the main diet of the urban fox." Stubbing out his cigarette underfoot, he stopped by a tree and dropped into a bizarre press-up position to sniff the turf. "Ah, their earth is near here." He raised his head, sniffing again. "Yes, it appears to be in those bushes that border the main road over there, in that dense area of brambles."

"What?" The youth shook his head. "You can actually smell it?"

"Olfactory, my dear Watson." The detective stood up smiling broadly. "I believe you mentioned my keen nose earlier?"

"Yeah." Watson eyed his employer's face. *Keen* was the last word he'd use to describe *that* huge nose. "To be honest, I don't know why I'm surprised."

"Calista intended to bring in a pest control firm to shoot the animals and poison their den. She mentioned it in passing when I interviewed her at the office, and I managed to talk her out of the idea. I promised I'd clear them off the course without harming them."

Watson frowned. "At the museum she asked you how, but you didn't..."

"Well..." Quist removed his wristwatch and signet ring, placing them in his pocket, before shrugging off his leather trenchcoat and passing it to his assistant to hold. "I couldn't really tell her *that*, now could I?"

"Oh, you're joking?" Watson watched uneasily as the detective unbuttoned his shirt and pulled down his trousers next to the tree. "Don't tell me you're going to..."

"I am indeed," confirmed Quist.

The youth gulped. *This probably wouldn't be the first time a middle-aged man had stripped naked with a young guy on a Yorkshire golf course at night, but it would be a definite first for what was about to happen next.* He'd witnessed this many times and knew he was in no danger, but he still experienced the unavoidable tingling of fear. It was a primal, inbuilt fear, printed into the human genes, that warns us to avoid snakes, big spiders and much *worse* things.

His pale nudity almost translucent in the starlight, Quist dropped into a squat, grimacing and groaning, as the transformation began and his bones crackled and lengthened. The six-second metamorphosis was agonising, but he was used to the pain.

Watson took an involuntary step backwards. The night air was already cold, but he felt the temperature drop even more as the supernatural change drew ethereal energy from the surrounding atmosphere. He watched, wide-eyed, as his boss's face extended into a hideous lupine muzzle – broad, like a crocodile's snout – the human teeth falling to the grass and turning instantly to dust as large fangs replaced them. Thick black fur sprouted to cover an increasing body mass and his eyes changed to gleaming amber. Taller and far bulkier than Bernard Quist, the huge wolf arose from the squat to stand erect on its rear legs.

"*Lovely,*" muttered Watson, gulping to clear the nervous dryness in his mouth. "Hello again, Mister Wolf."

The youth had long since come to terms with the sheer enormity of his employer's dark secret. Scary as this supernatural monster was, Watson was now fine with it. Not many people of his young age could say they worked in a private detective agency and fewer still could say they worked for a two-hundred-year-old werewolf. Both were pretty cool claims, but only one could actually be mentioned when chatting up girls.

Unlike all the legends and full moon myths, Quist and his kind were able to shapeshift *any* time between the hours of sunset and sunrise. Watson had often commented on his appearance in this lupine form, claiming he looked nothing whatsoever like a *normal* wolf. The wolves he'd seen on television resembled big scruffy dogs and he'd witnessed scarier animals strutting around his council estate. Quist was far larger and sleeker, but *this* creature really was the stuff of nightmares and resembled the thing that had attempted to tear apart *Little Red Riding Hood*.

"So this is the plan, I take it?" Watson's breath clouded on the freezing air. "Like all animals, such as those rabbits that ran away back there, the foxes will sense you and leave the golf course?"

"Yes," growled the wolf, looking around, twitching its pointed ears and sniffing the night air. Quist's senses were greatly augmented in this form and he could easily detect unwelcome observers. "Rather than killing them, the plan is to have them find a new home away from here. As I said, urban foxes are a good thing and, as you're aware, I'm an animal lover."

"Yeah." The youth nodded. "Shame they don't love *you.*"

Quist grinned, presenting his assistant with an unnerving set of sharp fangs that wouldn't have looked out of place on a great white shark. "My being in their vicinity will certainly send them running, but they'd return once I'd left. I'm afraid we require a more permanent solution." He wagged his tail and shrugged. "This is going to be somewhat embarrassing, but oh, what the hell."

Watson stared deadpan as the wolf dropped onto all fours, cocked up a hind leg and urinated on the tree in a steaming gush.

"Er... *okay*," drawled the youth, clearing his throat uncomfortably. "You're er, going to leave your, um... *scent* on the golf course."

"Exactly." Quist nodded. "A supernatural scent that will linger for several days. By doing this – marking my territory, as it were – the foxes will believe that I've moved in. They certainly won't remain with *me* around. Wait here with my clothes; I need to go mark this entire area, especially around their den."

"Um, right..." Watson looked puzzled. "So are you able to hold your piss and just squirt out a bit at a time like a dog?"

The wolf frowned. "I must admit, I never expected to be discussing my urinary behaviour with you, but yes."

"*Wonderful*," muttered Watson. "Okay, have fun, Guv."

He watched as the wolf flexed its muscles and bounded across the dark fairway, calling momentarily at each of the many trees to leave a steaming deposit. Quist was unable to see in pitch-blackness, but like an owl, his lupine eyes collected moonbeams and starlight to enhance his night vision; to him, this would be almost like daytime.

Watson could see the lupine eyes glowing amber, grateful that they weren't red. He was always reminded of the old cowboy movies where heroes wore white hats and villains wore black. Antisocial, it might be, but devouring humans was the norm for most werewolves and their eyes were bright red. His boss had never taken a human life – these yellowish eyes were the proof – and because of this, he was able to control the supernatural blood lust and predatory instincts that raged within all lycanthropes. Watson had met red-eyed werewolves before and really hoped to *never* meet one again.

The werewolf attack, that changed Bernie Quist's life forever, had taken place in 1790 and his boss hadn't aged a day since. His hair and nails didn't grow and there was little point in him buying a razor. He didn't grow ill either. Watson watched the creature and smirked to himself. *He didn't even suffer from mange, distemper and kennel cough.* Even in human form, his boss was much stronger and faster than most men and his augmented senses were far keener. Fully aware that many people are only two or three beers away from forming a lynch mob, Quist hid his supernatural immortality by moving around and changing identities on a regular basis.

The lycanthropy was the reason women found him so attractive, his lupine pheromones stimulating them sexually on a dark paranormal level. It was unintentional, but also unavoidable.

Watson wondered if the girls would find him quite so attractive if they could see him right now – *running from tree to tree and pissing everywhere.*

"Brilliant," he murmured, secretly praying that this territorial *marking* didn't progress to anything more *solid*. "Rather than kill them, we scare the foxes away with the stink of monster piss. It's nice to know that *some* werewolves care about natural history and the environment."

* * * *

Chapter 4

Gated communities are a perfect habitat for the ultra-wealthy and privileged. The rich can create poverty with profitable dealings, whilst remaining safely and luxuriously insulated with their swimming pools and security guards. Many assume gated communities are an American concept, perhaps originating in Florida or California, but they appeared many centuries before in the guise of European walled cities. For defensive reasons, most of these were constructed in prominent positions – clustered upon a high hilltop – but for some reason, the architects of York built *their* walled city on the flattest of rural plains: the Vale of York.

The foundations are Roman, but the picturesque limestone walls, that rise above their embankments to encircle York, date back to the early thirteenth century. Several gateways are set at intervals along the two-mile circuit – Micklegate, Bootham, Walmgate and Monkgate. Resembling miniature castles, these fortifications were constantly guarded to control access to and from the city, but along with the Shambles, Clifford's Tower and the Minster, they now form compulsory photograph stops for the hordes of international tourists.

With its original portcullis and 15th century doors, Walmgate Bar is the most complete and the only gateway tower to retain its barbican, a wall-enclosed "killing ground" that juts out twenty feet from the entrance. Unlucky attackers were trapped here and showered from the battlements above with arrows and cauldrons of boiling oil. An ornate Elizabethan extension protrudes from the bar on the internal face. This timber addition appeared five-hundred and fifty years ago. The figures on its roof – a half-naked girl and a werewolf – appeared fifty minutes ago.

"Magnificent, isn't it?" murmured Quist, gazing up. An array of filming floodlights illuminated the building. "This place was set on fire during the rebellion of 1489 and battered by cannons during the

1644 civil war siege, yet here it still endures in all its proud glory."

"Are you for *real*?" Watson glanced at him disbelievingly. His boss had amassed a wealth of knowledge over his supernaturally extended lifetime. "There's the gorgeous movie star Kitten Maye up there and you're talking about a frigging pile of stones?"

"Yes, well…" Laughing quietly, the detective studied the girl in the torn nightdress, noticing her lengthy black hair extensions, the sullen pout and fake globular breasts. "I'm possibly not quite as starstruck as you."

The two men stood on the crowded street that leads south from the city centre to this impressive gateway. An archway beside the barbican allowed traffic through the perimeter wall, but this had been closed off for the filming, enabling the nighttime gathering of onlookers to spread out across the road. Most were holding up phones to video the activity. A chest-high plastic cordon fence distanced them from the production, where a local security team, hired to police the shoot, stood guard in high-visibility jackets.

Watson smiled to himself at the shaven scalps and serious expressions on display. *With their brawny folded arms, microphone earpieces and suspicious eyes scanning the crowd, it looked as if, in their minds, they were expecting an attempt on the president's life. Many security firms were quite professional these days, but the youth guessed this bunch had been chosen from the cheaper end of the company list. Some of these scowling thugs had almost certainly spent time in a cell. He could easily imagine them insisting upon the upper bunk and performing that surreal magical trick of producing an illicit mobile phone from the nether regions.*

"I intended to drop you here and then leave," said Quist. "But when you told me the name of the movie I changed my mind."

"I had a feeling you would." Watson grinned at him. "*Howl of the Wolfman*. Brilliant title, eh? Who knows, Guv? Keep your eye on their werewolf up there and you might pick up a few tips on how to carry on."

"Yes, you never know," agreed Quist, laughing. He watched the stuntman in his furry suit on the roof, then checked the time. "I'll watch with you for a short while. The *Red Lion* pub is just up the road and Katie is working late today. I don't have to meet her there for thirty minutes or so."

"I've got to say…" Watson gestured to the stuntman and lowered his voice. "Out of the two werewolves I've seen tonight, you're probably the most convincing one."

Knowing that the protruding timber structure had been built in Elizabethan times, Quist hoped it could cope with the weight of everyone. Six members of the film crew clustered on the roof with the raven-haired actress and the wolfman stunt performer, all remaining out of shot on the left-hand side. These included the director, a portable camera operator and a young man wielding a lengthy boom microphone. Another camera had been set up on the hydraulic platform of a "cherry picker," with a third positioned at ground level beside the fleet of vehicles, all sporting the company name: *Candlemass Productions*.

"Wow, just look at Kitten," sighed Watson, as the filming paused for a short break and a blonde-haired make-up girl moved forward to touch up the actress's pouting features. "I've always had a big thing for her. I'm hoping she'll come over here to the barrier later for a few photos and autographs with her fans. Honestly, every time I see her, I could just eat her up."

"I rather think you'll need to join the queue," said Quist. "From what I've observed so far, that would appear to be the primary objective of her lupine companion."

Watson laughed. "Did you see her in her other *Candlemass* films, *Scream of the Vampire*, *Scream of the Vampire 2* and *Scream of the Vampire 3*? They're absolute classics."

"I must have somehow missed those," drawled Quist. "I can't

imagine how. I was possibly watching *Citizen Kane* instead."

"Never heard of that one." Watson didn't spot the sarcasm. "Joanna Marsh directed her in the three *Screams* and now she's doing this movie too. That's her up there – the middle-aged woman with the big specs."

"I suppose many would view Kitten Maye as an attractive young lady." The detective gazed up at the tower. "Especially those people with a penchant for fake silicon bosoms."

"Whatever." Watson laughed. "As we're on the subject of the good old fairer sex, how's it going with your lady cop? Is it getting serious yet?"

"Such things are somewhat challenging for me," sighed Quist. "Because of my um, *situation*, you're aware of how difficult it is for me to maintain meaningful relationships. Katie and I have been seeing each other on and off for some time, but who can say where it will all lead?"

"But she's spent the night at your cottage a few times," pointed out Watson. "So it's safe to say that we're past the kissing cheeks and holding hands stage."

The detective frowned slightly. "You know me well enough by now to appreciate that I'm a British gentleman and certainly not one to kiss and tell."

"Right." Watson nodded. "But I have to ask…"

"If it's your usual stupid enquiry about whether or not werewolves do it *doggy style*…"

"No." The youth smirked to himself. *That was indeed the question that he really wanted answering.* "No, I was wondering how she feels about the supernatural? I mean, she went through some pretty weird shit with us a while back. She accepted it then, but how about now? If things *did* get serious, could you ever tell her about your *situation*, as you call it? Hey, Katie, luv, you know how some guys have ingrown toenails? Well, I have a condition too that you should maybe know about…"

"I really don't know about *that*." Quist laughed quietly. "She doesn't speak much about those supernatural events. I suspect it may be a form of denial."

"Still…" Watson lowered his voice again. "Over two-hundred years old, but you can still pull the girls, eh, Guv? It's good to know you've still got it at that age."

"Okay, everyone," called out one of the crew, listening to his radio earpiece. "They're going for another take, so it'd be really appreciated if everyone watching could please remain quiet when they shout *rolling*."

With filming about to resume, the wolfman clambered up onto the rooftop handrail and raised his arms high in a menacing pose. Gasps and appreciative murmurs ran through the crowd of onlookers. The monster was probably readying himself to pounce upon the girl, but no one would ever know for certain if this were the case. The stunt performer's furry werewolf boot suddenly skidded off the slippery woodwork and he toppled backwards into space.

"*Fuck!*" hissed Watson, clamping a hand over his mouth.

Attempting to snatch hold of the rail and missing, the wolfman plummeted, his flailing body slamming into the cobblestones below with a sickening crunch.

* * * *

Chapter 5

Quist winced as the falling stunt performer hit the ground hard and, without a thought, grabbed the top of the fence and effortlessly vaulted the cordon. His open trenchcoat flapped behind him like a cape as he raced towards the injured man. Light and wiry, Watson scrambled over to follow, as one of the security team rushed forward to bar their path.

"Hold it right there," growled the muscular skinhead, grabbing a fistful of Quist's lapel. "Where the hell do you twats think you're going?"

"Get out of my way," snapped Quist, wrenching the man's hand from the leather. "I'm a doctor and I need to help that man."

Watson knew this was true. Many decades ago, his boss had worked as a general practitioner with Edinburgh's poor and destitute. He'd never officially retired and technically he still *was* a doctor. The youth ran behind him to the crumpled furry heap at the base of the tower, noticing how bizarre the monster looked lying motionless on his back with his big feral wolf grin.

Quist crouched by the man's side and turned to the film crew members who had gathered around. "How do we remove the head of this costume?" he demanded. "Quickly, someone. I need to check his breathing."

"Be careful." A young girl appeared from the crowd and knelt beside the detective to snatch his hand away. "We could hurt his neck if we start tugging at it." She clicked open a concealed catch in the thick fur at the rear. "There, that's it. Now we should be able to ease the mask forward and…" She moved back, startled, as the werewolf suddenly sat up.

"There's no need for that," he said, pulling off the lupine head himself to reveal a good-looking man of around thirty. Steve Lyle laughed at the terrified onlookers. "Wow, just look at all your frightened faces. I'm fine."

"Steve, you need to stay still," said the girl, anxiously. "You can't possibly be *fine* after a fall from that height. It must be over thirty feet. Don't try to get up until we get you properly checked out."

"You weren't moving," said Quist. "Everyone assumed you were unconscious and you..."

"Oh, my God," squealed a female voice. "Oh, my God, Stevie. Is my babes okay?"

The blonde make-up artist from the roof had hurried down the tower steps to join them. She barged past Quist and Watson to grab the stuntman's huge clawed hand.

"Oh, my God, Stevie Babes," she stammered again. "Tell me you're okay?"

"Will you listen to all this fussing?" chuckled Lyle, climbing to his feet and kissing her. "Don't worry yourself, Hayley. Take a look at me. Like I've just told everyone, I'm absolutely fine."

Joanna Marsh the director had followed Hayley down from the battlements. "*Jesus*," she gasped. "Is he actually standing after *that*?" Running a shaky hand through her hair, she turned to the gathered crew. "Please tell me that one of you has phoned for an ambulance."

"Ambulance?" Lyle gave her a broad white smile. "Oh, come on, Joanna, please. I'm a professional stunt performer, remember. I know how to roll with a fall and this monster costume is thickly padded. It took all the impact."

"I'm pleased to hear that," said Quist, watching him thoughtfully. "I was certain you'd been badly injured."

"I don't know who you are," said Lyle, Velcro crunching as he yanked off his clawed wolf gauntlet. "But thanks for your concern." He shook the detective's hand, stiffening slightly and gazing at him. "As you can see, my friend, there's no need to worry."

"Stevie, for God's sake," whimpered Hayley. "I'm sorry, but I don't care what you say, Babes. You need to see a doctor before…"

"Yes, he *does*," snapped a furious man striding over to them. "I want a medic to examine him right *now*. This shoot is finished for the night."

Sixty years old, bald and bespectacled, Brandon Massey wore an expensive camel hair overcoat and a wristwatch that cost more than a family car. His red face and bulging neck veins hinted at anger management problems, hypertension and impending strokes. The Cockney accent is said to be "cheerful and chirpy," but this stocky Londoner sounded permanently aggressive. Joanna, the director, knew that Massey had every right to be angry. As the producer of this movie, he was in charge of the finances and shareholder investments. Where some people look upon the filming process as the creation of art, Massey looked upon it as the creation of shit-loads of cash.

"*Professional stunt performer* or not," snarled Massey, "this is your second major accident in the same fuckin' week and you're daring to make light of it? You're openly laughing at a thirty-foot fall, but I've got the insurance to worry about."

"These furry wolf feet are the problem," said Lyle. "They have no grip and that handrail up there is polished and…"

"Seriously?" said the producer, sarcastically. "That's *your* department and all that should have been taken into account when you planned out the stunt. That's assuming you *do* actually plan them."

"Of course they're planned," snorted Lyle, gesturing to the tower. "How can you close down the shooting? What about my big leap from the handrail?"

"What about it?" scoffed Massey. "Do you *really* want to try it again after that fiasco? No, you could easily have internal injuries disguised by the pumping adrenalin. The filming is definitely over for tonight and we're going to get you examined."

Watson listened to the gruff Cockney accent, unable to decide whether this character belonged in a Guy Ritchie movie, or on some

East End market, yelling about fruit and veg.

"Joanna…" Massey turned to the director. "You already have three takes of that attack scene, so you can work with your editor and use the best one of them. Steve, you're coming to the control unit to sit and wait until the medic arrives."

"Intriguing," murmured Quist, watching curiously as the stuntman followed the director and producer to the nearby van. "*Very* intriguing."

"What is?" asked Watson.

"I'll tell you later," said Quist.

Watson was far more *intrigued* by the petite young woman who had helped his boss remove the costume mask. She wore a padded yellow puffer jacket against the cold night air, zipping it up snugly as he ran an eye over her short black hair and waiflike features.

"So you're an actress?" he asked. "No, wait a minute; probably not. No, to be honest, you're far too pretty to be appearing in *this* horror film."

"Yeah, right," she laughed. "No, I'm the film editor. Toni Nelson is the name."

"It's great to meet you." The youth glanced at Quist and saw that he was still watching the stuntman by the van.

Toni also noticed the detective's interest. "Steve Lyle over there is our principal stunt performer," she said. "The angry guy in the tan overcoat is Brandon, our producer. We have first-aid officers on the crew, but as you just heard, Brandon is having Steve looked at by a *real* medic. He's in charge of the budget and constantly worries about the money and insurance claims."

"I've just seen the wolfman costume close-up," said Watson, grinning. "Just how *big* is this budget we're talking about?"

"I know what you mean." Toni laughed again. "The thing is, this accident will have really shaken Brandon. Steve had a similar fall during a stunt in Egypt just a few days ago. That one also appeared bad, but just like tonight, he walked away from it without a scratch."

"Did he *really*?" murmured Quist. "Mr. Lyle seems to be quite a fortunate young chap, doesn't he?"

"Did I hear you tell security that you're a doctor?" asked Toni. "I must say, it's lucky that you were here watching, but it seems he didn't need you."

"Actually, I *was* a general practitioner," said Quist. "But not any longer. I currently operate in York as a consultant detective."

"Er, right…" Toni frowned. "You mean like a private eye?"

"More like a consultant detective," smiled Quist. "This is my assistant, Watson."

"I hope you don't mind me saying this," said Toni, "but that's a peculiar change of jobs, isn't it? So, um, what happened? Were you stuck off, or something?"

"I can understand how some might arrive at that erroneous conclusion, but no." Quist thought it best not to mention that an entire century had passed between the two professions. "Suffice to say that various factors combined to facilitate the career change."

"Yeah," nodded Watson. "The female patients used to complain about his cold hands."

"You're wasted at my agency," sighed the detective. "With razor-sharp jokes like that, you'd be packing out the comedy clubs."

"Ah, you know what they say?" The youth winked at Toni. "Sarcasm is the lowest form of wit."

The girl ran a puzzled eye over the two men.

The distinct contrast in appearance and personalities often confused people, but the detective had deliberately chosen his young employee *because* of this. As a result of moving around under different identities to protect his supernatural secret, Quist had lived alone for many years, long-lasting friendships being a little awkward for someone who never aged a day. Constantly striving to remain unnoticed had left him feeling isolated and he'd needed someone to help him integrate more with modern society and to reconnect him to humanity. Someone with a lively, jovial outlook to coax him from his reclusive shell, and this colourful, streetwise youth had turned out to be perfect.

"Amazing," said Watson. "So, just a few days ago, you were shooting your wolfman film in Egypt and now you're here?" He winked at Quist. "The idea of a werewolf in modern-day York is a bit far-fetched, isn't it, Guv?"

"Absolutely," agreed the detective, glancing again at Steve Lyle, who was now peering suspiciously back at him.

"Hey," gasped the youth. "Just look who's here."

He stepped forward as Kitten Maye walked towards them, a warm overcoat covering her scanty filming costume. Two nearby security guards noticed his interest and instantly homed in, both excited and slightly aroused at the prospect of beating up a black stranger.

"Hi, Kitten," said Watson. "I've seen every one of your films and I can't wait for this one." He pulled out his phone. "I wonder if there's any chance of getting a selfie with you?"

"Dream on." The actress walked straight past, giving him a look that he found less inviting than a shat bed. "I wonder if there's any chance of you fucking off?"

Openly disappointed, the thuggish guards headed back to their posts.

Toni smiled apologetically at the young man. "Don't take it personally," she said, as Kitten strode across the cobblestones to join the director and the stuntman. "Believe me, that's how she treats all her fans. Well, how she treats pretty much *everyone*, actually."

"Nah, she's probably just playing hard to get, I reckon." Watson smirked at Quist, who shook his head. "By the way, Toni, do you have any raisins on you?"

"Raisins?" She looked puzzled. "Um, no…"

"Well, then how about a *date*?" he joked. "York is a gorgeous city, and if this is your first time here, what you need is a gorgeous black guy to act as your guide."

"Why, do you *know* any gorgeous black guys?" she asked, laughing. "Yeah, I'll think about your ever-so-kind offer. You know what? I like your sense of humour and…"

"Really?" said Quist, feigning amazement. "Are you sure you're not in a state of shock after witnessing the accident?"

Watson laughed. "So when are you filming here again?"

"We're scheduled to be here on Tuesday," said Toni. "A street somewhere near the Minster, I understand. The production is based at Beningbrough Hall, a few miles north of here, and we're filming various scenes there tomorrow." She smiled at them both. "Here's an idea, if you're not busy, why don't you two come on over and I'll get you into the set?"

"Eh?" Watson's face lit up. "Seriously?"

She held out a hand. "Pass me your phone and I'll give you my number. You can call me if you can't find me at the security gate there."

"Hey, thanks," he enthused.

The youth waited as Toni entered the digits. *He was attracted to her elfin, waiflike looks, but there was something else about this petite girl that he couldn't put his finger on. Whatever it was, he really liked it.*

"It's the least I can do after you tried to help Steve." Toni turned to leave and winked. "I'll see you both there tomorrow, maybe?"

"Well, how about that, Guv?" Watson watched her walk away. "Kitten might be playing hard to get, but Toni obviously has the hots for me." He glanced at the detective. "Ah, I see you've got that look what you get."

"*That look what I get?*" echoed Quist. "Good Lord! I don't

know which English language college you attended, but perhaps you should think about suing them for compensation?"

"Yeah, yeah." Watson pulled a sarcastic face. "But you know the look I mean. I noticed you watching the stunt guy. Why did you say he was *intriguing*?"

"I'll tell you why," purred Quist. "When he fell from the roof I heard several bones break inside that wolfman suit."

"Wow, really?" Watson glanced over at the control unit where Lyle was being helped out of his furry costume by Hayley. "Which bones did you think he…"

Quist tutted. "Watson, I have supernatural hearing, but it isn't *that* good. I can't pinpoint the actual fractures."

The youth nodded. "But it turned out he wasn't injured…"

"Exactly." The detective smiled enigmatically. "And yet bones *did* break. *Very* intriguing, wouldn't you say? Yes, I think we'll most definitely pay a visit to Beningbrough tomorrow." He turned to head back to his parked car. "Come along, it's time to go. I need to be at the *Red Lion* and you need a taxi to Acomb. You can charge it to your company credit card."

Watson laughed. "Whoo, the glamorous lifestyle of us rich guys, eh, Guv?"

"*Any raisins on you*?" scoffed Quist. "Do you find that line actually works on the young ladies?"

"She gave me her number, didn't she?" The youth held up his phone. "The same line worked on Linzi too."

"Ah, the girl you described as being *a bit dim*." Quist waited as one of the security guards opened a gate in the cordon fence to allow them through. "I have to say, I find it a little strange."

"What? That I'm God's gift to women?"

"No." The detective rolled his eyes. "Strange that this editor invited two complete strangers to visit the film set. She claimed it was because I attempted to help the stuntman, but it didn't ring true."

"A good looking guy like me?" Watson shrugged. "Come on, Guv, can you blame her?"

"But the strangest thing of all…" said Quist. "Didn't you notice? Toni Nelson seems to be a normal young lady, yet my lupine pheromones appeared to have absolutely no effect upon her."

* * * *

Steve Lyle left the control unit and watched Quist exit through the cordon gate, his thoughts racing.

Had this man simply been watching the filming or was there more to it? Whatever he was doing here, they'd touched each other, so he must know – he must. The prize was so close now, and whoever he was, this character couldn't be allowed to interfere and pose a threat. Nothing could be left to chance.

Keeping Quist in sight, the stuntman climbed into one of the company lease vehicles: a black Audi.

"What the hell do you think you're doing?" asked Kitten Maye, snatching hold of the door handle before he could close it.

"Do you mind letting go of that?" Lyle nodded to the car door. "We've finished filming, so I'm heading over to..."

"Jesus!" snorted the actress. "So the muscles are big, but definitely not the brain, eh? You're not supposed to be going *anywhere*, dickhead. You *do* know that Brandon has phoned a doctor to have you examined?"

"And I've told the producer that it's pointless; I don't *need* a medical examination." He gave her a sarcastic smile. "Why not close the door, sweetheart, and just stay out of this, huh?"

"Whatever." She slammed it shut and flounced away. "Brandon won't like this, but hey, it's your funeral. What do I care?"

A nearby security guard had overheard the exchange and tapped on the Audi side window. Lyle tutted with annoyance, but lowered the glass.

"What a girl." The guard stooped to the open window and

laughed dryly. "I've spoken to her twice tonight and both times she answered me as if I were a piece of shit. She acts like the big Hollywood film star, but her *actual* acting leaves a lot to be desired, doesn't it?"

"I take it you don't rate her talents?" asked Lyle, peering through the windscreen to keep Quist in view.

"What?" The guard sneered. "You mean all that screaming in those crappy horror films of hers? There's no talent there *to* rate, but I've heard how Brandon Massey rates her talents in the bedroom. Still, she proves that you don't need to be a brilliant actor to become rich. I certainly wish I was a pound behind her."

The stuntman narrowed his eyes. "That isn't an expression I'm familiar with."

"I think it's probably a northern saying." The guard shrugged. "However much money a rich person has, it'd be great to be just a pound coin behind that amount."

"Ah, I see." Lyle grinned broadly. "Say it again."

"Huh?"

"What you just said – *I wish I was…*"

"You mean…" The man frowned. "I wish I was a pound behind her?"

Walking to the control unit, Kitten paused as the vehicle lights momentarily dimmed and a metallic tinkle sounded on the cobblestones to her rear. She turned, but saw nothing.

* * * *

Chapter 6

York was named *Jorvik* by the Vikings. They ruled the city for more than a century, before William the Conqueror's army arrived in 1066 with its medieval version of a *Compulsory Purchase Order*. Little has changed topographically since the reign of the Norsemen. *Gate* was their word for street and the principal thoroughfares – Fossgate, Coppergate, Ousegate, Spurriergate and Gillygate – still follow the same routes and bear the same names. Connecting Walmgate and Piccadilly, Merchantgate is one of the centre's shortest streets, with the *Red Lion* public house and its outdoor beer garden making up the entire southern side of its brief length.

The ancient tavern comprised of three large rooms, each with its own open fireplace. Katie Bradstreet warmed her hands beside one of them, smiling to hear the comforting sound of crackling logs in the grate. She wore a dark blue suit and sat at a small table with Quist, their overcoats draped over their chair backrests.

The detective inspector was forty-three, but her short blonde hair, coupled with regular exercise and a wholesome vegetarian diet, left her looking younger. Katie had found that a healthy lifestyle was something of a necessity when combatting the aging effects of two decades in the North Yorkshire Police. Gory crime scenes, sexual offences, autopsies, and endless interviews with gum-chewing liars and their smug solicitors – these everyday scenarios all had a nasty tendency to create premature facial lines and wrinkles.

"I've never been in here before," she said, sipping her glass of Merlot and gazing around. The inn was quite busy for a wintry Sunday evening. "It really is a lovely old place, isn't it?"

Plaster daub and exposed timbers covered the exterior of this Tudor building and the indoor designers had clearly opted for a similar theme. Dark oak beams supported sagging ceilings, the wooden floors creaked like the decks of a Spanish galleon, and the walls were a jumble of antiquated panelling and rustic open brickwork. Temporarily dismissing his puzzled thoughts of high falls and broken bones, Quist looked around too, noticing two of the barmaids pouting sexily as they watched him. The lupine pheromones were clearly working their unwanted magic.

"It *is* lovely, isn't it?" he agreed. "The *Red Lion* claims to be one of the oldest inns in York." He gestured to the deep-set brick fireplace. "This dates back to the thirteenth century and you can possibly tell from the shape and the alcoves that it was originally constructed as a bread oven. American tourists pretty much queue to drink in here and soak up the atmosphere."

Katie smiled. "I suppose it's haunted? To be honest, I've yet to find a York pub that isn't."

Quist nodded. "Haunted by several ghosts, supposedly, and it's filled with history and folklore. One of the small rooms upstairs was a hidden 'priest hole,' built to conceal clergymen during the Catholic persecutions. Also, this was Dick Turpin's favourite tavern, or so they say. The highwayman was staying here and made a swashbuckling escape through the attic window when a group of constables arrived to arrest him."

"That's brilliant," said Katie, drinking her wine. "Whether it's true or not, it makes for a great advertising story. I can easily understand why the tourists come here. You too, what with your love of history."

Quist gave a lopsided smile. This was quite true – he *did* have a passion for history, although he'd actually *lived* through more than two centuries of it.

"From what I know of your assistant," said Katie, "I'm guessing this isn't *his* favourite watering hole?"

"Watson?" Laughing quietly, Quist held up his pint of beer. "No, I'm afraid he prefers banal lager to these delightful craft ales. I've attempted to get him to try them, but to quote him, *he'd rather crap in his hands and then clap.* He also prefers flashing lights, neon and loud rock music."

"Well, I can't fault that," admitted Katie. "I like nightclubs *and* olde worlde inns."

"I've brought him in here a few times," said Quist. "He always remarks upon how the black and white exterior reminds him of an iced Bakewell tart or a humbug. The boy is constantly hungry and forever snacking upon junk food. I've yet to determine where he puts it all."

"I've yet to determine why you employed him." She grinned. "I mean, I know he's really bright and sharp-witted, but he's hardly *Mister Tactful*, is he? I can't imagine what he's like when he's chatting with your clients."

"He does tend to speak his mind without thinking," admitted Quist. "But he's ideal for clandestine detective work because, quite frankly, no one ever suspects him. Imagine conducting an illicit affair in some remote hotel and seeing Watson at the bar, dressed in his bright red jeans and yellow trainers, and messing with the social media nonsense on his phone. You'd never imagine, for one second, that this youth had been hired to watch you."

"Hey, don't knock *social media nonsense*," laughed the inspector. "Since it first appeared, it's been a godsend for the police. You can't imagine how many thick criminals brag about their exploits on there. They even post pictures and videos of themselves driving at high speed and committing other offences."

Quist sipped his beer and smiled warmly. "Speaking of which, you've been working today. Did you come across any serial killers, or anything equally interesting?"

"Hardly," snorted Katie. "I've been catching up on a mountain of paperwork, if you're weird enough to call *that* interesting."

"About as interesting as *my* day then," admitted Quist. "I've been looking into yet another messy divorce case with a wayward husband."

"Sounds delightful," said Katie. "But you've also been watching the filming over at Walmgate Bar? What movie are they making?"

"*Howl of the Wolfman*," chuckled Quist, cringing slightly. "If you haven't already guessed from the title, it's one of those horror productions that Watson is really enamoured by. This one stars one of his favourites, the *top actress*, Kitten Maye."

"I've heard of her," said the inspector. "She's supposed to be quite sexy."

"I saw her." Quist gave a lopsided smile. "She wasn't exactly my type."

"And yet I *do* appear to be your type." Katie reached over the table to take his hand. "It's flattering to know you prefer me to some beautiful actress."

"It's highly doubtful that the choice you describe will ever be presented to me," he joked.

"So *I'm* your type," Katie squeezed his hand. "And we're the same age, aren't we?"

"Give or take a couple of years," said Quist, swiftly calculating that it was actually a couple of hundred.

"But you never fully drop your shields, do you?" She lowered her voice. "Emotionally, I mean. Even after all that we went through together a while back – those occultists, the entity and that magical dagger. You talking about this horror film reminds me of all that. That… um, *episode* really opened my eyes to the reality of the supernatural."

"Really?" Quist recalled his earlier chat with Watson about this.

"It was the most terrified I've ever been," whispered Katie, shuddering slightly. "At the time it all felt so real and I was absolutely convinced, but do you know something weird? As time goes by, I feel less and less scared when I think about what happened. I try to convince myself that it *couldn't* have been real."

"That's understandable," said Quist, stroking her hand. "It's how the human mind copes with trauma. But do you still accept the supernatural?"

She nodded slowly. "No matter how my head has rationalised it since, yes I still do. I remember what happened and, yes, I *have* to accept it."

Quist smiled. "So I assume you're open to the idea of werewolves, like the one down at Walmgate?"

"Oh, yes, werewolves and fire-breathing dragons." She laughed. "Joking aside, let's face it, you saved my life at least once back when all that occult stuff was going on."

"I'm a true English gentleman." Quist shrugged. "To me, saving the life of a lady is much the same as politely holding open a door for them."

"Yeah, I imagine so." Katie laughed. "I have to say, it's always fun when we're together and the sex is truly amazing, but I get the impression that you don't open up because you don't want to get into a fully committed relationship."

Quist sipped at his beer before replying to give himself a little thinking time. *It was true – loving relationships had always been difficult for him. Virtually every one of his past girlfriends was dead, but he couldn't tell her that. It didn't sound right and, to be honest, it also came across as bloody scary. It was impossible to explain how every girl he'd known had a normal human lifespan and his lifespan was quite a bit longer.*

"Fortunately, it doesn't bother me," said Katie, before he could answer. "Being a police officer with a busy and awkward work schedule, this... *whatever it is* that we have between us, suits me just fine at the moment."

"Um, okay," murmured Quist. "That's good to know."

The inspector leant forward. "You know what…" she purred, huskily. "As lovely as this old pub is, I have several bottles of good wine at my place. I've been working all day, so why don't we finish these drinks and go back home to relax properly and sample a couple?"

"That sounds like an excellent idea," he admitted.

He knew the lupine pheromones were working their uncanny magic. Katie's pupils had dilated, her lips were puffy and engorged, and he could see the firm peaks of her nipples beneath the cotton blouse. Undetectable to a normal human nose, her natural bodily scents had changed too, as they always did when she was aroused.

"And, of course," continued Katie, smiling sexily, "that might leave you over the legal alcohol limit for driving home. Being an officer of the law, I'd have to insist you stayed the night."

"Well…" Quist grinned. "There are these mechanical inventions known as taxis…"

"No." She squeezed his hand tighter. "As I've just said, I'm afraid I'd have to insist."

Sometimes he felt guilty about the wolf pheromones – it was almost like spiking a girl's drink – and he'd never taken advantage of his supernatural attraction. Fortunately, he knew that Katie really liked him even *without* this bizarre aphrodisiac.

"Very well," he said, taking his trenchcoat from the chair. "Let's go."

Emptying their glasses and leaving the *Red Lion*, the couple turned left onto the deserted street of Walmgate, deserted save for a strolling fox, that noticed Quist and shot off into the distance. Surrounded by stunning Georgian buildings, the cobbled thoroughfare changes its name from Walmgate to Fossgate as it crosses the River Foss via an ornate humpback bridge just ahead of them. Having wound south through the northern suburbs of York, this waterway flows through the city centre here on its way to the confluence with the Ouse.

"Where are you parked?" asked Katie, holding Quist's hand as she walked up the gentle rise of the bridge pavement.

"Pretty much next to you," said Quist, gesturing to the narrow road ahead. Stars spangled the black winter sky between the rooftops. "I know where you usually leave your car, just up here at the end of Fossgate. I saw your BMW earlier and left mine near it."

"Okay," she nodded. "You can follow me back and…"

Quist's entire body stiffened. His accentuated hearing had picked up the sound of a car accelerating on the road behind them, right before the brutal crunch of rubber told him its tyres had mounted the kerb. Without a backward glance, he snatched hold of Katie, scooping her in his arms and springing up onto the shoulder-high parapet of the bridge. A black Audi hurtled past, its nearside wing mirror scraping on the stonework as it missed them by inches.

"What the…" gasped the inspector. She twisted in his tight grip to see the car leave the pavement and vanish at speed down Fossgate. "What the *fuck*!"

Still holding the woman, Quist jumped down from the stone balustrade and set her back on the ground.

"Was he pissed?" stammered Katie, shaking. "Or did that maniac just try to run us down on purpose?"

"Oh, I'm certain it couldn't have been intentional," lied Quist.

He had recognised the Audi saloon as one of the vehicles parked on the film set earlier and, for a split-second, he'd glimpsed who was driving. The man had glared angrily at him. It was Steve Lyle, the stuntman from the movie.

"Did you get the registration?" quizzed Katie.

"I'm afraid not." Quist lied again. "It all happened so fast."

He'd seen the number, but he wanted to question this man himself. Broken bones that swiftly healed were intriguing, but attempted murder was something else entirely. *Why on earth would this stuntman try to kill him?*

"Not to worry." She shook her head angrily and pulled out her phone. "There are CCTV cameras at either end of this road, so they'll definitely have a recording. Hang on a moment while I ring the station."

"Ah, of course." Quist concealed a grimace by scratching his nose. "Yes, that's great news."

He waited as Katie asked for a check on the footage and for the patrol cars to watch for any speeding black Audis, knowing that the people of York had nothing to fear. Steve Lyle had targeted him and he wouldn't be running down anyone else tonight. *Why would this stuntman attempt to kill him?*

"That was *amazing*," gushed Katie, finishing her call. Her heart still pounded as the realisation of what had just happened finally sank in. "This bridge handrail is over five feet high and yet you leapt up there without any problem. How the hell did you do that carrying *me*? Your reactions were… well, they were just unbelievable, and I honestly had no idea you were so strong."

"Well, I *do* work out a little," shrugged Quist.

"Thank you. I think you just saved my…"

"Honestly…" he smiled. "Don't mention it."

Pulling him close, Katie kissed him, sliding her tongue deep into his mouth. "I'm still trembling from shock," she whispered, "as I'm sure you can feel. I really think you should get me back to my place and do something to calm me down."

"If you insist," smiled Quist. "I'll have a think about the problem and see if any solution pops up."

* * * *

Chapter 7

Glued permanently to their phones, even the thickest of British schoolchildren are aware that something vaguely historical took place in 1066, although many aren't entirely sure *what*. Following the conquest of England in that year by the Norman King William and his French pals, the post of sheriff had been created in each of the counties to act as the chief law enforcement officer. The Sheriff of Nottingham clearly had a phenomenal publicist on his staff, as he's the only one that most people still remember.

Sheriff was a powerful position back in the day, especially in Yorkshire. Before they sliced up the county into the more manageable North, West, East and South areas, the land was unfeasibly vast and wild and the sheriff had to manage it all. Although the sheriffs still exist, the role is now purely ceremonial, much like the town mayors, so much so that 99% of Yorkshire folk are completely unaware that they actually *have* one.

The job obviously paid quite well in 1716, as it allowed John Bourchier, the High Sheriff of York in that year, to build Beningbrough Hall, the large redbrick mansion six miles to the north of the city.

Encircled by a meandering loop of River Ouse, this baroque stately home stands in open countryside, surrounded by gardens and countless acres of parkland. The grounds were covered in a layer of frost this bitterly cold Monday morning. The sun shone down from a cloudless sky, but the weak winter rays were doing little to turn the stark white meadows to green. It was nine o'clock and the A19, running from York to Thirsk, was now mostly free of its morning commuter traffic. Quist turned off this main road in his blue Ford and onto the rural lane that passes through the village of Beningbrough. He puffed on a cigarette, with his side window cracked open to draw out the tendrils of smoke.

"So it was definitely the stunt guy?" said Watson, chomping his way through a bag of crisps in the passenger seat. "You're *sure* it was him?"

"Absolutely," nodded the detective, cruising along the twisting driveway towards the mansion. "The Audi he drove was parked with three other identical black saloons on the film set earlier. They're probably lease vehicles hired for the duration of the Yorkshire shoot."

"You're saying he must have followed you from Walmgate Bar and he tried to run you down on purpose?" The youth shook his head. "But why would he do that? He'd only just met you and you tried to help him. Maybe he recognised you from one of your past cases? Maybe you gathered together some nasty shit on him for a divorce or something?"

"No, I don't believe so," said Quist.

"So why would he try and flatten you with the car?"

"I have no idea," admitted the detective, "but I intend to find out very shortly."

Watson crunched thoughtfully on a large crisp. Attempted murder would probably alarm most *normal* people, but his boss was far from a normal person and this certainly wasn't the first time some stranger had attempted to kill him. Strictly speaking, Quist hadn't even been a *person* for more than two-hundred years. The werewolf was an immortal creature, and silver, fire and decapitation were the only ways to destroy it.

The detective turned left and entered a long driveway leading straight up to the splendid two-storey frontage of Beningbrough Hall. He smiled with serene pleasure to see how the morning sunshine highlighted the orange and cream colours of the brick and stone, then shuddered as Watson crammed seven crisps into his mouth and chomped down hard. The property had been acquired by the *National Trust* in 1958 and opened to the public as a museum. To supplement its income, the trust allowed filming both inside and around the great house. Various television series and cinema movies had used this attractive location and, arriving here just two days ago, the latest production was *Howl of the Wolfman*.

"Cool place, if you're into this kind of historical crap," said Watson, holding out his crisp bag. "Where are my manners? You want one of these, Guv? They're cheese and onion."

"Thank you, but no." Quist gave a quirky lopsided smile. "They may not be beef or bacon flavour, but I'm afraid they still contain whey and milk-derived flavourings."

"Oh, right." His assistant squinted to read the ingredients. "Well, you live and learn, eh?"

To control his dark supernatural side, Quist couldn't consume meat or *anything* containing animal products. A strict regime of veganism and yoga meditation allowed him to manage the ferocious lupine urges – veganism and the overriding rule of *never* taking a human life.

Just before reaching the mansion, the driveway swept left again and opened out into a large car park surrounded by trees. The entire eastern half of this had been taken over by the film crew and several deluxe trailers of varying sizes were parked beside a multitude of vans, electrical generator units and canteen trucks. A six-foot fence of metal mesh, far more substantial that the temporary cordon at Walmgate, separated this busy area from the "normal" section of car park.

"Look, there's Toni," said Watson, as Quist pulled up beside the fence.

Finishing his snack, he pointed to where the girl stood inside the production area leafing through a folder of notes. She wore the yellow puffer jacket from the previous evening and a black baseball cap sporting the *Candlemass Productions* logo.

"Cool," murmured the youth, his heart beating excitedly.

"Wow, doesn't she look sexy in that hat? Kind of like a gorgeous pixie, what with that little pointed nose and those big brown eyes."

Rolling his *own* eyes, Quist climbed from the car, stamped out his cigarette and tugged on his black leather trenchcoat.

"Oh, hello there." Toni beamed and walked over, nodding to the security officer who stood guard on the fence gateway. "It's okay, Matthew, you can let these two in. They're with me."

"Good morning," said Quist, blowing warmth into his hands as he walked through. He glanced up as a flock of yapping jackdaws passed by overhead. "A cold day for filming, isn't it?"

"You aren't kidding," grinned Watson, brushing crisp debris from his red denim jacket. "I just saw a brass monkey with a welding torch over there in the trees. It was fixing its bollocks back on."

"Charming," muttered Quist. "I really must apologise for…"

"No, that's funny." Toni laughed. "I told you last night, I really like your humour."

"Perhaps you'd *really like* him as your assistant?" suggested Quist.

"I could think of much worse things," said Toni, smiling at the youth. "You're very open and carefree, aren't you? You don't worry about what you say, so long as it's jokey. It's really good to laugh and sometimes it's nice to dream about what might have been."

"Huh?" said Watson.

"Nothing." Toni shook her head. "Like you, I'm talking without thinking."

Quist gestured to the fleet of trailers. "I have to say, Miss Nelson, it's very good of you to invite us here, although I can't imagine why you did. Won't you get into trouble for us being on the set?"

"It's Toni," she smiled. "Let's have none of that *Miss Nelson* nonsense, please. Depending on the schedule, we're allowed to invite guests and that's what you are – my guests. As I said last night, it's the least I could do after you raced over to help Steve Lyle." She handed over two lanyards with visitor passes dangling from them. "Pop these on, would you? It'll stop the security team, or anyone else, questioning who you are."

The detective slipped the tape around his neck, but knew she hadn't really answered his question. *Why had she invited them here? Also, why wasn't this girl reacting in any way to his lupine pheromones? He wasn't complaining, but by now, any female in his presence would normally be sexually aroused.*

Watson wasn't overly concerned with the reason. "This is brilliant," he gushed, excitedly. "I can't believe I'm on the actual set of a Kitten Maye horror movie... and with a stunningly attractive guide too."

"So, Toni, you're the film editor?" said Quist. "Clearly I'm no expert, but I thought the editor's work began when the movie was completed?"

"Not at all," said Toni, laughing at Watson's *stunningly attractive* description. "At the end of every day's filming, the director and I view the scenes and edit them down accordingly. To be honest, I'm not really needed on set, but I like to be there to watch and get preliminary ideas for this later editing process."

"What's happening today?" asked Watson, gazing at the girl. *Yes, there was definitely something about Toni Nelson and he really liked it.* "Last night was your first York shoot and today you're filming here at Beningbrough?"

"That's right," said Toni, "although we're still finding our feet and dressing the sets. This trailer camp and everything else you'll see was set up for us last week, but the main crew and cast only arrived here from Luxor two days ago."

"Is the hall closed to the public?" asked Quist, glancing at the empty car park beyond the cordon fence.

"For the moment." Toni nodded. "*Candlemass* negotiated a

deal with the *National Trust* and we have the place to ourselves for a full two weeks for the interior scenes. This morning we're shooting in the library."

"That makes a change," grinned Watson. "They usually shoot *outside* mansions like this. You know, blasting pheasants and grouse out of the sky with shotguns."

"Very true," agreed Toni. "As you're probably aware, this is a period drama, set in the year 1900, and it's great that we can use all those wonderful historic details inside the hall. In the story, Beningbrough is Lord Hardacre's house and his eldest son, Miles, is the werewolf. He returns to his ancestral home after being bitten in Egypt."

"Great," said Watson. "So that would have been Miles jumping around on Walmgate Bar last night? The werewolf who gracefully fell off the roof?"

"That was him," confirmed Toni, laughing again at his humour. "That accident scared the hell out of me. The actor Kris Horsley plays Miles the wolfman in his human form, with Steve Lyle in the costume when he becomes the monster."

"So how's he feeling today?" asked Watson, glancing at Quist. "I know he seemed okay after the fall, but all kinds of crazy medical shit can happen later – concussion and brain bleeds and stuff."

"Absolutely," agreed Quist, shuddering. "*All kinds of crazy medical shit*. Speaking of which, I'd like to have a chat with him this morning, if that's alright?"

"Steve?" Toni nodded. "What do you want him for?"

"I've always been interested in movie stunt work," lied the detective. "Is he around here somewhere?"

"Well, Hayley Eden is his girlfriend," said Toni. "She's the make-up artist that you saw on the set last night. They're sharing a trailer together. As there are no stunts planned for today, that's where you'll probably find him. I'll take you over there later."

"Right now would suit me better," said Quist. "If that wouldn't be too much trouble?"

"Bernard Quist and John Watson?" The dour voice came from beyond the security fence. "Well, I never expected to find *you* here, but where you two are concerned, nothing really surprises me."

The pair turned to see a young Indian man in a grey suit and black overcoat locking a Volkswagen saloon by Quist's Ford.

"Did you order a takeaway?" whispered Watson.

"Rather amusing," murmured Quist, smiling thinly. "But I believe that could also be construed as borderline racism."

"Only if he heard me," shrugged Watson.

They'd met Tariq Aslam several times in the past and knew that he was the sergeant on Katie Bradstreet's detective team. Quist concealed a bitter sigh. After last night's exhibition of stunt driving on Foss Bridge, he knew the police would be showing up at Beningbrough, but he'd purposely set off early this morning to question Lyle himself before anyone arrived. *Clearly, this wasn't early enough.*

"Good morning," said Toni. "Can I help you?"

"Hopefully." Aslam walked to the cordon fence, showing his police ID to the girl and security guard. "I'm looking for a vehicle. It's a black Audi lease car from a York company registered to *Candlemass Productions* at this address." Entering through the gate, he handed Toni a sheet of paper with a registration number.

"We have four Audis here on site," said Toni. "They're all black. But what's this about?"

"It almost killed a police officer," said Quist. "Not to mention myself." He nodded to Aslam. "As I'm sure Inspector Bradstreet will have told her sergeant this morning, the car was travelling at a ludicrous speed on the pavement."

"Good God," muttered Toni, her eyes wide.

"Oh, don't worry. We were both unharmed." Quist smiled at the girl. "It happened shortly after the Walmgate filming concluded yesterday evening. Sergeant Aslam here will have identified the vehicle on the street camera footage and he now needs to know who was driving."

"Thank you," said Aslam, sarcastically. "I don't know how I could possibly have explained that without your help."

"Hey, don't put yourself down," grinned Watson. "I'm sure you could have managed."

"Er, *right*," said Toni. Noticing the slight tension between the three, she cleared her throat. "Those lease cars are all parked over here."

Quist and Watson followed Aslam as Toni led the way past the canteen unit and through an assembly of large white vans.

The sergeant turned. "There's no need for you to accompany us," he pointed out, frowning. "You *do* realise this is official police business?"

"Don't worry," said Quist. "I've no intention of stepping on any toes. By the way, it's good to see you again. You should know that your inspector speaks very highly of you."

"Yes, she seems quite *enamoured* by you too," muttered, Aslam, dryly. "Each to their own, I suppose."

"Here we go," said Toni. Arriving at a line of black Audis, she checked the registration and opened one of the doors. "This is it."

"Indeed," agreed Quist, quietly. He noticed the wing mirror scratch marks from the stone parapet of Foss Bridge.

"Each vehicle has its own logbook." Toni took a book from the glove compartment. "Everyone who uses the car enters their details in here – name, date, mileage and…" She shook her head. "Ah, that's odd. Whoever took it out yesterday hasn't filled it in."

"Hello there," said Watson, all thoughts of logbooks erased by the sight of Kitten Maye walking towards them. She wore a warm

Candlemass Productions jacket over her Victorian filming costume. "Nice to see you again, Kitten. Could I say you're looking fabulous. It would be great if I could get a selfie photo with you."

The actress ignored him. "I overheard you talking," she said, smiling at Quist and treating him to a sexy pout. *Unlike Toni, the supernatural wolf pheromones were clearly working just fine with this girl.* "I can tell you *exactly* who was driving that car last night."

Two-hundred yards away, Steve Lyle stood watching grimly from the window of his trailer.

* * * *

Chapter 8

"Who the hell *is* this bastard?" muttered Lyle, shaking his head. "He's obviously come here searching for me with some cop." Staring through the tinted window of his trailer, he drew deeply on a cigarette and tugged down the blind. "They're speaking to Maye over by the car I used. I might have known that little bitch would open her mouth."

"What are you mumbling about?" asked Hayley Eden.

"I'm talking to myself," said Lyle. "Don't let it worry you."

"Are you okay, Stevie?" The girl wore a tight black T shirt and jeans, and rummaged through a drawer, searching for her phone charger. "You look like you've seen a ghost."

"No," he sighed. "From the way he's acting, one of them would appear to be a police officer, not a ghost. He's with the man from the film set last night and I believe they both want to speak with me."

"Huh? What man?" Hayley looked puzzled. "And what would a cop want with you, Babes?"

"I have a good idea." Lifting the corner of the blind to peer out again, Lyle pulled a sour face. "But it's nothing that should concern you."

"Um… *right*."

Knowing Stevie as she did, Hayley guessed this police matter would be something to do with the possession of white powder. *For someone who believed in really taking care of his gym body, Stevie was quite partial to a few lines of coke. Strangely enough, he'd recently started smoking too – something he'd always detested in the past.*

"I meant to ask you…" She took out a small device similar to an electric shaver. "What *is* this thing? I found it here in the drawer last night."

"Oh, that?" Lyle turned to see it. "It's a stun gun – a sort of handheld Taser. They're illegal in Britain, but he bought it in Egypt and thought it would be fun to smuggle it back in the film props."

"*He*?" echoed Hayley, puzzled. "*Who* bought it?"

"Sorry, I was distracted by the policeman out there. I mean *I* bought it." Stubbing his cigarette in the ashtray and taking the weapon from her, Lyle thumbed the switch and watched the electricity sizzle blue between the twin prongs. "Actually, I think this will come in very useful."

"Whatever," shrugged Hayley. "But if a cop's looking for you, maybe you'd better stay in here out of the way."

Pouting sexily, she swished back her blonde hair. *It was really weird, but Stevie had been acting and speaking differently over the last few days, ever since he was knocked unconscious in the Luxor accident. It was definitely a change for the better. He'd been far more charismatic and dynamic. Crazy as it sounded, and despite the new habit of smoking, he even appeared to be more intelligent and knowledgeable. Then there was his increased sex drive; the sex had always been good before, but now it was out of this world.*

Hayley walked towards him. "When the cop calls, I'll answer the door and say I haven't seen you, Babes." Smirking, she unzipped her jeans. "Now, Stevie, I wonder what we could do to pass the time while you're hiding out from the law?"

"Oh, I know precisely what we can do." The stuntman gave her a feral grin. "Sleep tight… *Babes*."

The girl collapsed in an unconscious heap as Lyle pressed the crackling stun gun against the side of her neck.

* * * *

Steve Lyle's trailer wasn't the largest on the car park, but it was definitely pretty cool, decided Watson. *It was certainly better than the Skipsea caravan on the Yorkshire coast where he'd holidayed as a kid with his mum and her various boyfriends. Instead of a plastic bucket in the wardrobe, this one looked like it probably had a fully functioning bathroom.*

Toni knocked on the door and Hayley Eden appeared in her blue jeans and a black *Candlemass Productions* T shirt. Massaging the side of her neck, she looked them over.

"Morning, luv," grinned Watson. "We're looking for the stunt guy you're dating. White teeth, muscles and tattoos – looks like he should be on an episode of that reality show: *Hunky Essex Dates*."

"If you don't mind?" snapped Aslam, stepping in front of him and producing his police ID. "I need to speak to Steven Lyle. I understand this is where he…"

"Toni, thank God you're here." Clearly flustered, Hayley snatched the girl's arm and hurriedly beckoned them all inside. "I was just about to go fetch someone. There's something wrong with Steve. He's acting really weird and I don't know what to do."

The three men followed the editor up the trailer steps to find Steve Lyle perched on the edge of a couch, his suntanned features now ashen and glistening with a sheen of perspiration.

"Whoo, are you okay, mate?" quizzed Watson, concerned. "You look like shit that's been warmed up in a microwave."

"*What?*" Lyle grabbed Hayley's hand. "Who are these men? Why are they here?"

"Don't worry," she reassured him. "They're here to help."

"How are you feeling?" asked Toni, dropping to her knees in front of the stuntman. She felt the temperature of his clammy brow and checked his pupils. "I've got to say, Steve, you really don't look good."

"Yeah, I feel kind of weird." Visibly trembling, Lyle shook his head. "No, I feel *really* weird. This is crazy and I don't know how to explain it…" He looked around. "But I don't know where I am."

"What do you mean?" asked Toni.

"I can't understand it." Lyle laughed, but the dry sound was devoid of any amusement. "It's like I've just woken up and I can't seem to remember anything. I'm trying, but it's making me dizzy and I just *can't*."

"*Anything?*" repeated Quist. He noticed how Hayley was gazing curiously at him. "Do you know your name or your…"

"Of course I know my name." The stuntman laughed again. "I'm Steve Lyle. I remember everything…" He frowned. "Everything except for the past few days."

"That's convenient," grunted Aslam, flashing his ID again. "So I take it you don't recall speeding through York last night in that Audi out there?"

"Do you think he's making this up?" snapped Hayley, sitting beside her boyfriend and taking his hand as she continued to watch Quist with interest. "He's obviously ill or something. I mean, just look at him sweating and shivering."

"I don't know where I am," repeated Lyle, looking around anxiously. "I don't recognise this trailer or anything outside that window. Oh, my God, this is really freaking me out."

"Please try to remain calm," purred Quist, seeing the man's escalating agitation. "Tell us, what would be the last thing you *do* remember?"

"Er…" Lyle concentrated for several seconds. "The temple in Luxor where we were filming. I remember preparing for the night stunt there and the accident when I slipped off the wall and…"

"The Luxor accident," gasped Toni. "But that was five days ago."

"*Five days?*" Lyle gripped his head in both hands. "This is impossible. Yes, I remember the accident and then just… and then just *blackness*. It's as if I fell asleep in the temple that night and then woke up here a few minutes ago. Wherever *this* is."

"Believe it or not, you're back in Britain," said Quist. "We're just outside York."

"I don't like this," said Toni. Still kneeling beside Lyle, she pressed her fingers to the side of his throat, checking his racing carotid pulse, before turning anxiously to Hayley. "This is exactly how Lisa was."

"Someone else was acting this way?" asked Quist, intrigued.

"Lisa MacNeil," explained Toni. "She was working with us in Luxor as the script supervisor. Lisa, Hayley, Steve and I used to hang out together. After Steve's accident there, Lisa suddenly found she couldn't remember anything from the previous week. She had the same dizziness and shivering fits too."

"Why would some other person's accident affect her in that way?" asked Watson, puzzled.

"Who knows?" shrugged Hayley. "But yeah, the producer called it a mental breakdown and flew her back home." Frowning curiously at Quist and Watson, she took a cigarette from Lyle's pack, broke off the filter tip and lit it. "Who are you, by the way? I noticed you were both on the York set last night."

"They're detectives," said Toni.

"I think you'll find that *I'm* a detective," snorted Aslam. "These two are private eyes."

"Consultant detectives," corrected Quist.

The sergeant sighed. "Well, I don't understand anything about amnesia," he said. "But I can see that you're not faking this, Mister Lyle, and you're obviously in no fit condition to be interviewed. I think you need medical help as soon as possible."

"He's right, Steve," agreed Toni. "We should explain this to the producer and then get you to a hospital." She took his arm. "Come on. If you're feeling dizzy, let Hayley and I help you up."

"I don't understand amnesia either," said Watson. "Probably because I've never had it." He nudged Toni. "Or maybe I *have* had it and I've forgotten."

"Yeah, very funny," smiled the editor. "I'm afraid I'll be

needing those visitor passes back." She led the unsteady Steve towards the trailer door. "Not for cracking poor jokes, but because I'm going to be busy with my friend here. I'm sorry you've had a wasted visit."

"No, not at all," said Quist, handing her his lanyard. "We fully understand; of course we do. I just hope Mister Lyle is all right."

"You go on ahead with Steve," said Hayley, drawing on her cigarette. "I'll follow in a moment, but first I need a quick chat with these two guys."

"You're smoking?" Lyle noticed her cigarette for the first time as he walked out with Toni and Aslam. He frowned curiously and nodded to the packet and lighter on the table. "What the hell? I've never seen you with a cigarette before."

"Seriously, Steve?" Hayley smiled thinly. "Haven't you just been telling us all about your weird memory loss?" She waited until the three had left the trailer before turning to Quist and taking his hand. "So you two are private investigators?" she asked, gripping firmly. "Well, how fortunate is that for me? As luck would have it, I need to find someone."

"You've come to the right guys," said Watson, winking. "So you're talking about a missing person?"

"Not exactly *missing*." Hayley puffed on her cigarette. "I'm aware that this man lives in Yorkshire, but I don't know where. I want to track down his home address as quickly as possible."

Quist wondered why she was squeezing his hand. No signs of sexual arousal were present, so it was nothing to do with his lupine pheromones. Her pupils hadn't dilated, her lips weren't engorged and her bodily scents remained normal. Just like Toni Nelson, Hayley Eden was weirdly unaffected by his close proximity. He watched her smoking, then glanced at the stubs in the table ashtray and raised a curious eyebrow.

"Have you tried the internet?" Watson felt silly the moment

the question left his lips. *A girl like this would be online almost permanently.* "You know – social media and stuff?"

"Of course," she said. "But there's very little information about him online and no sign of any address. It's a man named Slaney who…"

"Gabriel Slaney?" asked Quist.

"Ah." Hayley narrowed her eyes. "So apparently you know him?"

"I'm aware of him," admitted Quist. "He's certainly known to the police. He has…" He groped for a polite way to phrase it. "Strong *connections* with the organised crime fraternities of the north."

"So Slaney is a criminal?" said Hayley. "Damn, that will make him much harder to locate."

Quist nodded. "Those sort of people tend to have a limited internet presence and I doubt you'll find any home address online."

"Ooh, a shady character?" drawled Watson. "What do you want him for?"

The girl drew on her cigarette and smiled tightly. "It's a private matter."

"Okay." The youth shrugged. "Well, if he's a villain, maybe you should be speaking to the *proper* cops instead of us? The Indian guy out there, for instance."

"The police?" Hayley frowned. "Ah, yes, of course. They have extensive records on all the local criminals, don't they?"

"They do indeed," agreed Quist. "But I don't think Sergeant Aslam will give out any private information without a very good reason."

"No, I don't imagine he would," said Hayley, thoughtfully. Leading them out of the trailer, she gestured to the perimeter fence. "Well, thank you both for that. The security guard on duty over there will let you back into the public car park. Right now, I have to go and make sure my boyfriend Steve is okay."

Quist stroked his large nose. *Hayley Eden seemed far more articulate today than the shallow make-up artist they'd encountered at Walmgate Bar.*

"Fascinating," he murmured, watching her walk away towards the hall.

"Huh?" His assistant watched too. "You mean her arse?"

"I mean everything about her." Quist nodded slowly. "And Steven Lyle too. I must say, Watson, this is becoming far more intriguing than I could ever have imagined."

* * * *

Chapter 9

The two-storey Beningbrough Hall had no shortage of rooms. Most of the ones on the upper floor now served as public art galleries, but the ground floor had everything one would expect to find within a mansion – morning room, drawing room, evening room, library and even a *smoking room*. The majority of these would soon feature in *Howl of the Wolfman*, but one of the chambers at the rear of the mansion had been temporarily adapted for use as the central production office.

Opening onto the gardens, a pair of French doors supplied plenty of daylight and the producer's large desk stood in the centre of a vintage Indian carpet. Brandon Massey sat fuming in the leather chair behind this, alongside Tariq Aslam, with Toni Nelson and Steve Lyle sitting opposite.

"What the fuck are you talking about?" snapped Massey. His harsh Cockney accent always sounded intimidating, but now it was openly hostile. "You're telling me that you can't remember *anything* since you had your accident in Egypt?"

The film producer's wristwatch was Swiss, but his designer tinted spectacles, silver-grey suit and shoes were all Italian. Peculiar choices for a sixty year-old Londoner who firmly believed that all those bloody foreigners in Britain should be sent back to their *own* country.

"I'm told it's five days since that night in Luxor." Lyle shook his head. "I remember being on the temple wall and I can remember the sickening sensation as I fell, but that's it. To me, the days since then are a complete blank."

"You were only stunned for a short while," said Massey, scratching at his bald head. "Moments later you were okay. You've been acting perfectly normally ever since, so how come you suddenly have amnesia this morning?"

"I don't know," moaned Lyle.

"So you don't remember last night?" snapped the producer. "When you fell again at Walmgate Bar?"

"*What*?" Lyle trembled in his seat. "You're telling me I had *another* accident yesterday? Well, maybe that's it? Maybe I cracked my head and that somehow…"

"For fuck's sake," hissed Massey, human understanding and compassion outweighed by thoughts of production insurance and eye-watering law suits. "This is absolutely ridiculous. Have you been taking something? Prescription medication or something illegal?"

"No, of course not." Lyle sat shivering. "I'd never dream of using…"

"No, of course you wouldn't." Toni squeezed the stuntman's arm. "Steve could be right about hitting his head," she said. "Perhaps this is all something to do with yesterday's fall? Some sort of fugue state brought on today by the shock from the…"

"Fugue state?" echoed Massey, glaring. "Are you an editor or a doctor? What the hell is that medical shit supposed to mean?"

"I don't know," admitted Toni. "I don't understand these things, but you can see that Steve isn't making this up and I just thought that maybe…"

"And now the police are involved." Massey gestured to the sergeant. "He claims you were driving one of our cars in York last night."

"Driving dangerously at speed," added Aslam, nodding. "You almost ran down two people, but you can't remember that?"

Closing his eyes, Lyle shook his head.

"I see." The producer's eyes narrowed suspiciously behind his blue-tinted spectacles. "Come to think of it, that ginger continuity girl was there when you fell in Luxor. What was her name?"

"Lisa MacNeil," said Toni. "The script supervisor."

"That's right," nodded Massey. "In fact, she was the first

person to try to help you that night and she had her weird fit just afterwards. She was shivering like a shitting dog and moaning that she couldn't remember anything, exactly like you're doing now."

"That's true," said Toni. "You had to fly Lisa home, but what are you saying?"

"Who knows?" Massey shrugged. "Maybe Steve remembered how she was and thought that playing this fucking amnesia card might be a good way of getting himself out of a coked-up dangerous driving charge."

Lyle began to gently weep.

"I told you to get yourself checked by a doctor," snarled the producer. "But you ignored me. You took a car and set off driving straight after your accident. *Anything* could have happened. Someone could have been killed."

"Someone almost was," pointed out Aslam.

"I don't remember," sobbed Lyle.

Gritting his teeth, Massey sighed. "Actually, I'm inclined to believe you. There's obviously something mentally wrong with you. Do you have any idea how this will affect our insurance? What do you think the investors will say when they find out the main stuntman has had *two* accidents and he's now gone loopy?"

Toni placed a comforting hand on Lyle's back as the sobbing continued.

* * * *

Hayley Eden stood in the corridor outside the producer's office, listening quietly at the closed door with arms folded. Jordan Coley and Charlie Wilsden, two of the production electricians appeared by her side. These young men were always together, hanging around the female crew members and chatting to them whenever a break presented itself in their work. Both wore baseball caps and denim jackets. The grubby cap, coupled with his gaunt features, straggly hair and beard, gave Coley the look of someone who cooked

67

crystal meth in an Everglades shack.

"Well, helloooo, Blondie," he said, leaning on the wall and grinning. "We hear tell your boyfriend's up to his neck in the shit? Oh, dear."

"Yeah, what a shame," said Wilsden, smirking. He had the same greasy hairstyle, but had also cultivated a thick moustache that belonged on the upper lip of a 1980s porn star. "I always liked Steve."

"Me too," lied Coley, sliding a hand down the rear of his jeans to scratch at his rump as he spoke. "But when are you going to realise you're much too good for him. You deserve someone better, if you take my meaning?"

Hayley gazed icily at the two men. Ever since the filming began, both had been trying their luck with this make-up artist, but without any success. Hayley had explained that she was dating Steve Lyle, but this hadn't stopped them. Where good-looking women were concerned, this pair didn't take "no" for an answer, especially Coley, who had an upcoming court date to prove it.

"Hey Charlie." The technical supervisor popped his head around a door further down the corridor. "If you could leave the ladies alone for a few minutes…" He beckoned him over. "I need a hand with the sound system in the dining room. It's gone down again."

"Speaking of which…" joked Coley, as his friend left them.

"Yes, speaking of sexual acts," said Hayley, "why don't you go fuck yourself?"

"Hey, listen to all the shouting," chuckled the electrician, nodding to the closed door. "It sounds like your Stevie boy is getting a real bollocking from baldie Brandon. Wow, I wish I was a fly on the wall in there."

* * * *

Brandon Massey pushed his chair back from the desk and stood up, his stocky frame towering over the seated Lyle. "Okay, I've heard enough," he said. "You must know that you can't continue working on this production?" He glanced up as the office lights briefly dimmed. "What's the name of that other big guy on your team? He's the right size to fill that wolfman costume."

"Big guy?" muttered Lyle, flicking at his nose as a housefly danced annoyingly around it. "Do you mean Danny? Yes, Danny Rimmer is on the stunt team and he…" His teary eyes drifted down to the desk. "Hey, look at this."

"Huh?" The producer peered around. "Look at *what*?"

"This fly here." The weeping stuntman pointed a shaky finger. "It's acting really weird. It's been dancing about in front of my face and now it's running back and forth in front of me, like it's trying to get my attention."

"This is unbelievable." Massey snatched up a folder of papers and slammed them down hard, splattering the insect. "Memory loss, drunk driving and now we have hallucinations. Like I said, you're finished on this film, Steve."

Lyle began to sob harder, his body shaking more.

"Brandon, you can see he needs help," said Toni. "Instead of just firing him, maybe you should get him an ambulance."

"I agree," said Aslam, taking out his phone. "I'm calling one for this man right now and I'll follow it to the hospital."

"I wonder if I could tag along too?" Toni stared in horror at the squashed fly on the desk, then turned to the producer. "Steve's more than a colleague, he's a friend, and I want to make sure he's all right."

"Yeah, I suppose we can spare you," sighed Massey. "You're not really needed until the end of filming. Take one of the Audis, but try not to go driving it on any pavements, okay?"

* * * *

Chapter 10

The hardened jailbirds of Alcatraz, and those languishing in the disease-ridden penal colony of Devil's Island, could never have imagined that these hellholes would one day be popular holiday destinations. The inmates of York Prison would have been equally astounded to know that, along with the Minster and the Railway Museum, their bleak gaol is now one of the city's top tourist attractions. Parents take their children around the forbidding cells and play with them in the enclosed rear yard where more than 160 people were hanged on the scaffold that was once sited there.

The English language is notoriously difficult to master and sometimes it's easy to understand why. After hanging something like a painting, the picture is said to have been *hung*. Men executed on a gallows are said to have been *hanged*. A man being hung is something else entirely.

York Castle was built by William the Conqueror in 1086 following the Norman invasion, one of his many northern outposts designed to subdue the unruly Saxons. Apart from Clifford's Tower – a superb fortification of gleaming limestone on a manmade conical hill – and a few sections of ruined wall, very little remains of this medieval stronghold. The current structures on the castle site, one prison for debtors and another for women, were constructed in the 1700s using the stones from the fortress. Positioned around a wide circular lawn, both buildings are quite ornate and, externally at least, resemble classic mansions rather than gaols. One now houses the *York Crown Court*, but the remaining buildings were given over to the *Castle Museum* which opened its doors to the public in 1938.

Instead of following Lyle's ambulance to the hospital, Toni Nelson had driven straight here from Beningbrough, leaving her Audi on the museum car park and hurrying to the museum entrance.

"This can't continue," she muttered to herself. She pictured the dead fly crushed on the film producer's desk and shuddered with horror. *And last night a police officer had almost been killed.* "No, I have to end this as soon as possible."

The girl entered the glass-fronted lobby and looked around. The museum was busy for a Monday lunchtime in March, but although she'd visited this place once before, Toni had yet to learn that York is *always* busy, with international tourists flocking to the city and its many attractions throughout the year. Noticing the young couple queuing arm-in-arm in front of her at the cash desk, she watched the man fondly stroking the girl's hair and briefly wondered how it must feel to be so relaxed and happy. Her thoughts turned to the young man she'd recently met.

Watson seemed really nice. How amazing would it be to go out for an evening with him in the beautiful city of York? To laugh and joke freely with him, without a care in the world. Perhaps to spend the night making love? But no, that could never happen, could it? She'd had relationships, of sorts, before, but she'd never allowed them to become serious. How could she?

Purchasing a ticket, Toni rushed through the entrance corridor, ignoring the various cases of artefacts, to reach the museum's most famous exhibit. She paused to look around, smiling appreciatively.

Yes, nothing had changed here since her previous visit. It was almost as if she'd left the building and stepped outside through some sort of time travel portal.

This was the display known as *Kirkgate*, but the word *display* didn't do it justice. Dimly lit with antiquated gas lamps, an entire York street from the Victorian age had been meticulously constructed indoors. This large area of cobblestones had once been the prison's outdoor exercise yard for the women inmates, but now it was completely enclosed beneath a roof. A horse-drawn hansom cab, complete with a mannequin driver and an actual stuffed horse, stood in the middle of the street and countless Olde Worlde shops lined the pavements. Various members of the museum staff completed the scene, costumed guides who wandered around in period attire answering visitors' questions. Toni walked past a baker, a toy shop and a confectioner, to arrive at the apothecary with its collection of period jars, bottles and antiquated implements filling the window shelves. She was only interested in one item.

Thankfully, it was still there. Five inches in height, it stood on the top shelf amongst the other colourful containers, just as it had done when she tracked it down forty years ago – the small red bottle.

Toni took several photos on her phone, then walked inside the shop. The window shelves, she immediately noticed, were sealed off behind a glass partition and secured with a small padlock. It looked to be cheap and flimsy, and she wondered how difficult it would be to prise it off, slide back the glass and take the bottle. Such ideas were pointless. The man standing behind the counter would doubtless have something to say about her actions. Dressed in his white pharmacy coat, the middle-aged *actor* smiled at his visitor.

"Good day, young miss," he said, jovially. "And what can we do for you? Perhaps some opium-based laudanum for an aching back, rosemary for a skin condition, or maybe a nice herb poultice for an ankle sprain?"

"Er, no. I was wondering..." Toni gestured to the window. "Are any of these items for sale?"

"Everything's for sale, young lady," he chuckled. "Our job is to cure you of your horrible ailments and..."

She shook her head. "No, I mean could I actually purchase one of these items for *real*?"

"Oh, I see." Shrugging, the man dropped his pharmacist act. "Well, no, not really. It's a display, you see?"

"I appreciate that," said Toni. "But I'd be interested in paying a high price for one of the minor items. One of those little decorative bottles in your window."

"Well, I don't really know." He shrugged again. "To be honest, no one's ever asked me that before. The museum *might* be okay with it, but you'd need to speak to Karen Taylor. She's the manager who deals with all the acquisitions."

"It isn't *really* a museum acquisition, as such," said Toni. "I mean, it's simply window dressing... *literally* window dressing." She gave him a sweet smile and, although the shop was empty, she lowered her voice. "As I say, it's just a little bottle. I'm sure no one would ever miss it if you handed it to me right now. In return, I could hand you some money for the charity of your choice." She pulled a handful of banknotes from her pocket. "Um, shall we say two-hundred pounds?"

"I see." The man stiffened, suddenly offended. "Like I said," he snapped, "you need to go speak to Miss Taylor. The people on the front desk will contact her for you."

"Thanks for your time," muttered Toni, leaving the apothecary and heading back to the reception. "*Marvellous*. I've managed to find myself an honest man."

* * * *

Named after the thoroughfare that runs through it, the pleasant neighbourhood of Fishergate is filled with restaurants, Victorian inns, artisan bakeries, barbers and independent shops. Bernard Quist's detective agency faced the perimeter wall of York, standing just sixty feet across the main road from the white limestone ramparts. Office rental was more economical here than in the city itself on the other side of these medieval fortifications.

Checking her phone again for Quist's business address, Toni walked quickly along the busy street to the gymnasium that stood on the corner of Fishergate and Baker Avenue. *Jehovah's Fitness* claimed to be the only Christian gym in York and she peered wide-eyed at the poster on their glass door – a muscular Jesus performing pull-ups on the side bar of a large cross. Quist's detective agency plaque adorned the wall a few feet away, beside a second door that led to his office on the floor above.

Taking a deep breath to compose herself, Toni walked in, contemplating how best to approach this. *Ever since touching the detective's hand the previous evening, she'd known this moment would almost certainly arrive and she was unsure how things might go. Knowing she might need Quist's help, she'd invited him to Beningbrough today in an effort to ascertain his character. To be honest, he seemed okay – very different from others she'd met – but with someone like this, you could never be sure. Still, the time was ticking by, people were dying and this had to be done.*

Hearing the street door close behind the girl, one of the fitness centre staff members eagerly appeared in the passage like a trapdoor spider. According to his badge, this was Simon Baxter and *God loved us all.*

"Hi there," said Simon, with his usual *Stepford Wife* grin, the grin sported by all evangelical cults. "We're talking to people like yourself about Jesus."

"Sorry," said Toni, passing him by, "but I'm really not the sort of person you're looking for."

"I believe you'd be surprised," he said, smiling even wider.

"No, I believe *you* would be," corrected Toni, heading up the stairs. "If you knew me, you'd be *really* surprised."

"You won't find anything up there, but Godless heathens," he called out after her. Simon had failed miserably on his several attempts to bring Quist and Watson into the Evangelical fold. "Just heathens – trust me."

Toni reached the top of the steps and knocked on the frosted glass of the detective agency door. Watson opened it and his heart missed a beat.

"I don't believe this." Grinning excitedly, he ushered the girl inside. "So here you are again – my all-time favourite film editor. Did you follow us from Beningbrough or something? We only got back ourselves a short while ago."

"I'm afraid I need your help with something," she said, walking through the small reception area.

"Don't be afraid," said the youth. "I'm pleased to hear it."

Toni entered the main office where a Vivaldi concerto played on a small hi-fi, much to Watson's irritation. She saw the usual filing cabinets cupboards and central desk, and raised her eyebrows to see Quist sitting upon the latter, cross-legged with his arms outstretched behind his back.

"Hello again." She gestured to the detective's weird pose. "Er, are we practising yoga?"

Watson snorted. "Yeah, this is what passes for *normal* around here," he explained. "He's always doing it because it calms his mind apparently, just like this shit that he calls *classical music*. But let's talk about why *you're* here. Hey, you just can't keep away from me, can you?"

"How's your stunt performer colleague?" asked Quist, flexing his arms. "I assume Mister Lyle is still undergoing treatment at the hospital?"

Toni nodded. "I've just rung them for an update. They don't seem *too* worried about Steve's condition, but they've sedated him and he'll be kept in overnight for observation and tests." She cleared her throat. "Um, listen, I'm here because I have a problem and I really need your assistance. I wonder if you know of a lively pub or a coffee shop nearby? Somewhere we can talk?"

"*Lively?*" echoed Quist, slightly puzzled. He climbed down from the desk, stretched his slim body and slipped his shoes back on. "I know several places, but what's wrong with talking here in the office?"

"Shall I write you a list?" Watson grinned. "For starters, it's

75

small and grotty and we have no lager on draught."

"We have coffee over there on the windowsill," pointed out Quist. "Not to mention a bottle of single malt and glasses in the filing cabinet."

Watson nodded. "I refer my learned friend to my previous statement."

"Very well." The detective gave him a lopsided smile and reached for his trenchcoat. "A pub it is then."

* * * *

Chapter 11

According to the old rumour, perpetuated by those loud characters who prop up pub bars, a Freemason can walk into any English inn named the *Masons Arms* and receive a free drink. This is just an urban myth, of course, but that *other* rumour – about how Masons can escape drink-driving charges by giving the arresting officer a "funny handshake" – is another matter.

The *Masons Arms* in York stands at the northern end of Fishergate, hanging flower baskets decorating its Victorian frontage of brick, timber and limestone. Just a short walk along the street from Quist's office, the inn looked out onto the city wall and the medieval Postern Tower. The two large rooms inside were filled with Olde Worlde decorations and open fires warmed the lunchtime clientele. Quist paid for three half-pints at the lounge bar – a hoppy real ale for himself and lager for Watson and Toni – and carried them to the corner table where his assistant sat chatting to the girl.

"You need our help?" Watson smiled affectionately. "Well, to be honest, I could do with a little help myself and I'm wondering what you might suggest. Every time I see you, the hairs stand up on the back of my neck and I get a warm tingling in my tummy…"

"Those symptoms sound worrying," said Quist, passing Toni a drink. "Perhaps you should consult a doctor?"

"Thank you," she said, smiling awkwardly. "I could definitely use this."

Quist sensed an edginess that hadn't been present this morning and suspected it wasn't caused by his assistant's dire chat-up attempts. "Cheers," he said, clinking his glass against hers.

Watson frowned. "Where are the beef crisps I asked for?"

"I didn't get you any," said Quist, shrugging off his leather trenchcoat. "I don't want you loudly crunching away like a pig with an apple whilst we're speaking."

"Whatever," grunted the youth. "The sooner this detective agency gets an HR department, the better. Then I can report you for the mistreatment of your staff."

"So Mister Lyle is doing well?" said Quist, ignoring his assistant. "That's good news. Any change with his peculiar memory loss?"

"No, but there won't be," said Toni. "The amnesia that he's experiencing is exactly the same as Lisa MacNeil."

The detective nodded. "You mentioned this colleague of yours had a mental breakdown in Egypt?"

"That's how our producer referred to it." The girl appeared evasive. "He had her flown home and they hospitalised her in London. I've been keeping tabs on Lisa and, fortunately, she seems to be fine now, but a chunk of her memory remains completely missing. Over a week, in fact. Steve will be the same when he pulls through."

"I see." Quist sipped his beer. "It would appear that you know something about this odd condition?"

"I do," said Toni. "I have to tell you that Steve Lyle wasn't to blame for driving at you last night. He genuinely can't recall anything about…"

"Yes." The detective nodded. "I fully believed him when he told us that, but what exactly is wrong with him?"

"It's very difficult to explain," sighed Toni. "I can't really tell you too much about it at the moment, but let's just say he wasn't himself."

"You can't tell us?" said Watson. "Difficult to explain? This is all a bit mysterious, isn't it?"

"You say you need our help," pointed out Quist. "So why not tell us about *that* instead?"

Toni took a drink of lager. "You have a museum here in York," she said. "*The Castle Museum.*"

"It's just around the corner from this very public house,"

confirmed Quist. "It's housed inside the old prison buildings by Clifford's Tower."

She nodded. "Yes, I called there before coming to see you. There's a replica of a Victorian street in there with lots of old shops…"

"Kirkgate," said Quist. "It was named after the museum's founder, Doctor Kirk. It's quite atmospheric, isn't it?"

"Yeah, if you say so," mumbled Watson. "I'll be sure to pop this place on my bucket list."

"If you're familiar with it, then you must have seen the apothecary shop?" Toni took out her phone and showed him the photos she'd taken earlier. "This is in the front window – a little red bottle on the top shelf. It's one of the many items set out in there for colourful decoration."

"Mmh, it's quite ornate, isn't it?" The detective studied the phone images. "It looks like one of those Middle Eastern bottles sold in the markets and tourist outlets of Turkey and Egypt. For a few extra coins, the vendor will fill it with cheap perfume for you. But why would this interest you?"

"That doesn't matter." She took a deep breath. "I really need it urgently. I spoke to the museum staff about purchasing the bottle, but the only person who can authorise such a sale is away on holiday. The thing is, even if they agreed to sell it, the process would take far too long and I have to have it now. That's when I thought of *you*."

"Er, *right*…" Watson looked puzzled. "So what can *we* do about it?"

"Well…" Toni gestured to Quist. "I was rather hoping that *he* could, um, *acquire* it for me?"

"Oh, you mean *steal* it?" The detective smiled. "I must say, when you told us you needed our help with something, I certainly wasn't expecting *that*."

"Swiping things isn't the kind of stuff we do," chuckled

Watson. "We're private detectives, not burglars. Now if you've got a cheating boyfriend that you'd like us to follow, or..."

"This isn't a joke," sighed Toni. "It's very important. This bottle has no value to the museum. It's just one of the many similar items they bought in bulk – ornamental bric-a-brac to decorate those replica shop windows. They won't even miss it and..."

"Miss Nelson..." interrupted Quist.

"I'm certain you have the necessary skills to do this." The girl sat forward. "It's a fairly easy task and, believe me, you'll be paid *very* well for your help. More than you can imagine."

Quist gave her a lopsided smile. "You must know that there are several shops in town that sell ornate bottles just like this. There's an antique outlet on Stonegate, for instance, that..."

"Not bottles like *this* one," said Toni. "Just name your price."

"It isn't a question of money," said Quist. "You're asking me to do something highly illegal and, as Watson has pointed out, this isn't our line of work."

Toni sat for a long moment before gulping her drink. "I see," she said, quietly. "Time is pressing and I really *do* need that bottle. I was hoping you might help me willingly..."

"*Willingly?*" repeated Watson. "Um, that sounds a bit like a threat might be coming."

"Um, I wonder..." She turned to the youth. "I have to speak to your boss privately. I'm sorry, but could you leave us alone for a few moments?"

"Absolutely not," said Quist. "Anything you have to say, you can say in front of my assistant."

"Really?" Toni took a deep breath. "Even if I were to say something about your dark secret?"

"My *secret?*" Instantly stiffening, the detective paused for a long moment, his thoughts racing. "Yes, even *that*," he said, smiling tightly. *So this was the reason the girl had appeared tense.*

"As you wish." Toni glanced around the busy room and lowered her voice. "You're far more than you outwardly appear, aren't you, Mister Quist? You're a shapeshifter. Some would say a lycanthrope, or…" She leant closer. "A werewolf."

Watson laughed nervously. "Well, I reckon we can all agree he's a bit of an eccentric oddball, but what the hell makes you think *that*? Maybe you've been affected by that wolfman horror movie you're working on and…"

"No, I touched you," said Toni. "Last night, when we were removing that stuntman costume together, our hands touched and I could instantly sense it. Yes, Mister Quist, I know exactly what you are." She turned to Watson. "I asked you to leave us alone because I wasn't sure if you were aware or not."

"Er, *right*," said Watson, astounded. "So what are you? A psychic or some shit like that?"

"Some shit like that," nodded the girl.

"Ah, and this is why you wanted us to come here?" Quist looked around the crowded inn. "If I *were* a supernatural monster, then it would make sense to chat in the safety of a lively public place?"

"You seem really… *nice*," said Toni. "You're so different from the others like you that I've come across, but as you can imagine, I wasn't entirely sure how this conversation would go down. I assumed you wouldn't do anything, um *rash* in a crowded pub like this."

The detective smiled. "My dear young lady, I never do *anything* rash and I would certainly never dream of harming you in any way. Whatever I may or may not be, I'm most definitely not a monster."

"Yeah, you don't have anything to worry about," confirmed Watson. "He's just a big pussycat really… even when he's being blackmailed."

"Blackmail?" Toni grimaced. "What a horrible word."

"Oh, *right*," scoffed the youth. "So what would *you* call this?"

"I haven't threatened to expose his secret," said Toni, turning to gaze at the detective. "But if my possessing the knowledge of what you are can persuade you to help me, then I have to take the chance. I honestly don't like this situation one bit, but as I said, time is pressing and I really *do* need your assistance with this."

"You desperately need a worthless bottle?" Quist shook his head, puzzled. "But why?"

"I'm sorry," said Toni. "But I can't answer that right now."

"I love a good mystery as much as anyone," admitted Quist. "But if I were to put myself at risk in this way, then the least you could do is furnish me with some sort of explanation?"

Toni opened her mouth to speak, but thought better of it. "Look, it's imperative that I get hold of that bottle without delay. I apologise for the veiled threat, but will you please do this for me? I have to know... *please*."

"Very well." Seeing the girl's obvious distress, he nodded slowly. "Yes, I'll get you your enigmatic bottle and you can also forget about the fee. Truthfully, I can't imagine how I'd calculate a fee for such a bizarre service."

"Thank you," she sighed. "You really don't know what this means."

"No, we don't," grunted Watson, "because you've told us fuck all."

"Sorry." She shot the youth a tight smile. "As I said, I need it as soon as possible. Tonight would be ideal."

"As you wish," said Quist. "Tonight then, after the museum closes at five. I'll contact you as soon as I have it."

"Once again, thank you." Openly relieved, Toni climbed to her feet and tugged on her coat. "By the way, I believe you."

"Believe me?" echoed Quist.

The girl leant over the table, keeping her voice low. "You say you're not a monster and I know that to be the truth. Last night I sensed your secret and, after spending time in your presence, I'm now able to sense that you're not dangerous like the other shapeshifters I've met. But how can that be possible? How can you not be a killer seeing as how you're a, er…"

"A clean and healthy lifestyle," said Quist. "Something I would highly recommend."

"Um, okay." Toni smiled faintly. "And now I have to get back to Beningbrough. They think I'm with Steve at the hospital, and a certain person can't know that I've been here speaking with you."

"Unbelievable," muttered Watson, watching her leave and raising his eyebrows. "Well, that was all a bit unexpected, Guv."

"Yes, wasn't it?" purred Quist, stroking thoughtfully at his large nose.

"You agreed pretty quickly there. Are you really going to nick this bottle for her?"

"Don't be silly," said Quist, grinning. "Of *course* I'm going to steal it. This whole situation is incredibly intriguing, don't you think?"

Watson snorted. "Apparently *too* intriguing to charge her a fee for it."

The detective finished his beer. "She knows my *secret* and I'm very curious to see this mysterious bottle and to discover where all of this leads. What exactly *is* it and why would she need it so desperately that she has to go to such lengths?" He stood up and grabbed his trenchcoat. "Come along. I'll explain more on the way."

"Huh?" Watson drank his lager. "On the way where?"

"On the way to visit our good friend Lestrade."

* * * *

Chapter 12

Toni Nelson closed the front doors and walked through the entrance hallway at Beningbrough feeling decidedly uncomfortable.

Had she done the right thing? Bringing any outsider into this situation would be hazardous, but she'd just involved a werewolf. Unfortunately, she had very little time and nothing much in the way of a choice – she couldn't perform the robbery herself. Bernie Quist didn't feel in any way dangerous and his supernatural abilities should enable him to succeed at the museum. Being a lycanthrope, he might also be able to assist her further after this. What she had to do in the near future was going to be difficult and...

Toni shook her head. *No, it had been difficult the last time. This time, it would be close to impossible. Should she take the private detective into her confidence and explain everything to him?* She realised she may *have* to.

The entrance hall, with its collection of marble busts and sculptures, opened into a large adjoining hall that contained the mansion's main staircase. Toni found a small crowd gathered at the base of the wide oak steps, all tastefully illuminated by several portable spotlights. The film director, Joanna Marsh, and her female assistant stood talking with Kitten Maye and the young stunt performer Danny Rimmer. Kitten wore a blue Victorian negligée and the stuntman was dressed in the shaggy wolfman costume minus the fearsome headpiece.

"You're looking good, Danny," said Hayley Eden. The make-up artist held the toothy mask, combing the black fur into shape. "You're just as scary as Steve in that outfit."

Three lighting and sound operatives watched the dress rehearsal with interest, along with the smirking electrician, Charlie Wilsden. Wearing his usual baseball cap and chomping on gum, most of Wilsden's *interest* seemed to be centred upon Kitten's breasts and the way their fake pertness stretched the flimsy cotton nightie.

"Hey, how's Steve?" asked Joanna, as Toni approached the group. "What happened at the hospital?"

"Yes, how is he?" asked Hayley, gritting her teeth into a plastic smile. "I've been ever so worried."

"Er, yeah, he's okay," said Toni. Although she'd been too busy to actually visit the hospital, she'd gathered enough information on the phone. "The doctors still don't know exactly what's wrong with him, but the good news is they don't appear worried. They're talking about temporary amnesia brought upon by some sort of intense anxiety attack. He's been sedated and they're keeping him in overnight for observation." She gestured to Danny Rimmer. "I see you didn't waste any time in replacing him."

"Well, as someone once said…" shrugged Joanna. *"The show must go on.* In this particular case, it was someone with a Cockney accent and an eye fixed permanently on the film budget. We needed a man of Steve's size to fill the costume and we were fortunate that Danny was on the stunt team."

"I'll drive over to visit him later," said Hayley, smiling at Toni. "Tell me, where's that detective sergeant? I wanted to speak with him, but he left with the ambulance."

"Sergeant Aslam?" said Toni. "Why?"

"Oh, it's a private matter." Hayley's smile tightened. "Not to worry. I'll see him soon enough."

"Okay." Joanna turned back to Danny Rimmer. "Let's get the wolfman head in place and try a run-through to see how this looks. I'll need you to go up the stairs to the halfway turn, Danny. When I give you the cue, you'll walk menacingly down towards Kitten here at the bottom. Kitten can't move, as she's frozen to the spot in terror. I want to see arms and claws outstretched, kind of like an angler describing a really big fish."

"Er, okay… *right.*" The young stuntman frowned pensively.

"But as I'm filling in for Steve, you must know that I haven't yet learnt the part. I feel I ought to understand the wolf a little better. I'll need to know my motivation in this scene?"

"Your motivation?" The director gazed blankly through her large spectacles. "Danny, you're a junior stuntman in a fucking monster costume, not Olivier performing *Hamlet*. Your *motivation* is that you want to eat Kitten."

"Yeah." Chewing his gum on the sidelines, Charlie Wilsden grinned. "Don't we all?" he chuckled to himself.

Clamping the wolf head onto Rimmer's costume, Hayley combed the fur to conceal the fixings, and then left the group to take Toni to one side.

"Get ready," said the make-up artist, "because you're not going to believe this. I was going to phone to let you know, but then I decided to leave it as a nice surprise."

"A surprise?" quizzed Toni. "What do you mean?"

"This." Hayley nodded over the editor's shoulder. "A certain someone arrived here unexpectedly while you were away at the hospital."

"*Ryan*?" Toni turned, her eyes widening to see a young man appearing from the entrance hall behind her. "What the hell are *you* doing here?"

"What kind of welcome is *that*?" laughed Ryan Turpin, strolling over to hug her. Fair-haired and good-looking, he reminded most people of Freddie in *Scooby-Doo*. "What do you *think* I'm doing here, Baby? I'm working as a sound technician, of course."

"You know what I mean," sighed Toni, untangling herself from his arms. "You dumped me in Egypt. You flew back to England to work at the London studios, not the York locations."

Ryan pulled a pained expression. "Well, that was the original idea, but…"

"The *original* idea," snorted Toni, "is that you'd decided you wanted to be with your ex, Chelsee."

"Yeah, I hurt you, Baby." Ryan gazed with wounded puppy-dog eyes. "I know just how *much* I must have hurt you, but straight away, I knew that I'd made a stupid mistake – probably the worst mistake of my life. You're my fiancée and, even as I left Luxor airport, I couldn't stop thinking about you. Looking back now, it must have been some sort of temporary insanity that caused me to…"

"Ah, *right*." Toni nodded her understanding. "You mean Chelsee didn't want to know?"

"Look, we need to talk," grinned Ryan, softly stroking her face. "Of course we do. But the main thing is, I'm back. I'm here now to make it up to you. I've squared things with the producer, and I'm working here in Yorkshire to be with you. We're still engaged and I love you, Toni. I can't apologise enough for what I…"

"Yeah, yeah," laughed Toni, leaving the staircase hallway for the drawing room next door. "Be a good boy, Ryan, and just fuck off back to London, would you?"

Shrugging at the deflated man, Hayley followed Toni into the empty room. She found her at the trestle table that had been set out with refreshments for the cast and crew.

"Well, that was unexpected," said Hayley, watching the editor pour a coffee from one of the urns. "I thought you said Ryan Turpin was *the love of your life*? You were absolutely devastated when he left you in Luxor."

"Yeah, well…" Toni sipped at her steaming drink. "I suppose we all change, don't we?"

"I suppose we do." Eyeing her curiously, Hayley poured a coffee for herself. "But you were engaged to be married and I still can't believe you got over the relationship so quickly. It's only five days since you completely went to pieces. You even took an overdose because of him and…"

"Exactly," scoffed Toni, shaking her head. "What a ridiculous thing to do over a callous bastard like that. It was the third time Ryan had left me for another girl. He was supposed to be my fiancé, but this time, he told me he was going back home to ask Chelsee to marry him. To be honest, that stupid overdose was probably some sort of cry for help, but as soon as I'd puked up those sleeping pills, I realised I could have actually *died*. Believe me, Hayley, that really focuses the mind and I saw how absolutely crazy I'd been."

"Yeah, you *were* crazy, sweetheart," said Charlie Wilsden, who'd been listening in the doorway. Grinning widely, he walked over to the two girls. "After all, there are so many *other* guys that you could have your pick of."

Hayley laughed. "Ah, guys like *you*, you mean?"

"Full marks to Blondie," he grinned, twisting the peak of his baseball cap around to face backwards. "Yeah, guys like *me*. Here I am, ladies. I'm ready, willing and *very* able." He stroked his thick Velcro-like moustache. "The girls tell me this can really tickle, but I won't say *where* it tickles."

Toni shuddered slightly as a little vomit rose up in her gullet.

"By the way," said Wilsden, "you haven't seen anything of my mate Jordan, have you? The technical supervisor's been looking for him, but there's no sign of him anywhere."

"You mean the other electrician who always hangs around with you?" Hayley frowned thoughtfully. "Oh, Beningbrough is a big place and I'm sure he's buzzing around somewhere."

"You'll have to excuse me," said Toni, sickened by Wilsden's close presence. His warm body odour smelled a little like pork that had passed its sell-by date. "I have somewhere I need to be."

"Lovely," smirked Wilsden, turning to watch the editor's bottom as she left. "Just look at the way those cheeks move. It looks like her arse is chewing on a sweet."

"Nice observation," said Hayley, sipping her coffee. "So you like Toni, do you?"

"I like *all* attractive birds," corrected Wilsden, leaning casually on the table. "But, to be honest, she's definitely in the queue behind *you*. Listen, with Stevie boy gone, maybe you might see sense at last and come out for a drink with me?"

"Mmh, maybe," nodded Hayley. "Let's see how things go, eh? Tell me, where might our leading actress be in this queue for your sexual favours?"

"Kitten Maye?" laughed Wilsden. "Well, she's right at the front, of the line, naturally. But let's face it, there's more chance of me playing football for England than skewering *that*."

"Ooh, I wouldn't be too sure," said Hayley. "I've heard her asking about you."

"Yeah, *right*." The man's eyes narrowed as he realised she might actually be serious. "No, hang on a minute. You're joking, aren't you?"

"Not at all. When I have Kitten alone in the make-up chair, we always get to talking." Hayley lowered her voice to an erotic purr. "When us girls are by ourselves, we like to talk about men, if you take my meaning? Yesterday she asked me: who's the slim electrician with the amazing moustache?"

"Kitten Maye?" Wilsden glanced at the door and slowly licked his lips, like a lizard removing the debris from an insect lunch. "Jesus, what I wouldn't give to be inside *that*."

"Well, why not say it?" asked Hayley, stroking his chest. "You can't imagine how much I love to hear dirty talk. Why not say it for me – *I wish I was deep inside her*."

"Hey, I didn't know you were like this," chuckled Wilsden. "Yeah, you're a sexy little bitch, aren't you? Okay, just for you, Blondie – I wish I was deep inside her."

Outside the drawing room, Kitten waited at the bottom of the hall staircase, watching in terror as the wolfman approached her down the steps. The hall spotlights dimmed momentarily and the actress gasped, gripping her tummy with both hands.

"Hey, are you all right?" asked the director.

"Yes, it's nothing," said Kitten, stroking her midriff. "I just felt suddenly bloated, but whatever it was, the feeling's gone."

Inside, in the hot blackness of her abdomen, a tiny screaming electrician began to suffocate as the girl's stomach acid ate into his flesh.

Hayley Eden closed her eyes, took a deep breath and sighed with deep satisfaction. "Yes, soon," she whispered to herself, listening to the ever-present musical voice in her head. "I can hear you and I know you're very close. You're somewhere over to the west, aren't you? Soon we will be together at long last."

* * * *

Chapter 13

The famous thoroughfare known as *the Shambles* has wound through the heart of York for more than nine-hundred years, a narrow, cobbled route of enchanting timber-framed shops. *So* narrow, in fact, that the buildings perilously overhang the street below, allowing people to reach out from the upper storeys and shake hands across the gap. Medieval buildings were taxed by the crown on how much land space they occupied, meaning that many of the older York structures have small footprints, but extend out in lateral steps as they gain height.

Now a place of fairytale beauty, the original appearance of this street was horrifically different, especially for any vegans that may have been around back then. *Shambles* is an obsolete term for slaughterhouse meat market, and the raised pavements created a channel along which blood and offal once gushed downhill towards the River Ouse. These butcher shops are now ornate tourist outlets, and crowds of international holidaymakers fill the Shambles both day and night.

Quist and his young assistant made their way through the tourist throng towards St Andrewgate where Watson's friend Lestrade lived. York is such a compact city that it's easy enough to walk everywhere within the perimeter ramparts. This is probably just as well. Finding a teenage girl without a phone in her hand can sometimes be easier than finding a parking space.

"That was unbelievable," said the youth, shaking his head in annoyance. "To think I really liked her and she…"

"Watson," laughed Quist, "you like virtually every girl you meet."

"Yeah, well…" He shrugged. "I don't know why, but it felt to me like Toni was a little bit special, and then she tried to blackmail you. Well, if she thinks I'm going to sleep with her after that…"

"She seemed quite desperate, didn't she?" said Quist. "I don't mean with her friendliness towards you…"

"Yeah, yeah," chuckled Watson.

"But her desperation in wanting me to perform this peculiar robbery. To be truthful, I don't believe she *would* tell anyone my secret, but then again, who *could* she tell without them thinking her insane? Of course, the main question is *why*? Why would this young film editor be so desperate to acquire a supposedly worthless trinket? What exactly could it *be*?"

"Do you reckon she really *is* psychic?" asked Watson. "I mean, we've met genuine psychics before, haven't we? Do you believe she was able to touch your hand and know that you're a were…" Remembering he was in a busy street, he ended his sentence. "Then there was all that '*ooh, I can sense you're not dangerous*' shit."

"Well, she clearly knew *somehow*," said Quist. He slid his hands into the warm pockets of his trenchcoat as he negotiated his way through the crowd. "Yes, I believe our Miss Nelson has genuine empathic powers and she's able to sense such things. She also claims to have encountered other lycanthropes in the past, so one has to wonder where and when? Just who exactly *is* this young woman?"

Watson nodded. "Yeah, where *would* she have met your lot before?"

"This is all very intriguing," said Quist. "Especially the mystery of Steven Lyle and Hayley Eden."

The youth frowned. "What mystery?"

"Apart from the stuntman attempting to kill me, you mean?" The detective let out a dry laugh. "Didn't you notice how both their personalities had completely changed today? Both were acting very differently this morning to how they were last night. Even *you* should have spotted that."

"Even *me*? Cheers, Guv." Watson smiled tightly. "Well, last night they were obviously in a bit of a state. I mean, he nearly died, didn't he?"

"*They?*" echoed Quist. "Yes, Miss Eden was upset and quite shrill following the accident, but the fall didn't appear to concern Lyle one bit. Plus, he broke some of his bones, but apparently they instantly healed, in much the same way that I heal."

"True," murmured Watson. "Hey, do you reckon he could be one of your lot?"

"You mean could there have been an *actual* werewolf beneath that werewolf costume?" Quist smiled. "It's possible, I suppose, but I strongly suspect something else is going on here. He removed his glove to shake my hand and immediately gave me an odd look. Toni Nelson claimed she…"

"Yeah," broke in Watson. "She claimed she touched you and could sense what you were. So maybe *he* could too?"

"Exactly," said Quist. "Lycanthropes are unable to do that with one another. He discovered my secret and shortly afterwards he attempted to kill me. One has to wonder *why*, just as one has to wonder why they were acting differently. Hayley appeared quite shallow last night. She kept calling him *Stevie*, but as you heard, she now calls him *Steve*."

"I dunno, Guv." Watson scratched his head. "I'm just playing the Devil's Avocado here, but he was obviously ill in the trailer and again she was concerned with…"

"She didn't appear concerned to me," said Quist. "Toni was clearly concerned, but not his *girlfriend,* Hayley. Lyle was surprised to see her smoking too. She broke the filter from the cigarette before lighting it and it wasn't the first time that had happened; the ashtray was filled with discarded filters. More intriguing, however, Hayley had lipstick all over the cigarette we saw her with, but there was no trace of lipstick on any of the ashtray stubs."

"You noticed *that?*" The youth grinned. "I don't know why I'm surprised.

The detective narrowed his eyes suspiciously. "It was almost as if that cigarette was her first one and someone else had smoked those others."

"Er... *right*." Watson nodded slowly. "I've got to say, that's a pretty weird idea, Guv. Not the weirdest shit you've ever come up with, but still pretty weird."

"Another *pretty weird* thing that you clearly haven't noticed," said Quist. "My lupine pheromones have no effect whatsoever upon Hayley Eden or Toni Nelson."

Watson thought for a few seconds. "Hey, you're right," he gasped. "How can that be?"

"I don't yet know," murmured the detective.

The Shambles came to an end, its narrow route opening out into King's Square. Once the 9th century site of the Viking royal palace, this tree-lined open space is now the daytime haunt of opera-singing buskers, mime artists and other lively street performers. Watson's friend Gareth Lestrade lived on St Andrewgate, which led off here, his upmarket apartment situated on the top floor of a converted Victorian Granary, imaginatively named *Granary Court*. Followed by his assistant, Quist climbed the steps and pressed the doorbell, his acute hearing picking up the sound within – the iconic five tones from the film *Close Encounters of the Third Kind*.

"Watty. Great to see you." Pale-skinned, with blonde hair, a bespectacled young man answered the door and ushered them into the hallway. "Hey, and Quisty too."

"Good afternoon." The detective gave a taut smile. "How are we today, Gareth?"

Watson knew his boss wasn't keen on the *Quisty* nickname, but he'd be less enamoured with the name Lestrade used in private – *Agatha*, as in the detective novelist *Agatha Quisty*. He'd be even less pleased with Watson's secret nickname of *Cyrano*.

To term Gareth Lestrade a *computer expert* would be

something of an insult; the young man was so much more than this. He handled computers in much the same way that Mozart handled pianos, and could access encrypted websites faster than a weepy woman accessing a tub of *Haagen-Dazs*. Lestrade worked freelance, visiting companies to troubleshoot their software issues and technical problems, but his sizable income was occasionally boosted by payments from Quist. No-questions-asked payments for hacking and supplying the consultant detective with snippets of case information.

The *sizable income* was reflected in Lestrade's apartment. Clearly an aficionado of science fiction and comics, signed cinema posters and framed issues of Spider-man decorated his walls, and model starships rubbed shoulders with movie memorabilia and action figures in his glass exhibit cases.

"Watty, you're not going to believe this," gushed Lestrade, leading them into his lounge. "I've just been reading the online movie forums and Kitten Maye is working in York on a new horror film. If we go over to where they're shooting, we'll probably get to see her."

"*See her*?" Watson covered a fake yawn with his fist. "The thing is, Gazza, I've met her."

"*What*?" Lestrade's mouth fell open. "Seriously? When was this, you lucky twat?"

"Actually, I've met her twice," drawled Watson, proudly. "Last night when she was shooting at Walmgate and again this morning on the film set at Beningbrough Hall. Yeah, Kitten and I had a bit of a chat."

"True." Quist nodded. "A *chat* that amounted to you talking and her neglecting to answer. She did speak last night, however. I recall there were profanities, but remind me – what was it she said?"

Smiling sarcastically, Watson turned to his friend. "Needless to say, Gazza, we're here hoping for a bit of help."

Lestrade nodded. "Computer help?"

"No," said Quist. "We were wondering if you could fit us a

staircase carpet." He gave a friendly lopsided smile. "Yes, of *course* it's computer help."

"Of course," echoed the young man, laughing and heading for the spare bedroom. "Come on through."

Watson followed them, smiling to himself. *Since he began working for Bernie Quist at the agency, his boss had really come out of his reclusive shell. He used to be serious and aloof and now he was actually cracking jokes. Shite jokes, to be fair, but jokes none the less.*

Lestrade walked to a long table beneath the bedroom window, covered in the sort of hi-tech equipment that belonged in a NASA lab. He flopped into his office chair with Quist and Watson sitting on the stools either side of him.

"Welcome back to the cyber cave," he said, gesturing to the large computer screen. "So what do you need this time?"

"The *Castle Museum* here in York," said the detective. "I wonder if you could find the floor plans for the buildings? As detailed as possible, please."

"Shouldn't be a problem," murmured Lestrade, his nimble fingers a blur as he typed on the keyboard.

"Excellent," nodded Quist, as the architectural blueprints appeared. "Would you be good enough to print those out for me, please?"

"Sure thing." Lestrade tapped a button and sat back as a nearby printer whirred into life. "Well, that was easy enough. I'm sure you could have done it yourself without paying me."

"Yeah," agreed Watson, bemused. "Is that why we came?"

"Not quite," purred Quist. "Can you possibly access the museum security systems?"

Lestrade grinned. "Ah, now *this* is more like the jobs that you hire me for." He typed again, swiftly working his way through several webpage menus over the next two minutes, before entering the root pages of system text. "Yes, it's hardly a bank, so it wasn't too tricky.

These are all their alarm systems and CCTV. The cameras just record footage on a loop. In a place like this, it isn't as if they need security guards constantly viewing live screens."

"Very good." Quist leant forward to peer at the unintelligible computer language. "I'll take your word for it that this is what I asked for. What I really need to know is whether or not these alarms and cameras can be remotely switched off from here?"

"Of course," confirmed Lestrade. "It's just a machine. Now that I'm inside its system, it doesn't know who I am, or if I'm here or in the museum office."

"I see." Nodding slowly, Quist climbed to his feet. "Will you be at home for the next couple of hours, Gareth?"

"If you're paying me to sit here on my arse watching the new *Star Wars* film?" The young man shrugged. "Yeah, I reckon I can manage that."

"Then I'll ring you later." The detective gestured for Watson to follow him. "You can switch everything off when I call."

"So I take it you're going to break into this place?" Lestrade sat quietly for a long moment. "And you want me to kill the alarms to let you do that? Um, yeah, no problem, I suppose."

"Don't worry, Gazza," said Watson. "Believe it or not, it really isn't anything *too* criminal."

"Quite true." Quist gave him a lopsided smile. "And you'll be adequately reimbursed as usual."

"Yeah, yeah," grinned Lestrade. "You know, with you it's always something weird like this, isn't it? Just *once* it'd be nice to retrieve a forgotten password, or erase some dodgy porn from your hard drive."

* * * *

97

Chapter 14

Watson peered up at Clifford's Tower from Quist's car as the detective drove around the base of the fortification and onto the wide expanse of tarmac below. Like most of the historic buildings in York, the tower is elegantly illuminated after sunset, its circular limestone walls reflecting an array of spotlights. Standing more than one-hundred feet high on a manmade defensive mound, the imposing structure reminded Watson of a pork pie, whilst the overall effect, with the conical hill beneath, was more like that delicious confectionary treat, the *Walnut Whip*. As usual, the youth was feeling peckish.

The *Castle Car Park* looked to be fairly full, but Quist cruised slowly to the furthest corner where he knew he'd find a space. The majority of people don't like to walk far and invariably leave their vehicles as close to the town as possible. A wire mesh fence and bushes separated the car park from the River Foss and he pulled up beside the higher security fence that surrounded the rear grounds of the *Castle Museum*. It was darker here, away from the streetlamps, and the perfect spot for what he had planned.

Quist checked the time – it was seven o'clock – then handed his watch and ring to Watson for safekeeping.

"You really think this is the best way, Guv?" asked the youth. He glanced uneasily over his shoulder at the other parked cars. "Breaking in there in *wolfy mode*, so to speak?"

"I'm faster, stronger and more agile in my lupine form," said Quist, ringing Lestrade on his mobile. "The museum windows are old and probably won't be too secure, but they're barred on the inside. Having studied the blueprints, I've concluded that the optimal point of entry is via the roof." He gave his assistant a wink. "Plus, a jet-black wolf blends into the shadows, doesn't it?"

"I'm sure you know best," murmured Watson.

"Hello again, Gareth." Quist spoke into the phone. "Yes, if you could deactivate the alarm system and cameras now, please?" He waited a few moments. "Thank you. I'll be in touch again shortly for you to switch them back on."

Watson turned away as Quist shuffled down his trousers and began to quickly undress. Not wishing to make eye contact with anything sausage-shaped, he stared out of the car window, focussing instead on the side of the prison building beyond the fence. A pair of white-painted doors were set into the wall and most people would understandably wonder why this entrance was several feet above ground level. Thanks to his boss, Watson knew all about the macabre history.

It wasn't an *entrance*, but an *exit*... of sorts. The inmates here had originally been taken to the Knavesmire for public execution, the expanse of grassland on the southern outskirts of York. A gallows had stood beside the main road there and, over the years, hundreds of bodies had been left dangling on display. The executions moved here to the castle in 1801 and the condemned were brought out through these elevated doors and hanged through a platform trapdoor. The last public hanging took place before crowds in 1868 and Watson shook his head grimly. *This kind of thing was obviously what passed for Yorkshire entertainment before televised football.*

His scary thoughts of the past suddenly became an actual scary *present*. The sharp drop in temperature told him that his boss had finished stripping and was now transforming. Watson had heard women complain about going through the *change*, but hot flushes and irritable mood swings would be far preferable to having your bones agonisingly stretch and the front of your skull crunch outwards to form a wolf muzzle. Shapeshifting sucked ethereal energy from the surrounding atmosphere, which instantly froze the air in this enclosed space. Seeing a layer of frost form across the car dashboard, the young man shivered.

"You know what?" Watson laughed nervously, his breath clouding and teeth chattering. "The temperature out there must be around zero at the moment. When you've gone, I think I'll open a few windows and let the winter air heat up the car."

"Right, let's get it over with," growled Quist, switching off the courtesy light before opening the door. He flashed Watson a mouthful of horrifying stalactite fangs, which the youth guessed was probably an encouraging smile. "Don't worry. This shouldn't take me too long."

"Happy bottle hunting, Guv," said Watson. "Have fun."

The enormous wolf slipped quietly out of the car and stood on his hind legs, sniffing the icy night air and peering around the multitude of parked vehicles to ensure he was alone. Satisfied, Quist dropped onto all four paws, tensed his lupine muscles and sprang over the high security fence to land in the museum grounds. Darting into the inky shadows, he ran straight around to the back of the building where an old cast iron fire escape was bolted to the rear wall. A ladder was usually needed to access the bottom gantry, but a swift supernatural leap rendered such things redundant.

He looked around, realising he had to climb these metal steps as quickly as possible. This face of the building was normally obscured by the mature riverbank trees, but thanks to the season, they were currently leafless. He'd be partially visible through the skeletal branches to anyone looking over the Foss from the throughfare of Piccadilly on the opposite side.

Taking a deep breath, Quist raced upwards, bounding from gantry to gantry, his front paws crackling to form large clawed hands as he reached the top. He jumped up to snatch hold of the stone ledge above him, hauling his furry bulk onto the flat expanse of roof and then pausing to check for unwanted observers across the river. Bright stars filled the sky and he glanced up to watch a meteor zip past overhead.

Quist had already identified several potential entry points on the museum blueprints and internet satellite images, and the nearby skylight was ideal. This rooftop window was antiquated, and by slightly easing up the base of the old wooden frame, he was able to slide a furry finger inside and use his curved claw to flip aside the securing catch. The wolf smiled shrewdly on noticing the two metal plates as the skylight opened. It might be an old-fashioned window, but the plates breaking contact with each other in this way would normally have activated the alarm system.

"Well done, Mister Lestrade," murmured Quist.

Leaving the window open for later and climbing through the aperture, Quist lowered himself from the frame and dropped into the blackness below. He landed quietly on all fours, then immediately froze, his lupine heart pounding to see a group of waiting men standing on either side of him.

The fur rose on the back of Quist's bulky neck, then quickly settled again as he realised these *men* were only mannequins. In *this* darkness it was an easy enough mistake to make, even for someone with supernatural night vision. His mind had been focussed on more pertinent matters, such as not being seen, but he now recalled this room from past visits here. Clad in army uniforms, these figures were soldiers in a scenario from the *First World War*. This upstairs area of the museum was devoted to this historic period and he'd landed in the middle of a simulated trench.

The wolf trotted through the display of machine gun posts, sandbag piles and barbed wire, recalling how he'd managed to escape this 1914 conflict by sailing to America two years earlier. He'd been aboard the *Titanic*, so in actual fact he hadn't sailed *all* the way there. Avoiding fighting in this and the following *Second World War* wasn't down to cowardice – he couldn't possibly take a human life and risk how the killing might affect his darker bestial side. He'd considered joining up as a doctor, or some other non-combat role, but no matter *what* post he'd opted for, there was always a chance he could have been shot, blown apart by a mortar, or slain in some other way.

Someone returning from the dead would be quite the talking point amongst frightened young soldiers in the tense confines of a trench. Quist had always maintained that many folk are only two or three beers away from forming a lynch mob, and Germans would be temporarily forgotten as everyone rallied together to organise a cheery game of *Burn the Werewolf.*

Quist shuddered at the thought, leaving the warfare section and running down a staircase to reach a lengthy room devoted to the 1960s. He ran straight through, glancing at the Lambretta scooters, the Mary Quant fashion and the Beatles memorabilia. Some elderly people still referred to the post-war era as: *the good old days* and the wolf smiled at some of the nonsense he'd heard.

Back then, you could leave your door unlocked night and day – no, of course you couldn't. Burglary was a lucrative career choice in the 1960s, as locks were so flimsy, windows were single-glazed and house alarms were non-existent. *Children could play out in our parks unharmed.* No, of course they couldn't. There were far more paedophiles and murderers around back when they didn't have to fear DNA testing, CCTV cameras and number plate recognition software. Older generations always look back through rose-tinted spectacles and block out the tuberculosis, scarlet fever and other ailments which had yet to be conquered. Even the horrific wars were remembered fondly – wonderful times, when everyone came together filled with the *British spirit.*

Shaking his head, Quist left the 1960s and walked through a pitch-black tunnel to reach his objective, the *Kirkgate* street. He turned the corner and paused, gazing with admiration at the horse-drawn hansom cab parked on the cobbled roadway and the lines of Olde Worlde shops with their ornate frontages of wood and glass. These windows were tastefully lit when the museum was open, but now stood in darkness. The wolf padded along the pavement on all fours, remembering the time when all the city streets of Britain looked like this for real.

"What the…"

The street lights were suddenly switched on and Quist stiffened, his keen senses alerting him to a human presence. He silently cursed, looking left and right and sniffing the air. Someone was approaching around the street corner up ahead and it was a man; his lupine nose could easily detect the difference between the sexes. Like most York museums, this place closed at five, but certain staff members might work late.

The wolf grimaced. Clearly, there was no *might* about it. *Perhaps he should have waited another couple of hours before attempting this*, but it was too late now for such considerations.

The hansom cab stood on the cobbles beside him and, praying that the chassis didn't creak under his weight, he hurriedly jumped inside as a cleaner appeared carrying a bucket. The cab was open-fronted, but Quist squinted slightly to conceal his glowing eyes and sat well back in the padded seat, his black fur blending into the shadows beneath the roof. The man strolled past without even a glance and the wolf let out a quiet sigh of relief.

Thankfully the driver standing on the rear of the cab was a mannequin and, more importantly, the horse in front of him had been stuffed by a taxidermist. Back in 1845, when Quist had been stupid enough to hail one of these cabs in London, the animal had sensed him climb inside and had bolted in fright along the full length of Oxford Street. The breakneck ride had been his one and only trip in this mode of transport and he'd been extremely grateful when motorised taxis finally appeared in 1903.

A door closed somewhere to the rear of the cab and the street lights were extinguished once again. Kirkgate was obviously a short cut between two of this particular cleaners areas of work. The wolf sniffed the air to ensure the man had definitely left, then climbed quietly down from the carriage. Walking on his hind legs, he found the apothecary halfway along the pavement and peered through the small glass panes in the corniced window. Although it was dark, he could make out Toni Nelson's coveted bottle, five inches in height, standing on the top shelf.

This was truly bizarre. It didn't look much, and certainly no different from the other ornamental bottles and jars in there, so why did the girl need this particular one so urgently? Such questions would have to wait.

Once again transforming his front paws into furry hands and trying the door, Quist found it to be open, but he guessed there would be little point in securing *any* of these shops once the museum visitors had left. The window display was separated from the shop interior by a sliding sheet of glass, but the small padlock snapped easily in his powerful fingers and he eased back the partition to take the bottle. The wolf rearranged the remaining items on the shelf to disguise the empty space, then replaced the lock before leaving, carefully positioning the shank to leave it looking undamaged.

Quist paused on the Kirkgate pavement to briefly examine his stolen wares with a puzzled frown. Middle Eastern in appearance, the little bottle was manufactured from red glass, with a diamond-like glass stopper that screwed tightly into the threaded neck. Once again, he wondered why on earth Toni would want this ornamental trinket so desperately. Shaking his head, the wolf retraced his steps, making his way back upstairs to the skylight.

Outside on the parking area, Watson sat quietly waiting in the darkness of the car, his face illuminated by the dim glow of the social media on his phone. He didn't notice the werewolf springing back over the fence, and caught his breath sharply at the sound of claws scratching at the window and the unnerving sight of two gleaming eyes.

"*Shit!*" Sucking in a deep breath in an attempt to steady his racing heart, he watched as the creature climbed into the driver's seat. "Why the hell would you *do* that? Don't you know that those kind of scares can kill people?"

"Just a little joke," growled the wolf, grinning. "Besides, aren't you a little young to be worrying about cardiac arrests."

"So how did it go, Guv?" quizzed Watson. "Did you manage to get it?"

"I did indeed." Quist passed him the small bottle as he began to swiftly transform.

"What? You mean this is *it*?" Frowning with disbelief, Watson examined the red glass, as falling lupine fangs and thick fur turned instantly to dust in the car footwell beside him. "Toni had you rob a museum to get her hands on *this* cheap piece of shite? What the hell could she want with it?"

"I honestly don't know," admitted his naked boss, grabbing his clothes from the rear seat.

"Weird." Watson looked away politely as Quist swiftly dressed, praying that no one walked past the parked car and jumped to the wrong conclusion. "So, are you going to ring her?"

"Of course," murmured Quist. "But tomorrow morning will be soon enough. I need a little time to look at it first."

"So, in and out without any problems." Watson glanced up at the museum. "That was all a bit tense, wasn't it?"

"It was certainly tense for *me* in there," said the detective, awkwardly reaching around the steering wheel to lace his shoes. "Probably not quite so much for *you*, staring at that garbage on your phone."

The youth grinned. "Hey, let's face it, you couldn't have done this without me. I was waiting here like a coiled spring, guarding the getaway car. How about we call somewhere for a few drinks to calm our nerves and talk about all this? Better still, a nice big vindaloo curry?"

"I'm afraid not." Quist studied the bottle. "As I said, I need some time to myself. I want to see what I can discover about this thing before handing it over. I'll drop you off at home and then I need to head back to the cottage to conduct a little research."

"You can drop me at *Poppadom Preach*," said Watson, stroking his tummy. "It's the Indian takeaway near my place. After all that excitement, I'm absolutely starving."

* * * *

Chapter 15

Stars encrusted the black winter sky above Beningbrough Hall where the film crew busily prepared for the upcoming night shoots on the main staircase and in the library. Kitten Maye sat in the make-up trailer with Hayley Eden preparing her hair. Apart from the two young women, the trailer was empty and a mix tape of pop music played at low volume over the hi-fi speakers. The actress wore a lacey white Victorian dress and chatted on her phone in front of a large mirror, with Hayley working behind her in jeans and a dark blue T shirt.

"Yeah, of course I'll let you do that," purred Kitten. "I know it's naughty, but I want it so much. I'm all yours, Baby, and I honestly can't wait. If only you were here with me right now. Okay, see you soon." She let out a little giggle and ended her call. "Bye, Baby."

"You'll have to forgive my eavesdropping," said Hayley, combing and spraying Kitten's long black locks. "I wasn't actually listening to the conversation, but from the way you were giggling, that had to be a guy, right?"

"Wow!" The actress snorted. "How incredibly perceptive and clever is our make-up girl?"

Hayley ignored the rude sarcasm. "A pretty sexy guy too, I'd say."

"A pretty *rich* married guy," laughed Kitten. "Apparently, he really missed me while I was filming out in Egypt and he's bought me a *welcome home* present. A black Porsche with the registration KITT3N."

"Some present." Hayley let out a low whistle. "Wow, that must have cost a fortune."

"He won't even notice it." The actress laughed again. "The cash will come from one of his tax-free offshore accounts and the interest will replace it in a couple of days."

"Amazing." Hayley whistled again. "So what car do you drive

at the moment?"

"You ask me that like I have just *one* car." Kitten grinned cruelly. "My favourite has to be the Bentley, but only because it was my ex-husband's pride-and-joy. My lawyer won it for me in the divorce settlement."

"Right," said Hayley. "So what does this boyfriend of yours do for a living?"

"He's a London financier," shrugged Kitten. "He manages a series of hedge funds, whatever the fuck *that* means."

"Again, forgive me..." Tilting Kitten's head back slightly, Hayley applied light foundation to her face. "But I thought you were seeing the producer, Brandon Massey?"

"That's right," she scoffed. "How do you think I got the starring role in *Howl of the Wolfman*? I've talked Brandon into putting my name above Kris Horsley on the credits. I'm *seeing* quite a few guys, if I'm to be honest, but obviously none of them know about the others. Guys tend to get upset about that kind of thing."

"I like your attitude," chuckled Hayley, gesturing to the hi-fi speakers. "There's a song somewhere on this music tape that sums you up – *Girls Just Want to Have Fun*. Have you heard it?"

"Have I heard it?" laughed the actress. "Are you joking? That song's been around for about half a century."

"Really?" Hayley ran a sensual finger down Kitten's cheek. "You know something, you have really superb skin."

"Do you think so?" Kitten smiled at herself in the mirror, turning her head from side to side. "Yeah, I guess it *is* pretty good, isn't it?"

"Don't you ever wish it was perfect skin?" asked Hayley.

"What's that supposed to mean?" The actress frowned slightly. "Are you trying to tell me it *isn't* perfect?"

"Well..." Hayley shrugged. "Let's be honest here, very few people have *perfect* skin, but yours certainly *could* be. If you wished for it, I could easily make it perfect."

"Huh?" Kitten shook her head, puzzled. "*Wished* for it? What do you mean?"

"Well, it's really quite simple." Hayley smiled sweetly. "Why don't you just say those words? *I wish I had perfect skin.*"

Kitten turned in her chair to peer curiously at the make-up artist, wondering if this was some sort of game. "Okay, why not?" she laughed. "Yeah, I wish I had perfect skin."

The trailer lights flickered and dimmed momentarily. The girl's face instantly darkened to a deep brown colour and her hair fell out from the roots, leaving her head resembling an avocado pear. A covering of tough leathery scales spread over her shocked expression, swiftly expanding over her bald scalp and down her neck to encase her entire body.

"*What the fuck!*" whispered the actress, pushing her chair back from the mirror and gaping in total disbelief. She lifted her arms to see the ghastly transformation. "What is this? How has this… What the hell have you *done* to me?"

"Well, isn't it obvious," said Hayley. "I've fulfilled your wish. You now have the skin of an alligator, the most perfect skin known to man."

"This is impossible," croaked Kitten, beginning to retch. "How can this even be possible?"

"The skin is still fresh at the moment," continued Hayley, calmly. "But it will soon grow much tougher and it can't be damaged by scratching or penetration. Your new, *perfect* skin can actually withstand the bullets of small calibre pistols and…"

"How the fuck did you *do* this?" Kitten leapt to her feet, knocking over the make-up chair in her panic and hoisting up her dress to gaze in terror at her dark scaly legs. "I don't know what's happened, but you have to get this skin off me right now. Get this off me…"

"Well, if you're sure," shrugged Hayley. "You just need to wish for it to be removed."

"I wish this skin was off me," she screamed, shaking uncontrollably. "I wish it was off me right now…"

Hayley nodded. "Certainly."

The lights dimmed again and Kitten stood petrified with fright as she stared wide-eyed at her skinless features reflected starkly in the mirror. Vivid red and glistening, every vein, tendon and facial muscle was exposed.

"Not like that," she croaked. "I want my original skin back, you crazy fucking bitch. I wish I had my original skin back."

"That's no problem," smiled Hayley.

The make-up artist left the trailer as Kitten's original skin immediately reappeared, folded neatly over the fallen chair in front of her. Rooted to the spot in horror, the flayed actress began to scream and scream.

Closing her eyes, Hayley breathed in deeply, turning her head from side to side as if savouring a rich aroma. She took a cigarette from her jeans pocket and snapped off the filter before lighting up.

"I need to speak with a police detective," she laughed, puffing smoke as she walked towards the mansion. "I could drive into York, but this was far more fun and I needed a boost. If *this* doesn't bring a detective here to me, then I don't know what will."

* * * *

Chapter 16

The village of Askham Richard lies in the lush open countryside four miles to the west of York. A jumble of cottages cluster around an old inn, a 12th century church and a village green complete with a duck pond. Set back from the rural lane, Briar Cottage stood isolated on the outskirts, with ivy covering the frontage, rambling roses around the porch, a tangle of wisteria draping the eastern gable and a walled garden at the rear. People often picture this sort of place when imagining the twee homes of the *Beatrix Potter* characters. A furry character did indeed live here, but instead of *Peter Rabbit* or a well-dressed mouse, Briar Cottage was home to a werewolf detective.

Quist sat in a leather armchair by his open log fire, smoking a cigar and thumbing through an old book. There was no shortage of volumes to read in the cottage; one of the lounge walls was covered by oak bookcases. The remainder of the beamed room was cluttered with paintings, antiques and bric-a-brac. A grandfather clock ticked in the corner and a classical CD played on the detective's hi-fi system – Rimsky-Korsakov's symphonic suite *Scheherazade*.

Quist's acute hearing was still able to pick up the melancholy hooting of a tawny owl above the music. The night bird was in the nearby trees to the west of the house, but with a resigned smile, he knew it would never alight upon his roof or the fruit trees in the garden. Like all animals – with the exception of *actual* wolves and a few breeds of ferocious dog – birds could sense his supernatural vibrations and kept well away from Briar Cottage.

It was quite disheartening for someone who loved wildlife, but the detective was used to it. Then again, the house was free of mice and cockroaches, and in the summer months, he was never troubled by buzzing flies, wasps or mosquitoes, so that was a minor consolation. As Watson would say: *It was a case of swingers and roundabouts.*

Quist turned to the coffee table by his side, pouring more single malt into his glass – *Bowmore* from the Scottish Isle of Islay – and puffing again on his cigar, before examining the stolen bottle. He unscrewed the glass stopper from the tapered neck to peer inside and sniff – it was quite empty and there was no scent of perfume, aromatic oil, or anything else for that matter. Replacing the stopper, he marvelled at how tightly it fit. With glass upon glass, it was impossible to achieve an airtight seal, of course, but the manufacturers of this had come pretty close.

He turned it in his fingers and picked up his magnifying glass to study it more closely. A faded figure was etched into the surface of the red glass, beside a symbol that looked to be possibly Asian. The figure was humanoid and depicted in profile, with an eagle's head and stylised wings. Frowning curiously, he sipped his drink and took one of his history books from the pile on the table.

Many of the decorative bottles and jars that are sold to tourists in countries like Turkey are mass-produced in Chinese factories. These pretty items are made to *look* Middle Eastern, but the faded designs suggested that *this* bottle actually *was* from the Middle East. Drawing on his Cohiba cigar and leafing through the book, he eventually found the same symbol and figure in an illustration.

Yes, the design was Persian, apparently from around 480 BC, the time of Darius the Great. Surely this bottle couldn't possibly be an artefact from back then? If so, why on earth was it being used as a mundane decoration in the museum window display?

Thumbing the switch on the magnifying glass to turn on the built-in light, he peered closer.

"Intriguing," murmured Quist, realising for the first time that this object *wasn't* manufactured from glass, as he'd originally assumed. This was some sort of natural crystal. "Highly intriguing."

He grabbed his laptop and quickly searched the internet for

crystal bottles, then *red crystal bottles*, before trying *Persian red crystal bottles*. Several minutes of searching passed by before he finally found what he was looking for on a geology website – it was *Cainite Crystal*.

The detective sipped slowly at his peaty drink, reading intently as *the Young Prince and the Young Princess* began to play over the speakers. This was his favourite piece of music from *Scheherazade* and Rimsky-Korsakov had been quite pleased when Quist told him so over dinner back in 1890. Cainite crystal was extremely rare, found only in certain parts of Asia, but Quist had heard of this red borate mineral before and it wasn't in the sphere of geology – *no, he'd read about it in books of mythology.*

He peered even closer at the bottle, the lighted rim of the magnifying glass illuminating tiny, almost invisible, letters etched into the surface. He ran a gentle finger over them and raised a curious eyebrow to find he was mistaken; the ancient letters weren't on the *outside*. This script had been etched onto the *inside*, cleverly and painstakingly inscribed by some ingenious tool inserted down through the slender neck of the bottle. Although he couldn't understand the Persian language, he could see that the words were written the wrong way around.

It appeared this script was meant to be read from inside the bottle.

"What the hell…" whispered Quist.

Unscrewing the stopper once again, he examined the bottle neck to see more letters, almost microscopic, etched all the way around the twisting thread. The detective sat bemused for a moment, then headed to the bookcases, taking down several volumes from his extensive mythology section. Returning to his chair with them, he found the red crystal in one of the indexes and turned to the relevant chapter.

Oh, of course – now he remembered. Cainite crystal was

traditionally used to imprison a certain type of supernatural entity in a rather unique way. This was why the letters were on the interior; it was a magical containment spell.

He continued reading, cross-referencing with chapters in other books, before sitting back and finishing his whisky.

"Could it be?" he murmured, gazing into the fire and puffing his cigar.

He remembered Hayley Eden and Steve Lyle, both at Walmgate and then in their trailer the following morning, and how differently they had acted on these two occasions. Lyle, apparently, didn't smoke. His girlfriend *did* smoke, but the man she lived with appeared to be totally unaware of this, despite an ashtray full of stubs and a pack of cigarettes on the trailer table.

Quist turned to smile at the hi-fi as Rimsky-Korsakov's symphony swelled. "*Scheherazade*," he said, nodding slowly. He'd always found synchronicity fascinating. "Yes, the *Arabian Nights*. How very appropriate."

He drew again on the cigar and laughed quietly. "Could it be?" he repeated. "I wonder."

* * * *

Chapter 17

Tuesday morning was freezing cold, with gunmetal clouds darkening the heavens and a harsh frost covering the landscaped grounds of Beningbrough Hall. Toni Nelson stood in the makeshift production office at the rear of the mansion, gazing out through the French doors at the winter scene. A pair of jays pecked on the lawn, pink and bright blue against the stark white. Toni would normally have taken time to admire their beauty, but today she didn't even notice them. She waited in sombre anticipation as Brandon Massey spoke on his phone and paced the carpet behind her.

"*Fuck!*" whispered the producer, thumbing off the mobile and wearily massaging his bald head. "*Fuck! Fuck!*"

Hayley walked in, smirking at the volley of profanities and perching herself on the edge of Massey's desk. She wore her tight jeans and a black *Candlemass Productions* T shirt.

"So what did they say?" asked Toni. "Are you okay, Brandon?"

"Do I look *okay*? The trio of *fucks* should have been a clue as to how I'm feeling right now." Massey unplugged the stopper from the whisky decanter on his desk and half-filled a glass. "I just can't believe this shit. As you know, that was the hospital ringing me. Kitten Maye died during the night."

"My God," whispered Toni, closing her eyes. "Oh, no, this is horrible." *She hadn't particularly liked the actress, but Kitten didn't deserve what happened to her. No one deserved that.*

"I'm sorry to hear that, Brandon," lied Hayley. "I imagine you wish you'd been there with her?"

Shaking his head, he gulped down the drink. "There was no real point, was there?"

"Oh?" Hayley took his hand and gave it a comforting squeeze. "But I thought the two of you were seeing each other?"

"Well, kind of," he sighed. "Yeah, I suppose we had this sort of romantic understanding." *The understanding was that, if Kitten got the starring part in this film, then Massey would get a starring part between her legs.* "I meant there was no point in my being at the hospital because they had her under deep sedation. She wouldn't know I was there."

"So the cause of her death?" asked Toni.

"Apparently she died of traumatic shock." Massey glared at the editor. "Probably something to do with her having no fucking skin on her body. How the hell could that possibly have happened? How does someone lose their entire skin like that? *How?*"

"So far, no one seems to know," said Toni, quietly. "She'd passed out before the paramedics arrived here last night and the hospital filled her full of fluids and drugs. She was unable to answer any questions."

"Shock?" repeated the producer, angrily. "If anyone should be shocked, it's *me*. The star of our movie is dead. Dead from some unexplained... *accident*, but what kind of accident causes *that*? My phone hasn't stopped ringing since the shareholders heard about Kitten being hospitalised, and now I have to ring them back and tell them all she's dead." He poured another large whisky, slopping some over the side of the glass. "Everyone knows that, with the main actress gone, this film is as good as finished."

"Excuse me," mumbled Toni, feeling her own phone vibrate. She checked the caller identification and left the room to answer it in the privacy of the corridor. "Do you have it?" she asked.

"And a very good morning to you too," said Quist. "Yes, I have your bottle."

"Thank you so much," sighed Toni. "Did you have any problems? Is it undamaged?"

"Well, of course it's undamaged," chuckled the detective. "I would never dream of presenting a young lady with substandard merchandise."

"That's good to hear." Toni smiled faintly. "I'll head into York now and pick it up."

"Doubtless you'll want to meet in public again?" said Quist. "To ensure that I don't tear you to pieces?"

"As I told you..." said Toni. "I can sense that you're not dangerous to me."

"Nevertheless, I'll see you in a favourite inn of mine at eleven o'clock." Quist checked his watch. "It's the *Phoenix* and, like the *Masons Arms*, it's quite close to my office. I'll text you the postcode now."

Ending the call, Toni checked the address in the text before glancing at the closed door of the production office and heading for the entrance hall. Kitten Maye's death would plunge the production into chaos and no one was going to miss the film editor.

* * * *

Brandon Massey swigged his drink in one gulp, adjusted his spectacles with a shaky hand and poured yet another. He didn't know what could possibly have happened with Kitten Maye's skin, but he *did* know that this *accident* had occurred here on the production and he had no answers whatsoever for the inevitable police and insurance investigations. Her death would probably destroy *Candlemass Productions* financially.

"What an absolute mess," he grunted. "The cops will be coming here soon."

"I'm counting on it," murmured Hayley.

"I have to ring all the shareholders and then her fucking relatives." Slumping into his seat behind the office desk, Massey shook his head. "I really don't need this. I'm sixty years old with high blood pressure and I shouldn't have to deal with such stress. There are times when I wish I'd never gone into this business."

"Oh, come on," purred Hayley, casually seated on the edge of

117

the desk. "Stress or no stress, you know you love it most of the time. Anyway, what else would you have done?"

Glancing at the girl's pert breasts straining the T shirt, Massey noticed that she'd clearly neglected to wear a bra. He turned away and sighed heavily. He'd always had a sexual interest in this young make-up artist – more so since he sacked her boyfriend – but right now he just wasn't in the mood for such distractions.

"I don't know." He ran a finger around the rim of his glass and shrugged. "Maybe I should have been a scrote farmer like my brother. Years ago, he suggested a partnership and I was stupid enough to turn him down."

"I'm sorry?" Hayley frowned. "A *what*?"

"Well, that's what Brent calls it." Massey laughed dryly, his voice beginning to slur from all the alcohol. "My brother is friendly with some shady people and he took out loans to buy up lots of London slum tenements when they were cheap. He knows all the right palms to grease, and he cut corners to convert them into multiple tiny flats to pack full of immigrant families. The cash from that enabled him to pay off his loans, buy and convert more and more buildings and, on it goes."

"So you're saying he's a sort of slum landlord?" asked the girl.

"Some might call it that." Massey laughed again. "Others would call him an entrepreneurial property developer. As I say, Brent prefers *scrote farmer*."

"I see," nodded Hayley, a cruel smile forming. "So I take it your brother is much wealthier than you?"

"Yeah," scoffed Massey, "and unlike me, he doesn't have to work for it. Producing movies can be a huge gamble, whereas *his* millions are assured. The government and social services pay the rents into his bank and those monthly hundreds of thousands are transferred straight into his offshore accounts. Do I envy the bastard? Yeah, you could say that."

"Interesting." The girl's smile widened, like a cat spotting a fledgling bird that had fallen from its nest. "Are you saying you wish you were a slum landlord?"

"No, I'm saying I wish I had my brother's money." Massey looked up as the light dimmed, then jumped slightly as the phone in his pocket began to ring. He pulled out the mobile and saw the caller's name. "Wow, talk about coincidences," he laughed. "It's Brent – can you believe this? Hold on, I need to take it."

"No problem," purred Hayley, watching as he answered.

His complexion suddenly drained to the awful colour of prison porridge.

"Brandon?" she quizzed. "Are you all right?"

"Summer," whispered Massey, ending the call. "That was Summer, my brother's wife, on his phone. I don't believe this. She's at the hospital morgue and Brent is dead."

"Oh, no," gasped Hayley. "That's terrible."

"Summer sounds furious," slurred the producer. "She's just found out that he's left everything to me in his will. Why would he do that? I honestly can't get my head around this. We were literally just talking about Brent and now... No, no, this is *unbelievable*."

"Absolutely unbelievable," agreed Hayley. "You were just saying how you wished you had his money and now..."

"Yes, but not like this," stammered Massey. "Not like *this*. This is just awful."

The girl nodded. "So do you wish he was alive?"

"*What?*" Massey glared at her. "Are you fucking joking, luv? He's my brother. Of *course* I wish Brent was alive."

The phone rang again and, trembling with shock, he answered it. Even with the device pressed to the producer's ear, Hayley could hear the hysterical shouting on the other end.

"No, calm down," snapped Massey. "No, shut up, you silly

slag. That can't be right. What you're saying to me is impossible. It's imposs…"

"What's the matter?" quizzed Hayley.

"He's woken up," croaked the producer. "Summer is saying that he's woken up." He paused, staring blankly at the phone for several seconds, then began to weep. "His insides are in bowls, but half way through his autopsy, Brent woke up screaming."

Breathing in deeply with satisfaction and leaving him sobbing, Hayley walked out.

* * * *

Chapter 18

Nowhere near as majestic as the four principal gateways into York, Fishergate Bar still remains a splendid limestone fortification. Standing on Paragon Street, just around the corner from Quist's office, pedestrians and cyclists can use the tunnel to cut through from the busy main road onto the much quieter George Street inside the city ramparts. Quist walked under the archway with Watson to where the *Phoenix* stood, tucked away beneath the high wall.

"So you think you know what's going on here?" asked the youth.

"Not at all," admitted Quist. "But I believe I now know what we're dealing with."

"Which is?"

The detective gave him an enigmatic smile. "Why don't we speak to Miss Nelson?" he said.

The *Phoenix* has changed very little since it was built back in the 1700s and Watson shook his head grimly as he entered. *His boss had introduced him to this place several months ago and, with small rooms, creaky wooden floors and log fires, it definitely hadn't made his list of favourite pubs. There were no televisions, gaming machines or juke boxes here and the only music was courtesy of an upright piano and regular evenings of live jazz. Needless to say, Bernie Quist absolutely loved it.*

Several lunchtime customers chatted at two of the three bars, and they found Toni sitting in an empty room at the rear of the inn, her face pensive and a glass of white wine in her hand. Watson pulled up a stool beside her as his boss visited the bar.

"I can't believe you blackmailed the Guv," whispered the youth, irately. "I really liked you and I thought we were getting along so well and then you…"

"I apologised yesterday," said Toni. "To be truthful, I really like you too, and I didn't *actually* blackmail him, did I? I knew about his secret and decided to use that knowledge to show how urgently I needed the bottle. People are dying and I can't allow it to go on any longer."

"Eh?" The young man frowned. "What people?"

Toni sighed. "There have been others, but Kitten Maye is the latest and if I don't stop this soon…"

"Kitten Maye is *dead*?" gasped Watson. "You have to be joking?"

"How did she die?" asked Quist.

They turned as he walked into the small room with two half pints and passed one to his assistant.

"Yes, you were both whispering, but I have exceptional hearing," said Quist, shrugging off his trenchcoat and sitting beside them in his open-necked shirt. "What happened to this actress?"

"I'll explain," said Toni. "But first, can I see the bottle, please?"

"You can have it, but first I require answers." Quist produced it from his coat pocket to show her and then replaced it for safekeeping. "Allow me to tell you what I've already deduced. This artefact is ancient Persian – from the faded etchings, I would estimate 2000 years old – and it isn't glass. As I'm sure you know, the bottle has been skilfully carved from red Cainite crystal, using miniature files to hollow out and inscribe the interior with magical binding and containment spells. The museum believes it to be an ornamental curio and they clearly have no idea of its real age and historical importance."

Toni sat quietly, sipping her wine. "Yes, go on," she murmured.

"Your stuntman Steven Lyle," said Quist. "Something possessed him in Luxor and then left him at Beningbrough. I met Lyle at Walmgate, but his personality was totally different the following day in his trailer. He'd experienced complete memory loss, leaving a blank patch from the time of his Egyptian accident until yesterday morning. You knew about my... *condition* when you touched me at Walmgate and Lyle touched me at the same time. Shortly afterwards he tried to run me down. I presume he believed the empathy worked both ways – he thought that I'd be able to sense that he was *also* a supernatural being."

"What?" Watson choked slightly on his lager. "The stunt guy is a supernatural being?"

"He *was*," corrected Quist. "Whatever possessed him, it vacated his body and entered his girlfriend shortly before we visited his trailer. How am I doing with this so far?"

Toni nodded slowly, sipping again at her drink.

"I'm unable to do that, by the way," added the detective. "I can't touch people and sense such things."

"I *did* wonder," she said.

"Hayley Eden," continued Quist. "Her personality had also changed yesterday and she was immune to the lupine pheromones that I release. All women are unavoidably affected by my scent, but not her. At the night shoot she referred to her boyfriend as *Stevie*, but the following morning she called him *Steve*. She was far more assured and intelligent in the trailer, and she was smoking too, which surprised the man she lived with."

"Not *too* intelligent then," said Watson, looking pointedly at his boss. "If she was smoking."

Quist shot him a derisive glance. "The cigarettes on the table and the ashtray stubs were all Lyle's; he'd been smoking until just before we arrived. It was as if the two had swapped bodies, or should I say the *entity* had swapped bodies? It clearly prefers strong cigarettes, as it breaks off the filter tips before lighting them." He took a drink of beer and smiled at Toni. "I'm sure you could explain this so much better than I."

"You aren't doing too badly," she sighed. "Al; right, I'll tell you everything. Knowing what you *are*, I'm really hoping you'll be able to assist with what I must do. You've helped me once already, but what I have to do next is far more difficult and lethal than robbing a museum."

"*Lethal*," echoed Watson, gulping. "Ah, my favourite word."

"You're correct about the bottle," said Toni. "It *is* Cainite crystal and I tracked down many examples of these years ago in case I should ever require one. There are only three in Britain – one in the British Museum, one in Oxford, and the other was here in the Castle Museum. It had somehow ended up in a private collection of pretty bottles and was purchased from a junk shop by the museum to use in their displays. It was never examined and the curators never knew what they owned." She took a drink of wine. "Yes, you're right about the body swap too."

"From my research last night, I've been wondering…" said Quist. "Would we, by any chance, be dealing with a Djinn?"

"You're rather perceptive, aren't you?" Toni laughed quietly. "Yes, I think you may *definitely* be the one to help me."

"*Djinn*?" Watson looked puzzled. "I'm guessing you're not talking about the stuff you mix with tonic?"

Quist gave him a lopsided smile. "The Djinn are an ancient race of supernatural entities originating from the land of Persia. They're often depicted in ancient wall carvings and art as winged beings, or creatures with the heads of eagles. You've heard of them by a different name, when in a more *diluted* form they were incorporated into the *Arabian Nights* and then into children's stories as genies."

"Oh, come on, Guv." The youth laughed. "Is this a joke? You're saying the stunt guy had a fuckin' genie living inside him, and so did the blonde make-up girl yesterday?"

"It's no joke," said Quist, glancing at Toni. "Is it?"

She shook her head.

"Incredible," purred the detective. "I've encountered various supernatural beings over the years, but although I've read about the Djinn, I was never fully convinced of their actual existence. I assumed they may be a mythical race not dissimilar to mermaids." He gazed thoughtfully at Toni. "Egypt was once a part of the Persian empire, wasn't it? First under Darius the Great, and then his son Xerxes. Did this Djinn join your film production whilst you were working out there in Luxor?"

"Her name is Cyra," confirmed Toni. "She was incarcerated in Iraq for many years. I watched over the prison to prevent her escape, but a military explosion recently set her free and she travelled from there to Egypt."

Watson sat listening with his mouth hanging slackly open.

"Cyra is seeking something," said Toni. "A magical amulet in the form of a bracelet that was hidden in Luxor long ago. She soon discovered that this bracelet is now in England, which is why she possessed the body of Lisa MacNeil and joined the film crew. The production is British and she was able to fly back home with them to continue her search."

"You know a great deal about all this," said Quist. "I should point out that, like this Cyra, you *also* appear to be immune to my wolf pheromones. When you say you watched over her prison, for how *long* was this exactly?"

"More years than you could imagine," admitted Toni, sighing.

"Oh, *right*," grinned Watson. "So I'm guessing you're a genie too?"

"Djinn," corrected Toni, with a guilty smile. "You may as well call me by my true name: Kymina." She turned back to Quist. "I wrongly thought you'd be able to sense me when I touched you at Walmgate. That's why I invited you to Beningbrough, to find out for certain."

"Oh, bloody hell, Guv." The youth studied the girl's face and laughed. "I know we've come across some weird shit working together, but this has to be bollocks. If you're a genie, I take it you can do the famous *three wishes* thing?"

"Well, of course," said Kymina. "We can grant wishes to humans, but not necessarily in groups of three. Cyra uses the wish power in an extremely dark way and I have to stop her."

"She obviously doesn't recognise you in that body?" said Quist.

"Fortunately not," said Kymina. "Although the Djinn can sense other supernatural entities, such as yourself, we're unable to detect each other when in human bodies. When I tracked Cyra down to Egypt and found that she'd possessed Lisa the script supervisor, I joined the film crew myself to get close and secretly watch her."

"I'm not speaking to a girl called Toni?" murmured Watson, still attempting to take it in. "Every time we met, I've been speaking to a genie?"

"You took over some poor girl's body?" frowned Quist. "This film editor Toni Nelson? You claim your intentions are noble, but I have to tell you, I find that repugnant."

"Actually, I feel exactly the same," said Kymina. "Cyra invades any human that suits her plans. She refers to the host bodies as her *scabbards* and accesses their personal memories too, which is far too intrusive. I only access the necessary memories that allow me to blend in and perform my work. I use their language, accent and speech patterns, and with Toni I needed to know about *Candlemass Productions* and the process of editing film."

Quist shook his head. "But the fact remains, that you still *invaded* Toni Nelson."

"I've possessed countless human bodies over the centuries," said Kymina. "But I always adhere to a code and only choose those who are fading and close to death. Usually that means the elderly, but Toni had attempted to take her own life when I found her comatose.

She'd already stopped breathing from her overdose and she was technically dead, but not yet brain dead."

Watson looked aghast. "So when you eventually leave her body…"

"Oh, so you believe me now?" smiled Kymina. "No, this girl will be fine; the organic damage caused by the tablets has vanished. The Djinn are entities of astral light and whenever we enter a human, our light swiftly heals their body."

"Such as Steven Lyle's broken bones?" asked Quist.

Kymina nodded. "Having said that, the overdose will be the last thing that Toni Nelson recalls. Her fiancé left her for another girl and she'll awaken still feeling the same way – distressed and suicidal. I'll need to have some contingency plan in place for that."

Quist thought for a moment. "So this is why you needed me to steal the bottle? You couldn't possess one of the museum staff and obtain it yourself."

"As I say, I abide by a code," said Kymina. "I never possess people in the way Cyra does. In Egypt she was using Lisa MacNeil, but discarded her for Steve Lyle after he knocked himself out in the temple, presumably because his body was stronger and more useful to her. The Djinn exist invisibly on the ethereal plane and we can only enter a human when they're sleeping or unconscious."

Watson shook his head and gulped down his half pint of lager. *So he was sitting in a pub with a genie? He'd begun to develop feelings for an actual genie? After some of the supernatural cases he'd investigated with the Guv, he didn't know why he should feel so sceptical with this weird shit. Quist seemed to attract supernatural cases in much the same way that a late-night kebab shop attracts argumentative pissheads. He'd come across magical entities possessing bodies before, but this was a frigging GENIE, for crying out loud.*

"So this *three wishes* thing…" he said, clearing his throat.

"How does that shit work?"

"It's an ancient symbiotic magic," explained Kymina. "When a human is granted a wish, the Djinn are able to fulfil it by manipulating the reality around them. We then recharge our astral selves by absorbing the positive energy emitted by the grateful recipient."

"Sounds simple," scoffed Watson. "But it's a bit risky, isn't it? What if some nutter wishes for the sun to explode?"

"That's impossible." Kymina shook her head. "It's too huge a wish. The magical energy and reality manipulation can only work within a limited scope surrounding the human who makes the wish. For the same reason, you couldn't wish for huge *positive* things, such as the disappearance of cancer, or peace throughout the world."

"Amazing." Watson turned to his boss, slightly bewildered. "So do we believe all this, Guv?"

"Yes, we do," confirmed Quist, quietly. "Tell me more about this Cyra. You say she uses the wish power in a *dark way*?"

"I'm afraid so," sighed Kymina. "Negative energy is much stronger than positive and Cyra is addicted to it. She chooses the right humans for her wishes, then ensures that the results create intense darkness, fear and horror for her to feed upon. In Egypt, for example, she had someone turn into a snail and…"

"*What*?" frowned Watson. "Why the hell would anyone wish to be a snail?"

"Obviously, they wouldn't," said Kymina. "Cyra chats with people and quickly controls the conversation. She probably talked to this man about how hectic our modern lives are and then manoeuvred him into wishing that his life moved at a slower pace."

"Bloody hell," muttered the youth. "So she sort of traps them? A kind of psychic vampire sucking up bad vibes?"

"It's how I was able to track her after her Iraq escape," nodded Kymina. "She possessed an American soldier and left an obvious trail of dark wish horror between there and Luxor, before abandoning him to take over Lisa on the film set."

"You say she killed Kitten Maye?" asked Watson. "Was that with this wish magic?"

"Yes, the girl was skinned alive," confirmed Kymina. "When Cyra is present, you need to be careful what you wish for – *very* careful. Djinns are empaths and Cyra senses resentment, jealousy and hatred. She offers her wishes to those sort of people. Recently, she's been doing this more and more to build strength in her search for the amulet."

"I see." Quist sat forward. "Yesterday, as Hayley Eden, she asked if I'd heard of Gabriel Slaney, a wealthy individual involved in organised crime. She wanted his address, so I assume he has this amulet, or he can point her towards it?"

"Damn!" Kymina grimaced. "She certainly isn't wasting any time. Yes, Slaney is the current owner; he bought the amulet at an auction two years ago. From what you say, Cyra is clearly aware of that, but she still hasn't managed to track him down. That's good, but it won't take her long."

"So what *is* this amulet bracelet thing?" asked Watson, still mentally picturing the skinned Kitten Maye. "I'm guessing it's more than a girly fashion statement?"

"You could say that," admitted Kymina. "It's the most dangerous artefact imaginable and Cyra *cannot* be allowed to find it. The Koura bracelet enables the Djinn to manipulate their *own* reality, allowing them to wish for things *themselves*. We've never been able to do that, so can you imagine what it would mean? Any Djinn wearing this magical device would be like a God. The power-hungry Cyra can *never* have it."

"Koura?" repeated Quist.

"The supreme magical adept in ancient Persia," said Kymina. "The personal court magician of Darius the Great. Darius and Koura were in Thebes – the city that is now Luxor – and Cyra was out of control and lusting for power. Using the body of a beautiful princess, she seduced the evil Koura into creating a magical amulet for her in the shape of a bracelet. Fortunately, before he could present it to her, I was able to steal it and stop her plans. With my help, Koura was assassinated by his enemies immediately afterwards and entombed in a hidden chamber within the Karnak temple complex. I ensured the bracelet was safely sealed in there with him. My only regret is that I was unable to have him killed before he could complete it."

"*Wow!*" mumbled Watson, raising his eyebrows as he recalled asking this girl out for a drink in York. *All things considered, she sounded a little more interesting than the girls he usually dated.*

"Fascinating," murmured Quist. "And now this magical bracelet is here in Britain?"

"Koura's secret tomb was discovered in Victorian times," explained Kymina. "It was excavated by a freelance archaeologist who was only interested in gold. He had no idea who Koura was or what he'd found when he sold off the amulet. It arrived in England and I monitored its progress as the bracelet passed from collector to collector."

"I thought you were guarding Cyra's prison?" said Quist.

"Yes, I lived in Iraq for centuries," said Kymina. "I remained near her, but the advance of technology freed me from that. For many years, I've had several cameras positioned upon the underground site and I've been able to watch over her prison using my phone."

"Cool," grinned Watson. "You can't beat using the good old phone for everything. But if this bracelet's so dangerous, why didn't you buy it yourself and destroy it? Just sling it over the side of a cruise ship or something?"

"I could never trust myself to handle it." She laughed dryly. "The amulet is unbelievably powerful, with a basic form of awareness, and the magic would overwhelm me. It was created specifically for

Cyra and it calls out to her. With her safely imprisoned, for centuries I've felt it calling to me instead, a sweet siren song that I hear as background noise. If I listen, I can hear it very faintly right now. The bracelet wants me to take it to its owner."

"Fascinating," repeated Quist. "So now that Cyra is free, will she be able to *feel* this thing?"

"Absolutely," confirmed Kymina. "Like me, she'll sense that her amulet is somewhere close in Yorkshire and, given time, the calling would lead her to it. After her long imprisonment, however, she's far too tired of waiting – she wants it *now*. The bracelet power is capable of causing coincidence ripples in reality. It's aware of her closeness and I believe it was responsible for you meeting both Cyra and myself."

"Huh?" frowned Watson. "Why?"

"If this theory is correct," said Quist, "the bracelet must hope that a supernatural being such as myself could help to unite it with one of these two Djinn."

"You're aware that I'm an empath," said Kymina, "and you both feel like genuinely decent people. I'm hoping that you'll assist me with what I need to do to stop Cyra."

"But what's the plan?" said Watson. "Are you going to kill her before she gets her hands on the bracelet?"

"Djinn can't be killed," said Kymina. "As I told you, we exist as light on an ethereal plane." She took a deep breath. "Besides, I suppose you ought to know that Cyra is my sister."

* * * *

Chapter 19

Hayley Eden drew on a cigarette as she strolled across the entrance hall at Beningbrough. She'd been rebuked several times over illegally smoking indoors, but had ignored the warnings. Turning as the front door opened, the girl grinned with delight to see Tariq Aslam being shown inside by a member of the production security team.

"Well, hello there, Sergeant," purred the make-up artist, stamping out her cigarette on the marble floor. "I've been so looking forward to meeting you again and here you…" She paused as a smartly dressed woman followed him in. Hayley ran an inquisitive eye over her short blonde hair, grey suit and black raincoat. "Ah, it appears you've brought a colleague?"

"DI Bradstreet," said Katie, holding up her police ID. "Apparently you're already acquainted with my sergeant. And *you* would be…"

"I'm Hayley Eden." The girl smiled sweetly. "I'm part of the film production staff. I'm guessing you must be here because of poor Kitten?"

"You'd be guessing correctly," said Katie, gazing around the spacious entrance hall. "We've just come from the York hospital."

"I assume they've been in touch with you?" asked Aslam. "Are you aware that your injured actress passed away a few hours ago?"

"Yes, they rang us." Hayley shook her head. "It's terrible, isn't it? What on earth could have happened to her?"

"A very good question," said Katie. "We were rather hoping that someone here could help us with that. Miss Maye was admitted to the hospital in the early hours of this morning. My sergeant describes her as being *injured*, but it's difficult to understand how anyone could sustain an unbelievable injury of that sort. We need to speak to whoever is in charge."

"They claim the poor girl was *skinned alive*," said Aslam, grimacing. "No one seems to know for certain, but it supposedly happened in the make-up trailer here on your film set. They're talking about some sort of bizarre accident, but there's no sign of cutting, or any blade having been used."

"So what then?" asked Hayley, innocently. "Surely her skin couldn't just slide off like a snake?" She smiled at Aslam. "An Indian cobra, for example?"

"Who's in charge here?" repeated Katie. "I need to speak to whoever can..."

"Our producer, Brandon Massey," said Katie. "That's who you need, although I should warn you, he's in a bit of a state right now. His own brother recently passed away."

"I'm sorry to hear that," said Aslam. "But I wonder if you could just point us in the right direction?"

"Of course." Hayley led them into the central corridor and turned to Katie. "But speaking of being in charge, did you just say you were a Detective Inspector? So you're a higher rank than Tariq here with far more power? More clearance when accessing police records?"

"Er, that's right," confirmed Katie, slightly puzzled. "What's your point?"

"Ah, so you'll be far more useful," muttered Hayley. "Could I speak to you alone for a moment?"

"Why?" asked the inspector. "Do you know something about this *accident* with Kitten Maye?"

"Please..." Hayley strode quickly to the library and held open the door. "In here, if you would?"

"Okay." The police officer followed her into the empty room of mahogany bookcases and Hayley closed the door behind them. "So what's this about?" asked Katie. "What do you know?"

"I've been expecting your visit," smiled Hayley. "I could have driven over to your headquarters in York, but although it took a little longer, this way was far preferable. I never liked Kitten and I needed the energy boost."

"*What?*" Katie shook her head. "What the hell are you talking about?"

"Do you know a gentleman named Gabriel Slaney?"

"Strange question," said Katie, baffled. "Yes, I know Slaney, but why do you ask? What does this have to do with Kitten Maye and her…"

"Very good," nodded Hayley. "And I presume you know where this man lives?"

"Yes, but again why do you…"

"Excellent." The make-up artist smiled sweetly. "I don't suppose you'd care to share his address with me? That really would be the simplest option."

"Of course not," snapped Katie, angrily. "Now would you mind telling me what all this is about, or shall I…"

"Okay," shrugged Hayley. "Let's go for option number two."

"Option number…" The inspector glanced down and saw that the girl had taken a portable stun gun from her pocket. The electrical prongs crackled as she depressed the trigger. "What the hell are you doing with *that*?"

* * * *

A couple of minutes had passed since his superior left with the make-up artist, and Aslam still waited in the main corridor. He walked slowly up and down, gazing at the collection of oil paintings and marble busts, then looked around as the inspector returned from the library.

"Ah, Tariq," said Katie, grinning. "You're quite a good-looking man, aren't you? I really love that brown Asian skin. It's like smooth caramel."

"Ma'am? *Er…*" Aslam wondered how to reply and managed

another: "*Er…*"

"I do like the darker-skinned gentlemen," she continued. "Probably because they remind me of the land of Persia. Yes, you'd have made a very attractive scabbard, Tariq, but this one is far more useful to me."

"Ma'am?" he repeated, concerned. "Um, what are you talking about? Are you sure you're feeling all right?"

"What's going on?" stammered Hayley, following the inspector from the library. She held onto the door frame for support and looked around with wide frightened eyes. "I don't understand what's happening. I was in my trailer with Stevie and then suddenly I'm… no, what's happening?"

Katie ignored the confused girl. "I honestly couldn't be feeling better, Tariq." She smiled sexily at her sergeant. "Come along. We have to return to the station right now. I need to look up someone's address as soon as possible."

* * * *

Chapter 20

"Bloody hell," muttered Watson. "So this evil genie is your sister?"

"You're doubtless aware of the old saying?" Kymina smiled faintly. "*You can choose your friends, but not your family.* Also *evil* is the wrong word to describe Cyra. Her problem is, she has no real concept of human right and wrong – of morals, compassion and understanding. Added to that, her rage and resentment have grown alarmingly during her time locked away, making her a *very* dangerous individual indeed. I can't even begin to imagine the chaotic destruction she'd cause with the Koura amulet."

"Like I said…" nodded Watson. "An evil genie."

"You claim it's impossible to kill a Djinn," said Quist. "So how will you prevent her from obtaining the bracelet? I'm going to hazard a wild guess here – you intend to use *this*." He took the small bottle from his trenchcoat and passed it to her. "From my research, I believe it's known as a *Dugdana*?"

"That's right," said Kymina, examining the red crystal and securing the bottle in her own zipped jacket pocket. "Stealing this was the easy part. Just like the last time, all those centuries ago, I now need to trap Cyra inside it."

"Oh, now you *have* to be joking," laughed Watson. "This shit is straight out of a fairy story."

"A very dark fairy story," agreed Quist. "I was reading about this last night. The Persian legends of imprisoning the Djinn in bottles were told and retold and ended up as simple stories for little children. According to the mythology, Cainite crystal is the only material that can hold a Djinn and it needs to be inscribed with the right magical spells of binding and containment."

"Many Cainite bottles were produced back then," said Kymina. "You're correct, they were known as *Dugdanas* and, as you're now aware, some still survive in museums and collections across the world. The people of Persia were understandably frightened of the Djinn; humans are always scared of what they don't fully understand. They felt they needed a way to imprison us."

Quist nodded. "But I presume you can't wish for Cyra to be inside the bottle?"

"I can't wish for *anything*," shrugged Kymina. "The wish magic doesn't work for the Djinn. We can't manipulate our own reality, or that of another Djinn."

"Very well," said Quist. "But if you were to give me a wish, couldn't I..."

"Again, no," said Kymina. "The wishes don't work for supernatural beings like yourself, and even if I gave wishes to Watson here, they wouldn't have any effect upon a Djinn. No, the only way to imprison Cyra within the bottle is to trick her inside, or have her enter it of her own free will..." She laughed dryly. "Which isn't likely to happen."

"I see," murmured Quist. "So the first time you trapped her..."

"It's a very long story." Kymina took a drink of wine. "I used subterfuge, but she's wise to such things now. Once I had her contained inside the Dugdana, I entombed it in a secret underground crypt in the country that is now Iraq. It was well-hidden, but the Americans blew the place apart with an accidental drone strike a month ago." Taking out her phone, she showed them the CCTV footage recorded by her hidden cameras. "The bottle was destroyed in the explosion and Cyra was set free."

"Good old *Uncle Sam*," drawled Watson.

"Naturally, I was always prepared for such an eventuality," said Kymina. "I owned another Dugdana just in case, a Cainite bottle that I kept with me for many years. After her release, I guessed Cyra would head straight to Egypt to seek out Koura's tomb and, sure enough, I found her there. After speaking with her, I soon realised her insane plans hadn't changed. After all those years, she's still intent upon finding and using the bracelet. She killed the old lady I was inhabiting and smashed my Dugdana bottle."

"So this other prison bottle you had the Guv steal," said Watson, his scepticism resurfacing. "It just happened to be in a York museum? That's a bit of a coincidence, isn't it?"

"Yes it is," said Kymina. "What *isn't* a coincidence is the film being shot in York, near the amulet. This city was a last-minute filming choice after *Candlemass Productions* was unable to shoot in its preferred southern location due to a fire. The bracelet is here in Yorkshire and I believe it manipulated reality, influencing the location choice to bring Cyra and myself closer to it, much as it did in engineering our meetings with you."

"Well, Guv…" Watson glanced at Quist. "That all sounds straightforward enough."

Kymina nodded. "You're still sceptical about this and *any* doubt will be highly dangerous when we're dealing with my sister. Why don't I convince you by granting you three wishes?"

"Now wait a moment…" began Quist, knowing his assistant all too well.

"You're kidding?" laughed Watson.

"No, it will convince both of you," said Kymina. "But you need to keep the wishes simple and not ask for anything stupid. The magic is bound to the phraseology and can only work if you begin with the actual words: *I wish…*"

"Okay, I'll play along." Watson pointed to his empty glass. "I wish that was full of lager again."

A half pint of amber liquid instantly appeared and the youth recoiled with astonishment. Gazing open-mouthed at the glass, he drew his legs up beneath himself on the seat, as if to escape from it.

"Truly amazing," muttered Quist, glancing up as the lights

dimmed.

"The wish power causes that," explained Kymina.

"Yeah." Watson laughed uneasily and composed himself, his heart still racing from the shock. "The Guv and me know all about how supernatural changes take energy from the atmosphere. Bloody hell, that really *was* incredible. Er, okay, here we go again. I wish I had a bag of beef crisps."

The lighting flickered as a bag immediately appeared beside his drink.

"*Wow*," he gasped, then mumbled something.

"What was that?" asked the detective, suspiciously. "What did you just say?"

"Um, nothing." Watson felt in his pocket and gasped again.

Quist snatched his wrist and saw what he held – a car fob with a rearing horse design. "Oh, for crying out loud," he snapped. "I presume it's outside?" Standing and pulling on his trenchcoat, he headed for the front door. "Come on. *This* I need to see."

They left the *Phoenix* pub to find a sleek red Ferrari parked by the kerb on George Street.

"For God's sake, Watson," hissed Quist, glancing uneasily up and down the empty road. "She specifically instructed you to keep it *simple*."

"Sorry, but it just sort of happened." The youth smiled sheepishly at Kymina. "I've always wanted one of these. I mean, it's not as if I wished I was the King of England or something daft."

"That wouldn't be possible," said Kymina. "The reality strands with that wish would be far too numerous and complex. The magic only works if the wish is closely contained and the ripples in reality don't spread too far outwards."

"What about the paperwork?" asked Quist. "The registration documentation and suchlike?"

Kymina shook her head. "There won't even be serial numbers

on the engine or chassis. With a wish like this, the reality strands in producing the *object* aren't too complicated. The car is real, but don't expect to find it on any vehicle databases."

"Unbelievable," muttered Quist, glaring at his assistant. "You wished for a half pint of lager, a bag of crisps and…" He ran a weary hand through his hair. "And a *fucking* Ferrari?"

"Um, yeah." Watson gave a guilty smile. "You've got to admit, it's nice though, isn't it, Guv"

"Yes *very* nice," said Quist. "But you have no *nice* license or insurance, do you? Let alone a *nice* explanation as to how you acquired it. Kymina, are you able to grant him another wish?"

"Of course." She turned to Watson. "I think we both know how he'd like you to use this particular one?"

"Yeah, okay," he muttered, glumly. The young man gazed sadly at the gleaming supercar bodywork and then glanced left and right to ensure no one was watching. "Yeah, I wish this Ferrari was gone and it had never been here."

"Thank you." Quist peered at the empty space that the vehicle had occupied, before lighting a cigarette and gazing thoughtfully at the Djinn. "Alright, Kymina, I think it's safe to say that Watson and I are fully convinced of all this. I accept everything you've told us and I'll assist you in any way I can, but how?"

"Cyra is working fast in her search for the bracelet," said Kymina, bitterly. "I've been forced to watch from the sidelines as she killed several people with wish magic to strengthen herself; if I'm nearby, I can sense when she releases their life energy through a wish. I've been unable to prevent the deaths without exposing who I am. She chose minor members of the film personnel, the sort who wouldn't be missed for a while, and she always ensured their bodies vanished during the wish. One was transformed into a fly and…"

"But not Kitten Maye," broke in Quist. "Your sister has just killed the main star of the film in such a ghastly way that the police will obviously investigate the death and..." He paused and nodded. "Oh, of *course*."

"Of course?" echoed Watson.

"She *wants* the police to visit Beningbrough," sighed Quist. "They have access to Gabriel Slaney's details and, if she possesses an officer, she'll soon have the address she seeks from their records. You're right, she *is* working fast, but I wonder..." He debated for a moment. "Why don't I get to this Slaney character first? If I could steal a bottle for you, then I'm fairly sure I could steal his bracelet."

"That's a brilliant idea," agreed Kymina, thinking quickly. "Yes, of course. I can't possibly handle it, but yes, if you were able to get the amulet away from Slaney before Cyra can find him, then we could work out how to dispose of it. Slaney's house is outside Ilkley on the moors – Riding Thorp Manor."

"Here's a *more* brilliant idea," said Watson, puzzled. "I don't understand why you haven't already thought of it. Why don't you give me another wish and I'll simply wish for this bracelet to be here in my hand right now?"

"Oh, if only it were that simple," smiled Kymina. "But I'm afraid it's impossible. In the same way that the wishes don't affect the Djinn, they also won't work on the magical amulet or the Dugdana bottle. That's why I couldn't have you wish it away from the museum. Those prison bottles are all etched with Persian spells. They're infused with ancient magic."

"Very well," said Quist. "So it appears I'll have to do this the old-fashioned way and, obviously, as soon as possible. Ilkley, you say? I'll go get my car and drive over there now. You take your own vehicle and we'll meet in the car park of the *Cow and Calf*. It's a famous rock formation above the town."

"I'll be there waiting." Kymina nodded. "I'm driving a black Audi."

"One of your film production's lease vehicles?" Quist smiled, tightly. "Yes, I've seen one of them quite close-up. I'll meet you there, you can point out Slaney's house and then leave everything to me." He paused, stroking at his nose. "By the way, rather than steal the amulet, how easy would it be to destroy it there and then inside the house?"

"I don't see how you could," admitted Kymina. "But once you have it, we can throw it into a furnace…"

"Hey, cool," grinned Watson. "This has suddenly all turned a bit *Lord of the Rings*."

* * * *

Chapter 21

"Genies?" muttered Watson, walking quickly along Fishergate. "This is some really incredible shit, Guv."

"Djinn," corrected Quist, striding beside him. "But you believe it now?"

"After *that*? Well, yeah, obviously," shrugged the youth. "But I still can't believe you made me wish away my Ferrari."

"Don't be so bloody ridiculous," snapped the detective. "You couldn't possibly explain to anyone where it came from. Technically it never really existed."

"Ah, well." Watson shrugged. "Knowing all the scrotes on the estate where I live, if it was parked outside my mum's house, it'd vanish much faster than it did back there at the pub. Still, just for a few moments, I actually owned my dream car."

Quist smiled tightly. "Yes, but now we need to pick up my *real* car and follow Kymina to Ilkley. If this Cyra manages to possess a police officer, she'll soon have Gabriel Slaney's address. I believe everything Kymina told us and we really need to beat her sister to that amulet. I'll be going into Slaney's house alone, by the way. You can wait at the Cow and Calf car park with Kymina."

"Good idea, Guv," nodded Watson. "If this guy's a dangerous criminal, we don't want Toni Nelson's body or *mine* getting damaged, do we?" He thought for a moment. "But even without the spooky bracelet, Cyra's still out of her prison bottle and here in Yorkshire. She's still going to be killing folk with her *dark wishes* magic shit."

"Yes, and naturally I can't allow that," sighed Quist. "I don't know how, but I have to stop her somehow."

"Well it's obvious how we stop her," grinned Watson. "Like Kymina said, we trick the genie back into a bottle. Come on, Guv, with all the supernatural stuff we've dealt with, that's just a typical day's work for us."

"I appreciate you're joking," said Quist, "but trapping Cyra in that crystal bottle is going to be next to impossible. She's been tricked inside a Dugdana once before and I presume she'll be constantly watching out for any clever deceptions. She isn't going to let it happen again."

"I'll see if I can't think of something," said the youth.

The detective laughed. "Yes, you *do* that."

"By the way," he said. "Djinn or no Djinn, I still like Kymina."

"No, you like Toni Nelson," sighed Quist, "and weird as it sounds, you've never actually met this film editor. You've been speaking with the entity inside her."

Watson nodded. "And *that's* who I have feelings for. Yeah, I know it sounds kind of weird, but I like the person who I've been speaking with, not the body. Although, I've got to admit, that body *is* pretty nice." He pointed as they approached the detective agency. "Hey look who's here – your favourite lady cop."

Katie Bradstreet stood outside the *Jehovah's Fitness* gymnasium reading through a folder of papers as she waited. She wore a black raincoat over her dark grey suit and carried a large leather shoulder bag.

"Katie?" said Quist, smiling warmly. "This is unexpected. What are you doing here?"

"Ah, Bernard, there you are," she said, sliding the file back into her bag. "I've been trying your doorbell intercom. We need to talk inside."

The hair on Quist's neck bristled. "Well, I'm afraid we don't have long," he said. "Actually, we only came here to pick up my car from around the corner and…"

"Inside," repeated Katie, pushing open the agency door. "It's rather important."

Walking through, they found Simon Baxter from the

downstairs fitness centre fixing an evangelical poster to the passage wall. The illustration showed Darwin being kicked to death by several offended monkeys.

"Well, hello there," he said. "I'm speaking to people like yourselves about Jesus and…"

"Ooh, yeah, there are some really nice *cheeses*," smiled Watson, heading up the staircase. "I like a bit of Stilton myself."

"That's really funny," said Simon, with a not particularly Christian snarl. "Let's see if you're still cracking stupid jokes when you're screaming for eternity in Satan's fires." He turned to Katie. "Now you look like someone who would embrace the Christian message…"

"Here's a Christian message," she growled, walking past. "Screw you *and* your deity."

Quist followed her up the steps to unlock the agency door and lead the way into the main office. "Shall I pop the kettle on?" he asked. "Your usual milky coffee?"

"Yes, please," said Katie.

"No, you're not Inspector Bradstreet, are you?" snarled Quist. "She always calls me *Bernie*, not *Bernard*, and you have a different swaggering walk. Even when angry, Katie would never have spoken that way to the gentleman downstairs. Not to mention that she's lactose intolerant and takes her coffee black like me."

"*What*?" whispered Watson. "Are you saying that this is…"

"This is the Djinn." Quist looked the woman up and down. "This is Cyra."

"Oh, well done," she laughed. "Yes, you can call me by my real name. The fact that you're aware of this means you must have been speaking to my beloved sister?"

The detective remained silent, eyeing her angrily.

"I knew Kymina would have followed me from Egypt," said Cyra. "She had to be around here somewhere, watching and plotting. I know she wants to keep me from my amulet. I presume she told you all about that and she wants you to help her?"

"Something like that," admitted Quist. "She believes that you having this bracelet would be disastrous and, if it's as powerful as she claims, then I have to agree with her."

"I see," nodded Cyra. "So where is she? She probably told you how we're unable to recognise each other when we're inside our scabbards. Which one is Kymina using?"

Quist didn't answer and Watson stood frozen to the spot, his mind whirling as he attempted to process the enormity of this.

"Kymina never deviates from her stupid code." Cyra walked slowly around the office like a prowling cat. "She only possesses humans who are close to death. Her last scabbard was an old Egyptian woman and I've been watching out for a similar elderly person. To be honest, I've had more important things on my mind tracking down my bracelet, so I've yet to work out who she is."

"She chooses the elderly?" Quist trembled with fury as he lit a cigarette. "But you have no such qualms, I see? It's disgusting that you've invaded this woman's body. Can't you see that this is a violation?"

"Ooh, aren't we touchy?" laughed the Djinn. "Yes, I know you have feelings for the inspector here. I have access to her memories and you'll be pleased to know that Katie has emotions for you too. Mmh, and how about these sexual memories? Oh, Bernard, you really are an animal in bed, aren't you? And I'm not referring to your animal *other self*."

"Hey, come on." Watson cleared his throat. "A bit too much information there, luv."

"I'll take one of those..." Cyra gestured to the detective's cigarette. "If you don't mind?"

"As a matter of fact, I *do* mind," said Quist. "Katie doesn't smoke."

"She does now." Cyra plucked the lit cigarette from his fingers and broke off the filter. "I'll ask again, which scabbard is Kymina currently using?" She drew on the smoke and smiled sexily at Watson. "Mmh, I love that dark skin. You'll tell me, won't you?"

The youth backed away slightly.

"Don't worry," said Quist, lighting another cigarette. "Yes, she's a Djinn, but she can't harm you unless you're stupid enough to indulge her with her offer of wishes."

"That's not true." Cyra smiled again at the youth. "I could harm you in all the ways that Katie here could and the inspector would take the blame. I could push you under a bus, for example. I killed someone that way a few days ago, the old scabbard my sister was using. I could stab you, or perhaps I have a police-issue firearm in this bag…"

"You've made your point," snapped Quist.

"Good," said Cyra. "Because you need to fully understand the situation."

Watson gulped and backed away further. *He'd had occasional dealings with cops before in his teenage years. As a black youth, he was no stranger to smirking officers who would happily "fit up" people like himself for minor drug offences. Such police racists could be dangerous, but they faded into insignificance compared to this particular "police officer."*

"I've asked which scabbard Kymina is using," said Cyra, drawing deeply on her cigarette. "But let's talk about *this* scabbard instead. I shouldn't worry too much about me damaging Katie with tobacco smoke when I could damage her in far worse ways. For example, she doesn't need *two* eyes when *one* will suffice." Cyra reached up to her face. "This is going to hurt, but allow me to demonstrate how serious I am by digging my fingers into this left socket and removing…"

"There's no need for that," said Quist, quickly. "An old

woman approached us earlier today. I don't know her human name, but she explained how she was a Djinn called Kymina and she told us all about you. Naturally, I was sceptical, but it's fair to say that scepticism is quickly waning."

"There, that wasn't so difficult, was it?" said Cyra, puffing smoke. "That's so typical of my sister. I was curious as to her hiding place, but I don't suppose it really matters. Tonight I'll have my prize, and Kymina and her plans won't ever matter again."

Watson cleared his throat. "So the last time we spoke to you, you were using the body of that blonde make-up artist?"

"Hayley Eden, yes." Cyra grinned. "By the way, the other night at the Walmgate shoot I noticed you were wanting a photograph with Kitten Maye. Hayley worked on her make-up last night and you probably wouldn't want her picture *now*."

"No, probably not," mumbled the youth. "We heard what you did."

"So why are you here?" asked Quist, irately.

"Ah, straight to the point," said Cyra. "I like that. I'm here because you're going to help me retrieve my amulet."

"Am I now?" Quist drew on his cigarette and smiled tightly. "So it's probably just as well that you didn't kill me with your car on Foss Bridge?"

"Oh, yes, I'm sorry about that," grinned Cyra. "I assumed you'd be able to sense me inside the stuntman, just as I'd instantly sensed you when we touched skin. I didn't know who you were and I thought you could be a problem for me. I couldn't allow for *any* problems when I was so close to reaching my prize. I'm afraid I have trust issues, you see, Bernard? Simmering issues, caused by my beloved sister, which have grown and festered over the years… and years."

The Djinn walked to the window and peered out. "I was wrong, of course. When you met me again yesterday morning in that caravan, I squeezed your hand, but it was obvious you had no idea of my true self."

"You say you want my help?" Quist reminded her.

"I do," confirmed Cyra, drawing on her cigarette. "Thanks to my useful new scabbard, I've just called at the York police headquarters down the road there and accessed their computer. I also took this file." She pulled the hefty folder from her bag and thumbed through it. "At Beningbrough I told you I was looking for a man named Gabriel Slaney and I now know everything about him. He's fifty-one and something of a murderous criminal. The police have nicknamed him *the Count*, but your girl Katie didn't know why."

"Do *not* refer to her in the past tense," snapped Quist.

"Ooh, we're getting touchy again." Cyra ran a sensual hand up and down her torso. "Don't worry. The inspector's right here and she'll remain perfectly safe provided you do as instructed. Slaney purchased my bracelet two years ago and today we'll take it from him. Now, as you can probably imagine, I can be quite persuasive, but this man is the head of a crime group with hardened underlings. I need muscle of my own and that's where you come in."

"You want the Guv as your bodyguard?" asked Watson.

"What better bodyguard than a werewolf?" said Cyra. "Slaney may be reluctant to part with my amulet, but he'll soon hand it over when you turn yourself into a monster."

Watson frowned slightly, but remained quiet. *His boss could only transform during the hours of darkness, but Cyra was clearly unaware.*

"He divorced his wife last year." Cyra read from the file. "She's thirty-two now and it seems that Anastasia Slaney worked in one of his clubs before they married."

"Anastasia?" echoed Quist. "Like the Russian Princess."

"*This* Anastasia is Romanian," said Cyra, reading. "Police intelligence suggests she's far more vicious than her husband and had a big hand in running his criminal enterprises. Their money is laundered through the clubs they own, including one here in York, which is why our Katie has had dealings with them. They're both suspected of killing people, but the police have been unable to prove anything."

"Where does this Slaney live?" asked Quist.

"Riding Thorp Manor." Cyra turned a page in her file. "According to this, it's a large house above a town called Ilkley. Do you know where that is?"

"Yes, it's about an hour away." Quist nodded, knowing that Kymina was heading there right now. "All right, I'll help you, but only because I need to remain close to Katie Bradstreet. I don't want any harm to come to that body whilst you're using it."

"Oh, I *know* you'll help me." Cyra reached up to stroke her eye again. "You'll do whatever I ask."

Quist bristled. "Threats will *not* be necessary."

"Just a little joke," laughed Cyra. "I'm just keeping you on your toes, so to speak. At any time, I can easily damage this scabbard or even kill it. Remember, if you don't do everything I order you to, I can pick up a knife and slice open my own throat."

"I fully understand," growled Quist. "Believe me."

With his mouth dry, Watson gulped uncomfortably. *You go through life without ever meeting a genie and then two come along at the same time. The genie inside Toni Nelson seemed really nice, but her sister was clearly a total fucking nutjob.*

"An hour to reach Ilkley, you say?" Shoving the police file back into her shoulder bag, Cyra tossed Quist a BMW key fob. "The inspector's car is parked around the corner on Baker Avenue. We'll take it and you can drive. As you know, I have a nasty habit of veering onto pavements."

"Watson can remain here," said Quist, turning away from Cyra and praying that his assistant could lip read as he silently mouthed: *ring Kymina*. "There's no point in him getting in the way as we…"

"Oh, no, he's coming too," laughed Cyra. "I want him there with us. You'll do everything you're told, or it won't just be your beloved inspector who gets hurt."

Quist closed his eyes for a moment, controlling his rising anger. "Very well," he snapped, heading for the door. "Let's go."

"Um, sorry, but I need to wring the black goose's neck," said Watson. "I won't be a moment."

"What?" frowned Cyra.

"I don't know if you genies use toilets," explained the youth. "But I'm a bit scared here and I need to go. You don't want a wet seat in the car, do you?"

"Just *hurry up*," hissed the Djinn.

Slipping into the bathroom, Watson quickly pulled out his phone and rang Toni Nelson's number. "Hi," he whispered. "Er, the plan's changed a little."

"What's wrong?" asked Kymina, driving.

"Everything," he said. "Your sister is in my boss's girlfriend." He paused, grimacing slightly. "Yeah, I know that sounds like a porno film, but the Guv was right. She's picked a cop to possess, a detective called Katie Bradstreet, and she's taking us to Ilkley right now."

"*Damn*," snarled Kymina.

"Yeah, *damn*." Watson laughed nervously. "It looks like we probably won't be meeting you at the *Cow and Calf* after all."

* * * *

Chapter 22

For many years, *On Ilkla Mooar Baht'at* has been accepted as the unofficial anthem of Yorkshire. Watson knew this slang translated to *On Ilkley Moor Without a Hat* and had always wondered why anyone would write a song about strolling around outdoors minus headwear. *His brainbox boss would almost certainly know the full story, but he didn't feel much like asking him at the moment. Speeding to meet a murderous gangster in Katie Bradstreet's BMW, with two supernatural creatures sitting in the front, such light conversational topics seemed somehow inappropriate.*

Watson gulped uneasily. *One supernatural creature he knew to be safe enough, but the other was a touch more dangerous and, from what he'd seen in the office twenty minutes ago, batshit-crazy.*

Seated in the rear, the youth turned to scan the traffic behind, hoping for a glimpse of Kymina's black Audi.

There was no sign of her. Kymina had set off before them and this main A660 road was the most direct route to Ilkley; she would definitely have taken it. After his phone call to her, he thought she might have waited in a lay-by for them to pass by and then followed. Then again, she'd be unaware of the car they were using, so who could say where she was right now?

Watson had never been the bravest of young men and, not so long ago, he would have been petrified out of his wits right now. Whether or not it was a good thing, he couldn't say, but working with a werewolf on a series of frightening and dangerous paranormal cases had somewhat desensitised him to such things. Rather than being a useless, terrified wreck, he now felt merely apprehensive.

Ilkley was just over an hour away from York by car, but Quist was greatly reducing that time by breaking the speed limit wherever possible. Both anxious and angry over Cyra's possession of Katie, he drove the silver-grey saloon in silence, deliberating the grim position in which they'd found themselves. It was a hostage situation with quite a twist.

The detective turned to Cyra as they reached the town of Otley. "We'll soon be in Ilkley," he growled. "But where exactly is this Riding Thorp Manor where Slaney resides?"

"According to the police files, it's an isolated house on the moor," said the Djinn. "Now that we're close, I can feel the bracelet actually drawing me. It's been faintly singing to me ever since I was released from my prison, but the song grew after I arrived in England. It's so much louder and sweeter as we approach Ilkley. It will lead me straight there, so I'll direct you."

"Ooh, check out the supernatural Satnav," mumbled Watson, under his breath.

"I heard that," said Cyra. Turning around to face him, she smiled mischievously. "Hey, why don't we liven up this journey a little? How would you like three wishes?"

"Watson," hissed Quist, an image of a Ferrari in his head. "Be careful."

"Don't worry, Guv. I'm not stupid." The youth glared at Cyra. "Yeah, I've heard about what you can do with that magic shit. Three wishes, eh? No thanks, luv. I'd rather beat out a camp fire with my balls."

"What a quaint image." The Djinn laughed. "But you can't make much money working as a private detective. I'm sure you'd appreciate some *real* cash? Maybe a suitcase stuffed with a million pounds in tax-free used notes – right there on the car seat next to you? Most people would want that, wouldn't they?"

"Well, yeah…" he shrugged. "I suppose they would."

"Ah." Cyra's eyes lit up. "So you're saying you wish you were rich?"

"No," snapped Watson. "I'm saying nothing."

"Well, how about sex?" she continued, pouting sensually.

"You're quite attractive and I'm sure you have plenty of girlfriends, but how would you like it if *all* the women you met were literally drooling over you?"

"Careful," warned Quist again.

"I know," said Watson. "I'm sure if I went along with *that* wish, she'd probably turn me into a bar of chocolate."

"You must be a mind reader," chuckled Cyra.

"That's quite enough," snarled the irate detective. "I wonder if you'd be good enough to stop playing with my assistant?"

"Ah, we're getting touchy again." Turning in her seat and taking one of Quist's cigarettes from the pack on the dash, Cyra snapped off the filter and lit it, waving the lighter in front of him. "You really need to *lighten* up."

"So you began this smoking habit in the Middle East?" said Quist.

"Good guess," said Cyra, gazing at the old sandstone buildings as they drove through Otley's marketplace. "Yes, I tried a cigarette in Iraq and I quite enjoyed it."

"Guesswork has nothing to do with it," sighed Quist. "Smoking tobacco in hookah pipes was commonplace in ancient Persia, but not cigarettes. They didn't exist before your imprisonment, obviously, so you began smoking them after you were released from the bottle. The cigarettes are untipped and much stronger in that part of the world, so you're removing the filter here in an effort to replicate that same robust flavour."

"Clever boy," said Cyra, blowing smoke over him. "I don't know when you were bitten by a lycanthrope, but were cigarettes around back when you were human?"

Quist ignored the question. "Listen to me," he sighed. "I realise it's a little late in the day to be asking this, but do you really *need* this amulet?"

"Don't be stupid," snorted Cyra. "I'm finally about to wear

my bracelet and wield its power after all these centuries. I watched as it was constructed over ten weeks by Koura the magician and slowly infused with his dark energy. The amulet was formed from a silver metal found inside a meteorite and it's quite beautiful. Koura fashioned it in two segments – two spiral serpents that interlock together between the wrist and elbow – but when it was complete, my sister stole it before he could present it to me."

"But why do you *need* it?" Quist shook his head. "The Djinn have existed happily and peacefully for millennia. Why does *one* of them need all that limitless power?"

"The Djinn have always been a hidden race," said Cyra. "The few of us that exist live secretly in the shadows, feeding upon the residual wish energy of humans, like dogs eating scraps from their owner's table. We're unable to wish for anything ourselves and I saw an opportunity to change all that. I always yearned for wishes of my own."

"The ability to change anything with a wish?" said Quist. "To wish *anything* into or out of existence? Such *godlike* power would send you insane, Cyra. Instead, why not just live as a *normal* Djinn? Like Kymina, you could walk amongst the humans in this modern world without having to..."

"What?" snapped Cyra. "You mean by inhabiting the bodies of the decrepit and the dying like my *compassionate* sister. I really don't think so."

"Compassion should never be sneered at," said Quist.

"Whatever," she laughed. "Kymina's ridiculous code only allows her to choose human bodies on the edge of death to use as her scabbards. I thought she might have seen the error of her benevolent ways after all these years, but no. In Egypt she was using some ancient local woman and now you say she's picked a similar scabbard in York."

Watson nodded. *It was easy to see how Cyra had been*

working with the twenty-something Toni Nelson and hadn't suspected her. It was also easy to see that his boss was flogging a dead horse in trying to talk sense and compassion into her. This Djinn was definitely a can or two short of the proverbial six-pack

Billowing dark clouds filled the afternoon sky as the BMW reached the outskirts of Ilkley. Quist turned left before the suburbs, taking a rural lane that sloped upwards towards the nearby hills and moorland.

"So what's the plan?" asked Watson. "Once you get your hands on this bracelet and you have the power to wish for all kinds of shit yourself? Will you be looking at a six-bedroom dream house on the coast, an indoor pool, a few Lamborghinis, and..."

"Ooh, yes," purred Cyra. "A six-bedroom house is certainly tempting, but I think I prefer the Presidential Palace in Iran. It was the ancient Greeks who called my land *Persia* and I always liked the name; it had an exotic ring to it. I've decided I'll become the supreme ruler of the country and change the name back."

"A perfectly reasonable idea," said Quist, rolling his eyes. "But don't you think the Iranian government and their army might have something to say about that?"

"I'm sure they will," agreed Cyra. "And I look forward to all the fun. Anyone who opposes me will be burnt alive."

"Oh, *please*," sighed Quist. "You've been free from your prison for a few weeks, with access to television and the internet. You must have noticed how much the times have changed since the days of Darius the Great and Xerxes."

"I *have* noticed," smiled Cyra. "I watched the news this morning. The British Prime Minister has made some tax decision and crowds are protesting outside your Houses of Parliament. I don't recall anyone protesting when Darius issued such proclamations to his people. If anyone so much as politely questioned his decisions, their families were fed to his crocodiles. Come to think of it, that practise will probably be the first thing I reintroduce."

"I don't know about you, Guv," drawled Watson, "but she sounds like she'd make a great leader." He turned to the woman. "You're not involved with the Tory Party, are you?"

* * * *

Chapter 23

A rugged wilderness of heather and dark rocky outcrops, Ilkley Moor rises to 1400 feet, stretching over the hilltops between the communities of Ilkley and Keighley. Quist drove up a steep incline to reach it, negotiating a narrow rural lane that twisted in a series of perilous zig-zags. Watson peered out from the BMW on the final sharp bend to see Ilkley far below them in the River Wharfe valley. Resembling a heap of dark, soggy towels, brooding rain clouds filled the winter sky above the market town.

The youth turned to look over the moorland, his mouth dry with apprehension. Dotted with prehistoric stone circles and standing monoliths, this desolate, yet eerily beautiful, place is steeped in myth. *He knew there were local legends about ghosts, witches and goblins, although Ilkley Moor had probably never played host to a werewolf and a Djinn before. Not only was he sharing a car with a mentally unstable genie, but they were heading to meet an underworld crime boss who was suspected of murdering people. What could possibly go wrong?*

Puffing on one of Quist's cigarettes, Cyra pointed to a lane that snaked across the bleak terrain. "I can sense we're very close now," she said. "Turn right along there."

"Once again," said Quist. "You really don't have to do this. We could still turn back right now and discuss…"

"Oh, shut up," sneered the Djinn. "We're going to get my amulet. Try to remember that the precious Katie is relying on you."

A huge boulder loomed beside the road bearing a metal name plaque: RIDING THORP MANOR, along with a STRICTLY PRIVATE notice beneath. Taking a deep breath, the detective turned the car onto a tarmacked driveway to reach the isolated cluster of buildings up ahead. The Gothic hall, built from grey sandstone, had stood in this remote location for many years. The adjoining annexes –

the four-car garage, gymnasium and indoor swimming pool – although constructed using the same dark stone, were clearly more modern. The driveway opened into a wide parking area and Quist pulled up outside a large front porch.

"Bloody hell," muttered Watson, gazing up at the towers and balconies. "It's just like a haunted mansion from a horror film." Reluctantly climbing from the car, he noticed a black Bentley and a Porsche parked nearby. "What kind of weirdo lives on the moors in a horror film set?"

"I believe we're about to find out," said Quist, watching as Cyra strode into the stone porch and pressed the doorbell. He quickly removed his watch and signet ring and zipped them away securely in an inside pocket. "It's still daylight," he murmured to his assistant. "But who knows what may happen later?"

"The bracelet knows I'm here," whispered the Djinn, gleefully. "The singing has changed. It's louder and so much sweeter now."

"What song is it?" asked Watson, nervously attempting to alleviate the tension. "Anything I might know, because I enjoy a good old karaoke singalong with…"

The youth shuffled back as a man in a black suit swung open the door. *This had to be one of Slaney's bodyguards; a butler agency would never supply anyone who answered a door whilst chewing gum, let alone anyone who looked so terrifying. With his shaven head, broken nose and cage fighting scars, this huge character added to the haunted mansion resemblance. He might easily have been stitched together in a lab by Baron Frankenstein.*

"The sign on the drive back there says *Private*," grunted the bodyguard, aggressively. "So you'd better have a fuckin' good reason for ringing that bell."

"Detective Inspector Bradstreet." Cyra held up her ID wallet. "We're here to see Gabriel Slaney. Your employer, I presume?"

"What's this about, luv?" Chomping on his chewing gum, the man ran his piggy eyes over them. "Mister Slaney don't see no one without an appointment. That includes the cops."

"Oh, no," sighed a relieved Watson. "Well, we're sorry to have bothered you."

"I think he'll see *me*," said Cyra. "Go and tell him that our visit concerns his bracelet."

Frowning slightly, the bodyguard closed the door in their faces. They waited in silence for thirty seconds before it reopened and the man jerked his thumb, brusquely beckoning them into a spacious wood-panelled entrance hall.

"Thank you," said Cyra, caustically. "It was getting a little cold out there."

Quist glanced at Watson. "Stay close to me in here," he murmured. He tensed as the bodyguard began to run both hands over his clothing. "Really? Is this necessary?"

Another large man, bald, musclebound and battle-scarred, appeared in the hall and stood watch as his colleague searched the visitors for weapons. Watson peered uneasily at this second character, mentally removing the black suit to decide which mythical creature he most resembled – an ogre or a cave troll.

"Did I mention that I was police?" said Katie, sarcastically, as the guard ran his hands over her bottom and crotch. "You really need to improve your foreplay."

Quist's keen nose picked up the muted scents of cordite and gun oil. At least one these men was carrying a handgun.

"Right," said the bodyguard, completing his search. "You're okay to come on through."

The trio followed him along a corridor, with Watson looking at the wall decorations on either side. Some of these framed horror film posters and signed photographs of actors would have put his friend Gareth Lestrade's collection to shame. The passage led into a large lounge which complimented the exterior *haunted castle* look with a gigantic fireplace, four black leather couches, expensive rugs and an iron chandelier. Melancholy music played over speakers and more photographs and horror movie memorabilia covered the walls. Two girls in dark mini dresses sat on one of the sofas, both momentarily glancing up from their phones as the newcomers walked in.

Although the girls were in their late teens and highly attractive – probably sporting very expensive price tags at their escort agency – Watson was more interested in the stocky man standing by the log fire. *The cops had apparently nicknamed Gabriel Slaney 'the Count' and, seeing the long black cloak, the youth could now hazard a guess as to why. Weirdly enough, the vampire cape wasn't the most bizarre thing here. According to the police report, Slaney was supposedly around fifty, but this white-haired character looked so much older.*

The youth narrowed his eyes. *In fact, he looked incredibly old. More of a pensioner's scrotum than a face, his crumpled features resembled a pumpkin lantern – three weeks after Halloween, when the fruit had wizened and decayed.* He glanced at Quist and could see that his boss had been equally startled by the man's shocking appearance.

Cyra had also noticed and smiled knowingly. "Mister Slaney…" she said.

"Please, sweetheart, call me Gabe." Slaney's brash voice and Yorkshire accent belonged to a busker on a northern fairground stall. He ran a curious eye over Quist and Watson as he walked to a sideboard of bottles and poured wine into a silver goblet. "My man, Vic, tells me you're a detective, but who are *these* guys? They don't look like cops to me, especially the black kid."

"That's right." Slipping off her shoulder bag, Cyra settled herself on one of the couches and casually crossed her legs. "These are friends of mine."

"Okay," shrugged Slaney, raising a bottle. "So would these

friends care for a drink? I've got anything you might fancy." He turned to Quist, smirking. "I even have some German schnapps. You *do* realise you look like a Gestapo officer in that long leather coat?"

Watson briefly speculated whether someone, who wore a vampire cloak indoors, had any right to mention another person's choice of clothing. He and Quist declined the drinks offer with head shakes, but Cyra nodded.

"I'll have the red wine like you," she said. "I'm not on duty and this isn't an official visit." Glancing at Quist, she winked. "In fact, this afternoon, you could say I'm not a police officer at all."

"So the question is: Why *are* you here?" Slaney filled another goblet. "It sounds a bit odd, sweetheart, but Vic tells me you want to talk about my bracelet. Now, that really got my attention."

"Actually," growled Cyra, "I want to talk about *my* bracelet. I know it's here in this room; I can feel it's so close."

"You can *feel* it?" Slaney chuckled as he handed her the wine. "That's a weird thing to say. It seems we'll definitely need to discuss *who* owns *what* in a moment, won't we?" He nodded to the two huge men who'd taken up sentry positions by the lounge door. "Vic and Tony, will help with the discussion. I have another two business colleagues pumping the weights out there in my gym."

Loud, arrogant and vulgar, Slaney reminded Watson of those trashy lottery winners he'd heard of, the sort who move into upmarket communities, throw all-night parties in their hot tubs, and make life hell for the neighbours. Still fascinated by the man's hideously decrepit face, the youth cleared his dry throat.

"Tony and Vic don't look like they need to pump *much* weight," he pointed out. "Er, nice cloak, by the way."

"Yes, isn't it?" grinned Slaney, swishing it flamboyantly. "As you've probably noticed, I'm a big fan of horror movies and I have the cash to indulge myself. That's why I bought *this* place; it looks like a mansion from the *Hammer Films*."

"Very nice," muttered Watson. *He wondered how long Slaney would wear the cloak if he were a "normal" bloke, and not a multi-millionaire who had underlings on hand to punch anyone who was stupid enough to smirk at their employer's dress sense.*

"These silver goblets are from *the Vampire Lovers*." Slaney held up his wine. "And this was the actual cape used by the actor Christopher Lee. Some guys wear robes or dressing gowns indoors, but I prefer *this*. I always wear it around the house after sunset, especially when I'm in my home cinema."

"The *actual* cape?" echoed Watson. "I'd heard there were lots of them?"

"Gosh, really?" gasped Cyra, sarcastically. "Oh, how knowledgeable."

"The kid knows his stuff," confirmed Slaney. "I'm guessing he's a fellow fan? Yeah, *Hammer Films* made several cloaks for the *Dracula* series, but Lee wore this one in *Scars of Dracula*." He gestured to the hi-fi speakers. "Do you recognise the music?"

"I know it, but…" Watson's nervousness had prevented him from paying it too much attention until now. "Oh, right. It's the soundtrack to the 1992 *Dracula*." He reached out to touch the cloak. "I've got to say, this cape is brilliant."

"Good, eh?" Slaney nodded. "I always wanted to buy Bela Lugosi's cape for my collection, the one he wore in the 1931 *Dracula*, but there's no chance, because..."

"Because the actor insisted on being buried in it," said the youth. "Yeah, I read about that."

Walking quietly around and gazing at the film props, Quist shook his head in amazement. His assistant had been understandably anxious about coming here, and now he was chatting away with a dangerous gangster as if they were old pals. *If this continued, they'd soon be sharing a bucket of popcorn in the home cinema Slaney had mentioned.*

"You have an interesting home," said Quist, pausing at a framed poster. "I met Kitten Maye recently in York. Isn't this her beside the blonde actor with the crucifix?"

"*Scream of the Vampire*," said Watson, pointing to it. "That's the original cinema poster, illustrated by the artist Clive Barrett. I see it's been signed by the director and the main cast."

"As I said…" nodded Slaney, "you know your stuff. Yeah, the blonde actor shown there is Kris Horsley. He's far better looking than Brad Pitt and Tom Cruise when they were at their peak. Kris Horsley – now that's who I'd want to look like if I hadn't been blessed with *these* dazzling good looks." He grinned at the two escorts. "You call me *Gorgeous Gabe*, don't you, ladies?"

Puzzled, Watson glanced at Quist again. *Was this his idea of a joke? If not, when did this guy last look in a mirror*?

"Your poster will be worth a lot more now that Kitten is dead," said Cyra. "You ought to thank me, but enough about stupid horror films. We need to talk about the amulet."

Slaney swigged his wine. "My man, Vic, tells me you're Detective Inspector Bradstreet." Turning to the woman, he nodded slowly. "Yeah, you're based in York. I've heard of you, sweetheart."

"That's hardly surprising," said Quist, warily eyeing the man's silver goblet. "For the past several years, she's been attempting to arrest and incarcerate you."

"Well, that's not very nice of her, is it?" Slaney laughed dryly. "But let me show you something that *is* nice." Opening the cloak, he rolled up his shirt sleeve to expose a glittering serpent coiled around his wizened forearm. "Superb, isn't it?"

"It is indeed," whispered Cyra, reverently. "There it is, after all these years – my beautiful amulet."

* * * *

Chapter 24

Cyra let out an almost sexual gasp. She rose slowly from the couch to gaze at the bracelet on Slaney's forearm with wide excited eyes.

"An intriguing piece, Mister Slaney," admitted Quist, inspecting it. "You don't strike me as the sort of person who would wear jewellery, so what made you purchase this?"

"I've always loved the horror films about Egyptian mummies coming back to life," confessed Slaney. "I just can't get enough of their eerie atmosphere. Believe it or not, I have the actual sarcophagus from *Curse of the Mummy's Tomb* upstairs on one of the landings. Egyptian jewellery and statues remind me of those films and I collect the stuff."

"I'm into those films too," admitted Watson, peering again at the man's geriatric face and hands. *Presumably the rest of his body was equally decrepit. Speaking of ancient mummies, he'd seen scientists unwrap them in TV documentaries and, without their bandages, they looked a lot like this.*

Slaney nodded. "A London auction house was selling Egyptian jewellery and I bought the bracelet in a lot with a couple of scarabs and some other items."

"Amazing," chuckled Cyra. "You're telling me that the only reason you have that wondrous amulet is because of your liking for third-rate horror movies? That is truly hilarious."

"Whatever." He winked at her. "I wanted to see Anastasia naked and wearing nothing but this silver..."

"It's Persian," snorted Cyra, walking closer. "Both you and your auction house got it wrong. Also, it isn't silver, but a very rare metal from a meteorite. By the way, that's only *one* segment of my bracelet."

"You keep referring to it as *your* bracelet?" Slaney's eyes narrowed. "You've obviously seen it before if you know about the two halves."

"She *has* seen it before," confirmed Quist. "Apparently, it was quite a while ago."

"The bracelet consists of two spiralling serpents that entwine," said Cyra. "When the second serpent is squeezed over the wrist, the two interlock together on the lower arm. So *where* is it?" Her eyes blazed. "Where *is* the other half?"

"I divorced last year," said Slaney. "Speaking of *halves*, my *other half* took it with her." He laughed at his *joke*.

"You mean it isn't *here*?" hissed Cyra, angrily.

"No, it's with my loving ex," said Slaney, sarcastically. "The delightful Anastasia from sunny Romania." He gestured to the two pouting escorts on the couch. "She's Transylvanian, just like Pinky and Perky, my little playmates here."

Watson eyed the man's cloak. *With his love of vampire horror films, why was he not surprised that this wealthy oddball picked his wives and girlfriends from Transylvania? He'd heard about couples having to divide their possessions when they split up, but he'd never heard of anyone dividing an ancient magical amulet.*

"So you know all about this?" Slaney held out his arm. "That's good, sweetheart. You might be able to answer a few questions."

"Oh, I've waited for so long." Cyra ran a slow finger over the coiled serpent and drew in a deep breath. "That's the first time I've ever touched it. Let me hold it."

"Not a chance in hell," laughed Slaney. "I never take off my lucky charm, not even in bed. I've had the most unbelievable good luck since I began wearing this little beauty. For the past two years, I've found that I can't lose and *everything* has gone right for me. I get the feeling that, if I *did* remove it, I'd probably trip and break my neck."

"Amazing," said Watson. "I've always been nervous about flying, but I suppose I'd feel okay with you on the same plane."

"That's true," he grinned, drinking his wine. "Just two months after I began wearing the bracelet, I realised I didn't need to work ever again. I sold off my nightclubs and er, *other* businesses, and began to make all my cash from gambling. You can't imagine what I make at the racecourses and dog tracks, or how much I can make in just *one* night by gambling online. This bracelet really *is* a license to print money."

"What about the other half?" asked Quist. "Wouldn't wearing that, um, *double* your luck?"

"No, which is why I let my ex take it." Slaney laughed dryly. "The bracelet looked nice when it was complete, but wearing it like that was impossible. Anastasia put it on and got a raging headache that was so bad, she actually passed out. I tried it myself and the pain was unbearable. It felt like…"

"I'm not surprised," snorted Cyra. "It was never meant for your kind."

"What do you mean *my kind*?" Slaney bristled aggressively. "Don't you look down on me, darling. I've got more fuckin' cash offshore than you could even dream of."

"No, that wasn't an insult," said Cyra. "It was a simple fact. Had either of you worn the complete amulet for long, it would have killed you."

"I'm no idiot." Slaney marched to the sideboard to refill his goblet. "I don't know much about such things, but I *do* know that this bracelet must have some sort of supernatural power. I'm guessing *you* know that too, so what can you tell me about it?"

"Everything," she smiled. "It's far more than supernatural; it's magical and your incredible luck is a simple side-effect of it being on your arm. There's a further side effect which you clearly haven't noticed."

Slaney gulped his wine. "Which is?"

Cyra shook her head. "Before we go into that, I want to play a game. I'd like to play cards with you for the amulet."

The bodyguards by the door both began to snigger.

"You mean *gamble*?" Slaney laughed too. "Haven't you been listening to me, darling? I *always* win. Besides, what could you possibly offer up against the bracelet that would interest me?"

"How about this?" Walking to the couch, Cyra opened her shoulder bag and slid out the police file. "Our covert investigation into you, your ex-wife and your criminal dealings. You sold your nightclubs, but Anastasia still runs two, along with all the drugs and girls in them." She gestured to the escorts. "There's a good chance she trafficked your friends here."

"Very possibly," agreed Slaney, smirking. "The fact that we've never been arrested must tell you the trafficking is hard to prove."

"True," said Cyra. "The police know that both you and Anastasia murdered at least three rival drug dealers in the past few years and our evidence is here. Not quite enough evidence for the CPS, obviously, but it's all contained in this file and there are no digital copies. I've deleted them."

"Interesting," murmured, Slaney. "As I say, I make my living from gambling and everything is legit..." He laughed. "I almost said *now*, but that might suggest that my previous dealings *weren't* quite so legal."

"Merely a slip of the tongue," said Quist, smiling dryly.

"I just don't get it." Slaney shook his head. "You're a cop, so why the hell would you come here offering me a confidential file for a…"

"I told you," said Cyra. "Today I'm no cop, and what I'm suggesting won't take long. A simple, easy game for both the file and the bracelet. We take turns to cut a deck of cards and whoever gets the highest card wins both prizes."

"Oh, you're right," said Slaney. "This definitely *won't* take long and I suppose it would be interesting to have that bit of bedtime reading." Opening the sideboard, he took out a pack of cards and tore off the cellophane wrapper. "But before we begin, allow me to show you something." He placed the deck face-down on the coffee table in front of the Transylvanian escorts and nodded to Watson. "Okay, kid, go ahead and cut them."

Sitting beside the girls, the youth did as instructed and held up the Two of Diamonds. Smiling, Slaney cut the deck himself and showed him the Ace of Clubs. "Let's do that again," he said.

Seven shuffles and cuts of the pack later, Watson had produced an assortment of twos and threes and Slaney had seven consecutive aces.

"Incredible." Quist stroked his nose thoughtfully. "Yes, I don't believe you could have chosen a better way to prove this bizarre luck of yours."

"Exactly." Slaney turned to Cyra. "So, sweetheart, having watched that, do you *still* want to gamble with me?"

"Absolutely," said Cyra. "Who shall go first?"

"You're unbelievable," laughed Slaney, vigorously shuffling and placing the cards on the table. "Right, let's get this over with. I'm a gentleman, so it's ladies first."

Cyra cut the deck and held up her card without bothering to look at it.

"*What?*" mumbled Slaney. He stared silently at her Ace of Spades for several seconds and then cut the pack himself to produce the Two of Hearts. "What the hell is going on here?"

One of the escorts turned to Watson with a puzzled frown. "Is that a *good* card?" she asked. "Has Gabe won?"

"Er, not really," he murmured. "But he *did* come second."

"So…" said Cyra. "If you'd be good enough to slide off that

amulet?" She held out a hand. "I'll take it, thanks."

"Okay, Pinky and Perky…" Gritting his teeth, Slaney turned to the two girls and clapped his hands. "It's time to go upstairs and play with your phones. Uncle Gabe needs to have a grown-up chat with his guests."

Climbing to their feet, the escorts left the room as Slaney nodded to his bodyguards, Tony and Vic. Tony closed the lounge door behind the young women and Vic pulled a handgun from the concealed holster in the rear of his belt.

Quist tensed and swiftly stepped in front of Cyra and Watson.

"Oh, *shit*!" muttered the youth, frozen to the couch.

* * * *

Chapter 25

Gabriel Slaney grabbed the pack of cards and threw them into the fire, his cape flapping around him. "I don't know how you beat me," he snarled. "You obviously cheated in some clever way like a stage magician, but you wasted your time. I'm a poor loser and if you think I'm going to give you..."

"There was no cheating," said Cyra. "I beat you because that petty *good luck* power won't work on my kind. The bracelet was personally designed for me and infused with an ancient magic that you couldn't begin to comprehend. You lost because I'm here now and it wants to be united with its true owner."

"You don't talk like a cop," said Slaney. "In fact, you talk like a fuckin' lunatic. You've probably noticed that Vic has his gun out. He isn't pointing it at anyone at the moment, but that could soon change if you don't start to make sense."

"I believe we need to calm down," said Quist, eyeing the automatic pistol. "You know that we're not armed and there's no need for that weapon."

Watson sat motionless on the couch. "Absolutely," he agreed, gulping. "No need at all."

"Vic," growled Slaney. "You keep hold of that gun."

"I mentioned the side-effects," said Cyra. "Wearing my amulet isn't exactly healthy for humans. You tried wearing it whole and experienced an intense headache. If the complete bracelet had remained on your arm, you'd have been dead within minutes."

Slaney listened, peering curiously at the shimmering serpent coiled around his forearm.

Cyra continued. "Unfortunately, wearing just *one* segment like that is also destructive and it *will* kill you eventually – a terrible, lingering death. I knew it was on your arm the moment I saw your face. The two halves feed upon any human who tries them on. They suck out the life energy, preying upon you like the vampires in those films you enjoy so much."

"That's crazy," snorted Slaney. "I feel amazing. In fact, I've felt much better and more alive since I began wearing the bracelet."

"Ah, I see," said Quist, nodding his understanding. "I believe she's correct."

"Um, yeah," said Watson. "However you might be feeling, mate, I'm afraid you don't *look* amazing."

"What's *that* supposed to mean?" Slaney strode to the large gilt-framed wall mirror beside the fireplace. A plaque beneath claimed it had been used in *The Brides of Dracula.* "I look great..." He grinned at the youth. "As always."

"Idiot," laughed Cyra. "The amulet is protecting itself. It seduced you with the good luck magic so you'd keep it on your arm. It wants to remain there night and day in order to fully drain you. It's altered your personal perception and isn't allowing you to see and feel the *real* you. Take it off and then look again at your reflection."

"I've told you," said Slaney. "I *never* take it off."

"I strongly suggest you take her advice," said Quist. "Remove the bracelet for a moment and look at yourself without it."

Slaney moved closer to the ornate mirror, stroking his seemingly handsome and unblemished features. "This is total bullshit," he muttered, glancing at the bodyguards. "Hey, Vic, how does my face look to you? Do you or Tony see anything wrong with it?"

"Um, well..." said Vic, evasively. "Er, I don't really know, Mister Slaney."

"Yeah," nodded Tony. "Your face looks, er... I mean, well..."

Slaney stared suspiciously at the three visitors, then slowly eased the bracelet over his wrist for the first time in almost two years. He froze to the spot instantly, gazing again at his reflection, with heart pounding and mouth falling slowly open. "What the fuck is *this*?" he whispered. "What in the… I look like… I look like my fuckin' great-grandad."

"It isn't a pretty sight, is it?" smiled Cyra. "I don't know how much you've been paying your Transylvanian cuties, but I'd say they've earned every penny."

"How could I not see this?" Slaney ran trembling fingers over his wrinkled cheeks and scrawny neck. "Look at my hands; they're old and frail too. *Why* couldn't I see this? How is it possible that I didn't know?"

"The bracelet prevented it," said Quist, glancing at the bodyguards. "The aging will have been gradual and I suspect your people were too scared of you to mention the steady change. Besides, they probably had no idea *what* to say. I certainly wouldn't wear it again or you'll continue to deteriorate and die."

"*What*?" snarled Slaney. "Do you think I'm some sort of fucking lunatic? There's no way I'm putting this parasite thing back on my arm." Staring in horror at the serpent spiral in his shaky hand, he tossed it into Watson's lap. "I don't even want to touch it."

Sitting on the couch, the youth instantly tensed. *After seeing the state Slaney's face, he was decidedly uncomfortable with the amulet being so close to his genitals.*

"But just look at me," moaned Slaney. "Look at me, for God's sake. Even with the bracelet off, I still look like *this*. Jesus, I don't want to look like *this*."

"I can easily fix that," said Cyra, quickly. "Do you wish you looked young again?"

"What?" he croaked. "Young again?"

"Listen to me…" began Quist. "Shock has begun to set in and you're not thinking correctly. Whatever she says, do *not*…"

"Yes," he said. "Of course I wish I looked young again."

The geriatric man instantly vanished, an eight year-old child appearing in his place. The bodyguards rushed across the lounge to where their employer had been standing.

"*Wow!*" whispered Watson, jumping up from the sofa. "Just *wow*."

"Where is he?" snapped Vic, his gun frantically jerking from side to side as he pointed it at everyone including the child. "What the hell just happened? Where's Mister Slaney?"

"I'm right here?" said the little boy, staring in awe at his reflection and turning to Cyra. "Yeah, I remember how I looked when I was a kid. *You* did this? How the fuck did you *do* this?"

"Oh, didn't I mention?" said Cyra. "I'm a Djinn. A genie, if you prefer. I'm able to grant wishes and this is exactly what you just wished for."

"Fuck off," shouted Vic, somewhat unhelpfully.

"Try it," said Cyra, smiling sweetly at Slaney. "Wish for something. Anything at all."

Guessing this probably wouldn't end well, Watson gulped and moved close to Quist. He handed the half bracelet to the detective, who stowed it away in the deep pocket inside his trenchcoat.

"Okay, let's try this." The child laughed. "I wish I was adult, but an attractive and healthy adult."

"Mister Slaney?" stammered Vic, staring in total disbelief at the actor Kris Horsley. "Oh, this is fuckin' nuts. Is that *you*?"

"Yeah, it's me all right," whispered Slaney, peering into the mirror. "This isn't exactly what I meant, but I love it. I was expecting my normal older self, but yeah, this is definitely an attractive and healthy adult." He stroked his new face and began to laugh manically. "A genie, you say? You're some sort of fuckin' genie and you're telling me I can actually wish for *anything*?"

"Anything at all," confirmed Cyra. "Ah, that cloak of yours, for example. Didn't you say you wanted the cape worn by the actor Bela Lugosi?"

"You need to be really careful," said Watson. *This guy was giggling away like someone in a straightjacket. As his boss had just said, it was probably due to shock, but Slaney was obviously losing it.* "Whatever you say, she'll probably turn it to…"

"I wish this was Bela Lugosi's actual cape," laughed Slaney.

The cloak instantly changed to a stained garment covered in a greasy putrid mould. A hideous, sickening stench began to fill the lounge.

"Ugh, what *is* this?" Slaney began to retch. "This thing is an absolute mess and it stinks."

"What did you expect?" sighed Quist. "You knew that Lugosi was buried in that cloak. It's been wrapped around his rotting corpse for decades."

"*Shit*," coughed Slaney, gagging. "I need to get rid of it right now. I wish the cloak was back where it came from."

"Where did he go?" yelled Vic. Terrified and beginning to panic now, he aimed his pistol at Cyra. "Mister Slaney vanished into thin air. Where is he? What the hell have you done?"

"I haven't done anything," she said, closing her eyes to bask and drink in the ethereal energy released by the wishes. "He wished for the cloak to be back in Lugosi's grave in Los Angeles, but unfortunately he was wearing it when it returned there."

"*What?*" The bodyguard shook his head. "No, this has to be impossible. Are you seriously telling me that he's inside some guy's coffin on the other side of the fuckin' world?" He pointed the shaking gun at her face. "I want him back. Bring him back here right now, bitch, or you're dead."

"I'm afraid I'm unable to do that," smiled Cyra. "But you can do it easily. All *you* have to do is say the words: *I wish Mister Slaney was back.* I should do it quickly though, if I were you. There won't be any oxygen where he is."

"I wish Mister Slaney was back," shouted Vic.

Slaney reappeared in the lounge, minus the rotting cloak, but still looking like the actor Kris Horsley. Screaming hysterically from the horror, he coughed and heaved on the grave gasses that filled his lungs. Watson gagged too as the ghastly stench of human decay reached him.

"I wish Mister Slaney was okay," stammered the bodyguard, his mind spinning. "I wish he looked like how he looked an hour ago."

Slaney's face instantly changed and crumpled, transforming from the attractive actor to the aged mess created by the amulet over the past months. "You idiot, what have you done?" he screamed, lunging at Vic and grabbing his jacket. "I'm old and wrinkled again and…"

Already in a heightened state of panic, the bodyguard's trigger finger accidentally tightened and the gun fired. His employer staggered backwards, a crimson flower blossoming on his shirt where the bullet had torn into his stomach.

"Oh, bloody hell," stammered Watson. "I don't think anyone was expecting *that*."

"I wish…" gasped Slaney, slumping to the carpet. "I wish I hadn't been shot."

"Sorry," said Cyra, grinning. "I'm afraid I don't have any more wishes to grant you."

Both Vic and Tony twisted around to point their pistols at her.

"Put those guns away," snapped Quist, shielding the woman with his body. "Look at your employer; just *look* at him. You don't have time for threats or anything else. You can see he's badly wounded and you're responsible. You need to get this man to a hospital as soon as possible."

"Yeah, ring an ambulance for me," gurgled Slaney, glaring at Cyra before turning to Quist. "Take that fuckin' bracelet and get it out of my house. Genie, or whatever the fuck she is, get her away from me right now. Get out *now*."

The detective grabbed Cyra's arm and pushed Watson towards the lounge door before Slaney changed his mind. Out in the parking area, he quickly jumped into the BMW as Watson dived headlong into the rear.

"I believe you have something of mine," said Cyra, climbing in beside the detective. "I'll take it."

"No." Quist started the car and sped away from the hall. "I think it will be best if I hang onto this half for now."

"You'll do as I say…" began Cyra, angrily, before biting her tongue and pausing for several seconds. "Very well," she said, calmly. "You can keep it safe for now. We'll retrieve the other segment and then discuss this further."

Watson frowned. *He didn't need to be Einstein to know that Cyra was planning something here.*

The Djinn opened the folder in her bag and found Anastasia Slaney's address. "So where is Harrogate?"

"We passed close by it on the way here," said Quist, tearing along the moorland lane. "It's about thirty minutes away."

The *Cow and Calf* hotel appeared on their right and Quist pulled into the half-empty car park.

"What's this?" snapped Cyra. "What the hell do you think you're doing?"

"I'm dropping off Watson," said Quist, stopping the BMW. "He can get a taxi back to York from here."

"Not a chance," she hissed. "He's coming with us. I've already told you, the boy is insurance and he…"

"And I'm telling *you*," growled Quist. "Watson stays here. People were shooting back there and we could easily have a repeat of that at Harrogate. You want this amulet, don't you? Well, I can obtain the other half for you, but not if I'm trying to protect both the inspector and my assistant from flying bullets. Katie Bradstreet is insurance enough."

Cyra seethed for a moment, staring angrily at the darkening sky above the nearby rock formation. "Okay," she said, turning to the nervous youth. "Get out."

"Um, cheers, Guv," stammered Watson, climbing from the car. "Have fun."

* * * *

Chapter 26

Less than two minutes after receiving Watson's phone call, Kymina's car sped along the moorland lane and screeched into the hotel parking area.

"That was fast," said Watson, jumping into the passenger seat. "So you waited over there at the Cow and Calf rocks like the Guv told you? Am *I* glad to see you."

"The bracelet," said Kymina. "Where is it? Please tell me that Cyra doesn't have it."

"It's okay." The youth smiled reassuringly. "No, the Guv has it; well, half of it anyway. He dropped me here, which pissed off your sister, and they're going to try and get the other part."

"Slaney has split the amulet?" Grimacing, Kymina nodded slowly. "I was unaware, but it would explain why it suddenly changed. If I concentrate, I hear the bracelet calling to me, but last year the song became slightly different."

"That would be when Mister and Missus Gangster got divorced," said Watson. "Slaney's ex-wife has the other half in Harrogate, but I don't know exactly where." He pulled out his phone and tapped quickly at the screen. "Luckily for us, we don't need an address."

"Ah, you're able to track Bernie with your phone?" Kymina watched curiously. "Like a parent with a wayward teenager?"

"Yeah." Watson's teeth chattered. "I'm really glad my mum never used this app, not after some of the things I got up to."

"Are you all right?" asked Kymina. "You're really shivering and your teeth..."

"I'm not bloody well surprised." He took a few deep breaths to calm himself. "I'm still buzzing from being in that gangster's house back there. His guys were waving guns about and Slaney ended up getting shot. Everything's been happening so fast, but it's all sinking in now."

"Did my sister shoot him?" quizzed Kymina.

"No, one of his own guys, which isn't going to look good on his bodyguard CV." Watson laughed dryly. "Cyra stuck to harming people with her *bad wish* routine." He gestured towards Ilkley. "Okay, they're a few miles in front, but I've found them. You'll need to head downhill to the main road and turn right."

Starting the Audi, Kymina pulled out of the car park and onto the lane.

"The Guv and I can track each other," explained Watson. "My mate Gazza loaded the satellite programme onto both our phones, but his technology is more advanced than the usual phone apps. With some of the weird jobs we've had, it can be really handy."

"Like now, for instance?" Kymina nodded. "I'll drive towards Harrogate and you can guide me with the tracker as we get closer." She gave him a rueful smile. "So you've met my sister?"

"Yeah." He winced slightly. "Bit of a scary twat, isn't she?"

"Oh, she can be," admitted Kymina. "And you told me she's now using a police inspector's body? It sickens me when she callously invades a human in that way to further her plans."

"Listen…" The young man cleared his throat. "I was angry when you blackmailed the Guv into robbing the museum, but I can see now why you had to do it. You have that personal code about using human bodies and I know how you..."

"There's really no need to explain." Kymina reached the A65 and turned east towards Otley. "I completely understand how you felt."

"I'm sorry," smiled Watson. "I just watched someone get shot and that frightening shit kind of sharpens your senses and helps you to focus. It makes me want to tell you that I like you; I mean I *really* like you and…"

"Er, surely you're *aware*?" broke in Kymina. "It's a young

film editor named Toni Nelson that you like. Not me."

"That's what the Guv said, but…"

"Really?" The Djinn laughed. "You've been discussing your feelings for me with your boss?"

"No." Watson shook his head. "Well, yes, I suppose so. Look, I know it's Toni's body, but I'm speaking to *you*, Kymina."

"And it's this body that you're looking at." She gave him a shrewd glance. "I'm an empath, remember. I sensed how sexually attracted you were when we first met."

"Um, guilty as charged," grinned Watson.

"You instantly read people when you meet," explained Kymina. "It works on a subliminal level. You look at them and instantly analyse their hairstyle, clothing, tattoos, their tanned skin… All these things and more provide an immediate impression as to who the person is – their persona and intelligence. In a split second you decide whether you want to be with them. You did that with Toni Nelson and it's *that* impression that you're attracted to."

"I get all that," agreed Watson. "Yeah, obviously I took one look at Toni and really fancied her, but since then I've been getting to know *you*."

"Yes, we've been interacting," said Kymina. "But you still don't *know* me. You don't even know my name."

"Huh?" Watson frowned. "Are you telling me it's not Kymina?"

She shook her head. "Kymina is a Persian name that I adopted long ago in order to interact more easily with humans."

"I see." He shrugged. "So what's your real name?"

"I'm afraid you couldn't pronounce it."

"Don't worry; I'm pretty articulate." Watson winked. "Good with my tongue, you might say."

Kymina sighed and then spoke, but the sound was weirdly reminiscent of electricity crackling.

"Er… *right*." The youth stared blankly for a moment. "That's your Djinn name?"

She nodded.

"Okay," he smiled. "Well, articulate or not, I think we'll stick with the Persian name. I like it and, as I say, I really like *you*."

"Certain people are always attracted to the Djinn," said Kymina. "Just like your boss attracting humans with the lupine pheromones he gives out, some humans are attracted to our light."

"Some humans?"

"The more romantic souls amongst you," she explained. "They can subliminally sense the astral light and they're drawn to it."

"That's me," he grinned. "A romantic moth. Well, whether or not it's this invisible light nonsense, I still really like you."

Kymina laughed softly. "But you probably wouldn't like *me* if you really knew me."

"Why not?" Watson turned to her. "I mean, you seem like a really good Djinn. Probably the nicest Djinn I've met this week. Have you ever gone around killing people like your crackpot sister?"

"Of course not," she said. "What I mean is, it's almost impossible for your mind to comprehend that I'm an entity composed of ethereal light and, as such, I'm so unlike you. The Djinn are a benign, peaceful and cultured race. Many wonderful artworks, musical compositions and poems have been produced by our kind inhabiting elderly humans. Her yearning for power has made Cyra something of an anomaly, however. She's so different from the other Djinn and behaves more like a human."

"What's that supposed to mean?" quizzed Watson, taken aback. "We're a peaceful bunch too."

"Is that a joke," laughed Kymina. "All you do is fight and kill. It's all you humans have *ever* done."

"Don't talk so daft," he frowned. "We put men on the moon, we write brilliant rock music and we invented the *Cornetto* ice cream."

"All incidental," shrugged Kymina. "Every species fights its own kind over territory and kills to protect their young, but you're unique in that you enjoy killing. You're genetically hard-wired to kill each other over *anything*."

"Bollocks," laughed Watson.

"Really?" The Djinn glanced at him. "I've spent so long living amongst you, observing your violent behaviour, and it truly saddens me. Long ago, you invented various religions in an attempt to justify all the slaughter. The idea was to kill only people who followed a different creed, but that didn't last long."

"I can't accept that," said the youth.

"All right," sighed Kymina. "Let's take a look at this. You're English, so why don't we just concentrate on *your* nation and not go too far back in history? In the last five-hundred years, the English spent their entire time fighting and killing the Welsh, the Scots and the Irish. For century after century, you also fought and killed your closest neighbours, the French and the Spanish, sometimes teaming up with the Spanish to kill the French, and sometimes joining with the French to kill the Spanish. *Five* long centuries of non-stop carnage."

"Well, as you say, that's history," pointed out Watson.

She nodded. "After continuously fighting and killing the Spanish and the French, you fought and killed the Germans and their allies in two World…"

"Yeah, but come on…" he said, attempting a joke. "They were Germans."

"You even killed each other," continued Kymina. "In a break between killing your continental neighbours, the English killed the English. Over two-hundred thousand people died during your *Civil War*, which wasn't particularly *civil*, was it?"

"I know what you mean," conceded Watson. "But you claim that the violence is some genetic thing. During all those wars, the people were *ordered* to fight. We wouldn't just kill people if…"

"Open your eyes," said Kymina. "You do it all the time – fighting and killing anyone you perceive to be different. People with other religions, gay people, foreigners, people with darker skin, even supporters of rival football teams. In pubs and clubs, you'll beat and stab people who glance at you, or accidentally brush against you in a crowded…"

"Okay, okay," said Watson. "You have a point, but trust me, that isn't *everyone*. It certainly isn't *me*."

"I believe you," said Kymina. "But killing is built into humans. You English sailed to America, a fresh new world, and immediately began killing there. First the native inhabitants and then each other in yet *another* civil war. The white people enslaved and killed the black people, before heading to Viet Nam, Korea and…"

"Okay, enough," said Watson, quietly.

"I'm attempting to save human lives by stopping Cyra from getting that amulet." The Djinn sadly shook her head. "Meanwhile, the more powerful nations and, for some peculiar reason, Britain are spending countless billions on stockpiling atomic weapons. I still can't believe you haven't already fired them and destroyed this planet in a nightmare of thermonuclear fire."

"No, please…" said Watson. "Enough. You make us sound horrible."

"Not all of you." Driving the car into a layby, she pulled up and leant over to kiss his cheek. "Don't look so glum. I know that *you* aren't like that – I can feel it. In every baying homicidal mob, there are always humans who know right from wrong. Humans who have the courage to stand against their murderous peers and say *no*."

Unable to help himself, Watson gently kissed her mouth.

Responding warmly, Kymina ran her fingers through his curly hair to pull him closer. "No, I'm sorry," she muttered, turning away. "I'm sorry, but I can't do this."

"Like I said, I really like you," smiled Watson. "I suppose you think you're too old for me? Well, I may be a couple of thousand years younger than you, but…"

"This isn't my body," sighed Kymina. "You know I follow a code and it's just wrong."

"No, it's just a kiss." The youth kissed her again. "I'm sure Toni Nelson wouldn't mind that. Do the Djinn have kissing and relationships and, er…"

"And sex?" Laughing quietly, Kymina squeezed his hand. "Yes, of course we do. Just like humans, we have friendships, love and sexual relations within our small society. I've never had much time for these things myself. I felt responsible for Cyra and I've always had to watch over her prison. Besides, I rarely inhabit a young body like this. I've spent most of my years in very old people."

"That's so sad." Watson stroked her cheek. "The thing is, I kind of get the impression that you like me too."

"The Djinn fall in love with each other." Kymina hesitated for a moment. "And yes, sometimes we can have those kind of feelings for humans too."

"Humans such as me?" he asked.

"We need to find Cyra and your boss," she said, pulling out of the layby.

"Ah." Watson grinned. "A bit of clever question dodging there, I see?"

Kymina smiled at him. "When I met you, I could instantly sense all the fun, joy, freedom and excitement within you. I can't tell you how much I'd love to spend time with you, but it's impossible. Still, I can always dream about what might have been."

"But after we stop your sister?" suggested Watson, hopefully. "When we've destroyed this bracelet, do you really have to leave Toni Nelson straight away? We could maybe have the time to see each other and…"

"Yes, maybe," she said evasively. "Yes, we'll definitely talk about it again when this is over."

"Okay," said Watson, realising there was something she wasn't telling him. "Remember, that exclusive tour of York is still on offer – all the amazing pubs and clubs with a good-looking black guy as your free guide. I normally drink lager, but I reckon it'll be pretty cool to drink a gin and tonic with a Djinn."

* * * *

Chapter 27

A large North Yorkshire town encircling an expanse of open parkland known as *the Stray*, Harrogate lies on the edge of the Dales, roughly halfway between Ilkley and York. The 18th century discovery of sulphur-rich springs transformed the place into a celebrated spa resort where prosperous tourists flocked for the remedial waters. Grand hotels and other imposing buildings appeared in the Victorian era, along with streets of stately townhouses for the wealthy residents.

In recent decades, the *really* wealthy moved to the much greener outskirts. Stars were encrusting the early evening sky as Quist drove through Rossett Green, a suburb on the southern edge of the town, and turned the BMW into a tree-lined thoroughfare named Millbank Lane.

"It's doubtful that a prestigious locale such as this will have house numbers," said the detective, cruising along the quiet street. "What's the name of the place we're looking for?"

"Oh, we don't need the name," said Cyra. Drawing on a cigarette, she squirmed excitedly in the passenger seat. "I can feel it waiting for me up ahead. My amulet is calling so strongly to me."

"Up ahead," echoed Quist, nodding grimly. "Right."

He glanced at the detached houses on either side, estimating that anyone buying a property here would see their bank balance drop by at least two or three million. Most of the dwellings were positioned a hundred yards back from the road behind high hedgerows, lawns and landscaped gardens. He was aware that television personalities lived on this famous street, along with company owners, and two or three footballers with *Leeds United*. At some point last year, a less wholesome character had also made Millbank Lane her home.

"Just here." Cyra inhaled a last lungful of tobacco smoke and tossed her cigarette stub through the car window. "On the left."

An eight-foot wall appeared, running along the northern side of the lane, and Quist pulled up in front of the electronic steel gates that obscured the property beyond.

"It knows I'm here," laughed the Djinn, jumping out and heading to an intercom system. "It's singing in your pocket and it knows the other segment of the bracelet is here too. It's singing so sweetly to me."

Before she could reach the intercom buttons, the gates silently parted to reveal extensive grounds with mature trees, large decorative rocks and dense clumps of evergreen bushes.

"Intriguing," said Quist, peering around to check for cameras. "There doesn't appear to be any CCTV observing us, yet it seems someone *other* than the bracelet knows you're here."

Cyra climbed back into the car and the detective followed the curved driveway, skirting the shrubbery, until Anastasia Slaney's house came into view. At first glance, it appeared to be a bungalow, but the ultra-modern construction had been sited on the edge of a steep slope and built on various levels. The most noticeable feature was the glass – the house was almost entirely constructed from glass.

"Very nice," mumbled Quist, parking by the entrance. "One has to wonder how much her window cleaner charges."

"Come on," said Cyra, clearly in no mood for humorous chat. "Just remember, you're here to get my amulet. Once we're inside, you'll do whatever I tell you to."

"*You're* here for the amulet," corrected Quist. "Primarily, I'm here to protect Inspector Bradstreet, so let's attempt to keep things civil. Do *not* antagonise this woman."

"That sounded suspiciously like an order," chuckled the Djinn, ringing the bell. "You know you're in no position to dictate any terms."

Quist raised an eyebrow as a huge black man in white T shirt and tight jeans opened the door. *After their trip to Riding Thorp Manor, it was quite obvious that the Slaneys were partial to having big men around them.*

"Two visitors, just like she said." The bodyguard grinned. Six-foot four and musclebound, he politely stepped aside before Cyra could produce her police identification. "A man and a woman, like lambs to the slaughter. She says you can both come on in."

"Lambs to the slaughter?" repeated Quist. "A peculiar choice of phrase, but please lead the way."

They followed the bodyguard through a hallway and into a vast minimalistic lounge with three simple columns supporting the roof, a white marble floor and floor-to-ceiling windows in place of walls. One glass wall faced the gardens and, like many of the houses on the northern side of Millbank Lane, the other looked out over the lush valley of the River Crimple with its distant railway viaduct. Another oversized black man in a muscle T shirt waited for them, standing beside a bright yellow suite where Anastasia Slaney relaxed on one of the four leather couches.

From Katie Bradstreet's police file, Quist knew Anastasia's age to be thirty-two, but just like her ex-husband, this slender woman looked much older; perhaps in her late sixties. Lines and a mass of wrinkles covered a sunken face that, until recently, had clearly been highly attractive. Long black hair flowed over her withered shoulders, and over the straps of a dark blue dress that showed off her cleavage and long legs. Quist noticed Cyra staring gleefully at her wizened right forearm and the sparkling serpent that spiralled around it.

"Well, hello there," said Anastasia. Her sensual East European accent belonged in a 1960's spy movie. "I've been expecting you both and here you are, right on time."

"You knew we were coming?" Quist shrugged off his trenchcoat and draped it over his arm, ensuring the bracelet segment remained safe in the deep internal pocket. "Did your ex-husband contact you after we left him?"

"No one rang me," she smiled, gesturing to his coat. "One of my people will take that for you."

"No, that's fine; I'll hold onto it," said Quist, looking again at the size of the two men. "You say your *people*? Do you mean your private security?"

Cyra walked nonchalantly around the lounge, peering down a wide spiral staircase to see a further lounge and dining area below.

"Yes, they're bodyguards," nodded Anastasia. "Staff, hired help, lovers – you can describe them in any way you like."

"Lovers, eh?" said Cyra, running an approving eye over the bulging biceps on show. "Sorry to hear about your recent divorce, by the way."

"Are you serious?" she laughed. "If you met Gabriel earlier, then you must be aware of that bizarre obsession he has with old horror films. Five years of that nonsense was way more than enough for me." She smiled sexily at the bodyguards. "Gabriel's entire business is in my name now. I run everything and, in my line of work, these larger gentlemen are something of a necessity."

"Knowing the kind of business you refer to, I'm surprised they haven't searched us," said Quist. "Your ex-husband had us both checked for weapons before we could get *this* close to him."

"There's no need for that here," said Anastasia. "I know that neither of you are carrying guns or knives."

"Intriguing," said Quist. "And you say you were expecting us? If no one contacted you, then I presume this is something to do with that rather enchanting amulet?"

"That's right," said Anastasia, holding aloft her arm with the gleaming serpent. "So I assume you know about this bracelet and how it affects the wearer?"

"I know what it is," admitted Cyra, raising a curious eyebrow. "But I've no idea how it affects *you*. Why don't you enlighten us?"

"Why not?" The woman smiled. "It's not as if you'll be able to repeat it to anyone."

Quist's body tensed at the words, his heart beating faster.

"Gabriel bought the bracelet because of his weird liking for horror movies," said Anastasia. "It reminded him of those mummy films. It's made up of two parts and this is only one half of…"

"I know all that," sighed Cyra. "But I'll ask again – how does it affect you?"

"It's quite simple – I'm a psychic." The woman laughed loudly. "Believe it or not, I'm an actual psychic, *that's* how it affects me. I never had much time for such things, but ever since I began wearing this piece of jewellery, I've been gifted with the most amazing paranormal abilities. Empathy, extrasensory perception and precognition, I now have genuine psychic powers and you can't imagine how helpful that is in my *business dealings.*"

"Ah." Cyra nodded her understanding. "Just like Gabriel's good luck, this is another side-effect."

"Side-effect?" echoed Anastasia, puzzled.

The Djinn didn't answer, but stared longingly at the bracelet.

"Well, no matter," shrugged Anastasia. "I never remove the bracelet and the precognitive powers keep me safe with their warnings."

Quist nodded his understanding. *Just like Gabriel Slaney, this was the parasite protecting its host as it fed upon her life energy.*

"I knew about you," said Anastasia. "I knew that a man and a woman would visit me tonight at this exact time, but strangely, I couldn't tell *who.* I also know that you intend to take the amulet from me and that one of you will attempt to kill me. Obviously, I will be preventing *that* before it can take place."

"No, I assure you," said Quist. "Neither of us intend you any harm and…"

"The premonitions are never wrong." She shook her head. "But I don't understand. The bracelet isn't particularly valuable and I know Gabriel didn't pay much for it at the auction. So if you were unaware of the psychic power it bestows upon the wearer, why would you want it?"

"I want it because it's mine," said Cyra, icily.

"I see." Anastasia nodded to the closest bodyguard who moved nearer to her couch. "Another weird thing – now that you're here, I can't pick up anything from either of you. It's the first time this has happened since I began wearing the bracelet. I know that one of you will try to kill me, but I can't pinpoint which one. I just can't read either of you."

"Of course not," said Cyra. "Those psychic powers won't work on supernatural creatures."

"Supernatural?" Anastasia frowned. "What the hell is *that* supposed to mean?"

"It means that he's a werewolf and I'm a Djinn." Cyra smiled sweetly. "The Djinn who *owns* that bracelet. Now why don't you save yourself an awful lot of trouble and bloodshed and simply hand it over to me?"

* * * *

Chapter 28

Watson gazed around the upmarket neighbourhood as Kymina motored slowly along Millbank Lane on the edge of Harrogate. Night had fallen and the streetlamps illuminated the lengthy drives with their parked cars.

"BMW, Mercedes, Porsche and Audi," muttered the youth. "It looks like you need a German car to fit in around here." He spotted a Lamborghini. "Oh, or Italian." He turned back to the app on his phone. "Hey, here we go. The tracker is saying they're just up here on the left."

"Yes, I can sense the amulet," said Kymina, tensely. "The song has been growing increasingly louder and more powerful as we approached this street."

"Are you okay?" asked Watson, picking up on her edginess.

"It's the song," she explained. "It feels very different now and I don't like it."

She brought the car to a halt outside a pair of open gates and Watson peered up the curving driveway. A small part of an illuminated glass building could be seen behind the dense shrubbery, along with the rear end of a parked BMW.

"I guess we all have different tastes," he said, frowning. "But from what I can make out from here, it looks like this Slaney woman lives in a bloody big greenhouse. By the way, that's Katie Bradstreet's car."

"They're obviously inside." Kymina nodded bitterly. "Oh, no, that's why the bracelet's song has changed. Both segments are now together again and Cyra is there with them. I can sense that she isn't wearing it, but the amulet has finally been united with its owner and it feels ecstatic. We have to get it away from her before she has a chance to place it on her arm."

"But what the hell can we do?" Watson sighed. "The Guv

agreed to help your sister because she's possessing Katie Bradstreet and she threatened to harm her body or kill her. How are we supposed to get the bracelet without Cyra hurting her?" He thought for a moment. "And, more to the point, without *us* getting shot by some friggin' lady gangster?"

"One step at a time," said Kymina. "We can't see anything at all from here. We need to get closer."

"Er, yeah," agreed Watson, nervously. "We need to trespass on the dangerous gangster's property and get much closer to her house."

Leaving the Audi by the gateway, the two entered the grounds and, instead of following the drive, headed quickly across the lawn and into the bushes, quietly sneaking through the evergreen foliage to the parking area outside the rear of the building. Watson gently parted the branches to see the glass walls of the lounge.

"Well, how about that?" he whispered. "We needed to know what was happening and those glass walls certainly make things easier for us. There's the Guv and I'm guessing that must be Anastasia Slaney who he's talking to. The big black guys will be her security team and, if they're anything like her ex-hubby's bunch, they'll be carrying guns."

"There it is on her arm," said Kymina. "I can see that Anastasia is wearing part of the bracelet."

"Yeah, the other half is in the Guv's pocket," said Watson.

"I can sense it," she said, nodding. "At this close distance, I can feel the power radiating from both segments. So the fair-haired woman in the raincoat is the police inspector? My sister is using her body?"

"Yeah, that's the Guv's girlfriend, Katie Bradstreet," confirmed Watson. "Although, like you say, it's now Cyra." He gave Kymina a tight smile. "Hey, you know what they say about people who live in glass houses?"

She turned to him. "They shouldn't throw stones?"

"No," he grinned, uneasily. "They shouldn't have sex with the lights on."

* * * *

"So you're a Djinn and he's supposed to be a werewolf?" purred Anastasia, indifferently. "How truly bizarre. People have tried to frighten me many times over the years, but that has to be the strangest threat ever. It's also the most ludicrous."

Reclining on the bright yellow couch, she casually crossed her legs and nodded to the bodyguard who stood beside her. He reached behind a leather cushion and pulled out a silenced handgun that he'd concealed there earlier.

"Stop right now and *think*," snapped Quist, holding up a hand. "This woman is a police inspector and her people know that we were coming here. You can't just shoot a…"

"I told you," sighed Anastasia. "My precognitive powers are never wrong. The police are totally unaware of this visit. I know you came here secretly and I know that one of you is going to kill me. Annoyingly, I can't sense *which* one of you, but it doesn't really matter. There's an easy solution to that problem."

"*Very* easy," agreed Cyra. "You just give me my property and we'll leave."

"You claim the bracelet belongs to you," laughed Anastasia. "You obviously have some sort of history with it, but I don't particularly care what your story is. Gabriel became the owner when he bought it two years ago and I now own *this* half. It's *mine*. What on earth makes you think I'd give up the paranormal power that I now possess?"

Cyra shrugged. "I would have thought the threat of being torn apart by a werewolf would be adequate persuasion, but apparently not."

Anastasia suddenly jerked. The woman caught her breath and

sat upright on the couch, massaging her temple. "Something is about to happen," she muttered. "I just had a premonition and it was so vivid – thousands of glittering diamonds, my spiral staircase over there and blood; so *much* blood. Something is going to happen right here within the next few…"

"Oh, something is *definitely* going to happen," confirmed Cyra. "You're about to die unless you give me my amulet."

Anastasia sighed. "I can't process this vision with you making your tedious, empty threats. I don't know if you've noticed, but this floor is marble and very easy to clean. It certainly won't be the first time we've had to mop up blood." She gestured to her bodyguard. "Finish them both."

Cyra saw the silenced pistol being raised and turned to Quist. "It's over to you," she said. "You don't want poor Katie to get hurt, do you?"

"No, wait," snapped the detective, dropping his trenchcoat and leaping in front of the Djinn. "Don't do…" He grunted as the automatic coughed twice and two 9mm bullets hit him in the chest.

Fighting the pain, Quist launched himself straight at the gunman, bursting open his nose with a headbutt, before lifting him from the floor. He kicked the fallen pistol under the couch and hurled the struggling man into his colleague, slamming both of them to the floor. Anastasia jumped up from the couch, attempting to dodge past the fight, but Quist snatched her arm. Evading her frantic punching and scratching, he grabbed the bracelet and wrenched it off over her hand.

"No, you bastard," she snarled. "Give that back to me."

"Believe it or not, I'm doing you a favour." Quist stowed the amulet inside his coat with the matching half. "You need to go to a mirror and look at your reflection."

Cyra stood behind the detective, watching with delight as he punched both bodyguards unconscious. Quietly taking the taser from her raincoat pocket, she turned up the electrical charge. "Full power for a big strong boy like you," she murmured, pressing the crackling prongs against Quist's neck.

He crumpled to the floor instantly and, stooping to grip his wrist, the Djinn vacated Bradstreet's body and entered the stunned detective.

"Oh, yes," she grinned. "Now *this* feels powerful."

* * * *

"That was some sort of Taser stun gun," hissed Watson, watching anxiously from the garden shrubbery with Kymina. "The Guv has both halves of the bracelet in his coat pocket, but if your sister has electrocuted him unconscious, he won't be able to stop her taking them from him."

"It's far worse than that," stammered Kymina. "I saw Cyra squeeze his arm. She's left the police officer and entered Bernie's body instead."

"Are you sure?" Watson shook his head. "No, we'll never be able get your bracelet off the Guv; he's far too strong and fast. *Shit*, this is a total nightmare."

"She's possessed a werewolf," moaned Kymina. "Oh, Watson, I'm sorry, but I don't know what to do."

Trembling, the youth glanced over his shoulder and made a snap decision. "Okay, come with me... quick." Giving the girl a frightened smile, he grabbed her arm and yanked her towards the gates. "Like I said, people in glass houses shouldn't have sex with the lights on. They should *also* watch out for people doing what I'm about to do."

* * * *

"Bernie, where *am* I?" stammered the dizzy and disorientated Katie. Gripping the wing of a couch for stability, she looked around the vast lounge and saw a furious old woman standing over her two unconscious bodyguards. "Is that Anastasia Slaney? But she looks so old. What's *she* doing here with... I don't understand this. Where are we, Bernie?"

"I'm afraid Bernie isn't here," said Cyra. The blood from the bullet wounds had turned to powder on leaving Quist's body and she brushed it from his shirt. "You've served your purpose, my dear, and now you need to stop whining before you annoy me."

"Bernie?" Katie shook her head, bewildered. "What do you mean?"

"I mean *shut up*." Cyra closed her eyes for a moment and laughed quietly. "Ah, Bernard's recent memories are interesting, to say the least. So my sister was hidden away in my editor friend Toni? Well, I would never have guessed that."

Annastasia stood watching in angry confusion. She felt strangely naked without the amulet, not to mention her two security men. "What are you talking about?" she demanded, glaring at the Djinn and edging towards Quist's trenchcoat on the floor. "You seem somehow *different*. What did she do to you with that stun gun?"

"You can shut up too," chuckled Cyra, rolling her neck and running exploratory hands over her new body. "Yes, this is just as I expected. Even in its human form, this Quist scabbard is exceptionally powerful."

"Bernie?" pleaded Katie, again. "You're really frightening me. You aren't making any sense and I don't understand what's happened to me."

Noticing Anastasia moving for Quist's coat, Cyra swatted her away with the back of her hand and picked up the garment. "Oh, yes," she whispered, smiling gleefully to see the two amulet segments inside the deep pocket. "After all these centuries I can finally…"

Her smile became a frozen grimace as the entire glass wall to her right disintegrated in a deafening explosion. A black car burst into the lounge, thousands of glittering diamonds showering down around it, spilling over the vehicle and the marble floor. Watson slammed the

Audi's grille into Cyra as he braked hard, propelling her broken body across the room and down the spiral staircase.

"What in God's name…" began Katie.

Kymina flung open the passenger door and leant out to grab Quist's coat from the marble tiles where Cyra had dropped it.

"Get in," shouted Watson. Knowing all about Quist's supernatural fast-healing, he was aware that Cyra could return any second. "Get in here *now*."

Katie stood rooted to the spot in wide-eyed terror, completely frozen until Kymina snatched an arm and roughly dragged her inside. Still reeling from Watson's rather dramatic home invasion, Anastasia dropped to her knees and groped beneath the couch for her bodyguard's gun.

"You ran him down," screamed the inspector, squirming on Kymina's lap. "What the fuck were you thinking? You ran Bernie down."

The young man changed gear and reversed out of the lounge with the car roof still showering glass diamonds and the door flapping open. He skidded the Audi into a tight turn and heard Anastasia's bullets tear into the bodywork as he sped along the driveway and into the lane.

"Trust me," he yelled. "Knowing the Guv, he won't hold it against me."

* * * *

Chapter 29

Climbing slowly to her feet at the bottom of the staircase, Cyra ran her hands over Quist's body. "Amazing," she muttered, feeling down the outside of the trousers. "The broken bones and other damage to this scabbard healed almost instantly. Yes, I knew the lycanthrope would be a good choice."

"I'm ready for an explanation," snarled Anastasia, behind her. Anger had accentuated her East European voice. "I want the names and addresses of that loathsome bitch you came here with and the black kid who drove the car. Who were they and where will they have taken my bracelet?"

Cyra turned, stroking thoughtfully at Quist's large nose and smiling sweetly. The furious woman had followed her down the steps into the dining area, albeit in a more conventional and far less injurious manner. Her bodyguards were now fully conscious again and stood on either side of their employer, both holding silenced handguns and glaring indignantly after their beating from Quist.

"No need to concern yourself with any of that," said Cyra. "I'll be retrieving my amulet from them very soon." She ran an eye over Anastasia's aged, wrinkled body. "So I guess you still haven't looked in a mirror?"

"You mentioned that upstairs," said Anastasia. "What are you talking about?"

"You look a little *rough*, to say the least," laughed the Djinn. "But it doesn't really matter; you'll soon be looking far worse. To be honest, I thought you might have taken the opportunity to flee after that car hit me. My skull was cracked and my spine was fractured. This body was out cold for over a minute as they healed."

"Your broken spine healed?" scoffed Anastasia. "And why would I run from my own home? Haven't you noticed the guns pointing at you?"

"Oh, I have," confirmed Cyra. "But haven't *you* noticed the two holes in this shirt? Everything happened pretty fast up there, but your boys shot this body twice in the chest. A few more bullets aren't going to make much difference. You'll be delighted to know that your psychic powers weren't wrong, my dear." The Djinn gave her a wide grin. "One of your visitors tonight *does* intend to kill you."

"I'm tired of listening to you. I'll find the bracelet without your help." Anastasia turned to her men. "Go ahead and kill this man."

The silenced pistols coughed three times each and Cyra tottered backwards.

"*Ugh*, that hurt," she mumbled, massaging Quist's torso and seeing the spilt blood turning to powder. "I really dislike being hurt. Now, let's see how this transformation process works."

She held out Quist's arm, peering curiously as the crackling bones began to lengthen, the fingers shrank and the hand expanded into a large furry wolf's paw.

"Ah, it seems that shapeshifting is *also* quite painful. I really ought to warn you – this won't leave me in the best of moods."

Cyra began to transform fully and the terrified bodyguards started firing again. Several more bullets tore pointlessly into Quist's growing body as his shirt and trousers were ripped apart.

* * * *

Watson sped out of Harrogate along Leeds Road, nervously checking the car mirrors to ensure no one was following.

"Do you think you could climb into the back?" grunted Kymina, wriggling awkwardly beneath Katie. "We can't possibly travel like this."

Still disorientated, the inspector scrambled from her lap and over the backrests to curl up shivering on the rear seat.

"We need to check Bernie's coat," said Kymina, nodding to the pile of leather in her dark footwell. "We saw him put that woman's segment in the pocket and I can feel the energy calling to me, but you need to take a look. You have to make sure the complete bracelet is definitely in there."

"I'm driving and it's right by your feet," said Watson, puzzled. "Can't you check it yourself?"

"I can't look upon it." She smiled weakly. "The amulet is too powerful for me to see it close up like this. As I say, I can sense the power, but you need to confirm we have both halves."

"Okay." Watson stopped by the kerb and leant over to rummage inside the trenchcoat. "Yeah, both curly snakes are in here."

"That's good. We managed to get it away from Cyra." Sighing with relief, Kymina averted her eyes. "But when you opened the pocket, it began calling louder to me. It wants me to take it from you and deliver it to her."

"Bad bracelet." Watson jokingly slapped the coat. "Naughty bracelet."

Her spinning mind still recovering from the possession, Katie wasn't listening. "I remember Beningbrough," she muttered, rubbing her eyes. "I remember calling there with Tariq. I was speaking to a make-up artist when she took out one of those stun guns. She must have used it on me, because the next thing I remember is waking up back there in that house."

"You'll be groggy for a short while, but you'll be fine," said Kymina, turning to Watson. "Cyra was only using her body for a few hours. The after effects won't be as debilitating as they were with Steve Lyle; she was using the stuntman for days."

"What?" stammered Katie, running a shaky hand through her short blonde hair. Her senses began to quickly return, like snapping out of a dream. "I'm sorry, but what the hell are you talking about? Come to that, who *are* you?"

"This is Toni Nelson," said Watson, pulling away from the kerb and continuing along Leeds Road. "She's the editor on the new movie they're filming in York as…"

"Is that supposed to make sense?" shouted Katie, angrily. "Yes, but who *is* she and what the fuck is going on? Why did you ram the car into Bernie and then leave him? He could be badly injured and we need to go back there… wherever *back there* actually was."

"Um…" mumbled Watson. He had no idea what to say, or how much to tell her… or *not* tell her.

"Ugh!" The inspector grimaced. "And what's this foul taste in my mouth?"

"Where else would you have a foul taste?" asked the youth, grinning nervously.

"*What?*" Katie glared at him in the rear-view mirror. "Was that supposed to be a fucking joke?"

"Sorry," he sighed. "Just trying to, um, ease the tension. The taste is from all the cigarettes that you've been smoking."

"*What?*" she repeated.

"This is no time for secrecy," sighed Kymina. "My sister can sense the amulet calling out in song. Because it belongs to her, she'll feel it far more than I and she'll follow the song like a beacon. We need to explain everything before Cyra tracks us down."

* * * *

Cyra stood panting in Anastasia Slaney's dining room, the shaggy black fur of her body soaked in scarlet gore.

"Well, that was truly exhilarating," growled the werewolf, its red eyes gleaming brightly as it licked the dripping blood from its lips. "Oh, yes, I could easily get used to this feeling of raw power; such a beautiful, savage power."

Ragged body parts, steaming intestines and other internal viscera lay all around the huge creature. Cyra knew how many she'd just slaughtered, but looking at the crimson carnage, it was almost impossible to tell that this horrific scattering of arms, legs and lumps of flesh had belonged to just *three* people. Smiling with satisfaction, she shapeshifted back into the form of a naked man.

"Well, it's been fun," she laughed. "But if you'll now excuse me, I have a few people to shred and an amulet to retrieve."

Heading up the spiral staircase, back to the ground level, Cyra left the building through the wide opening where the glass wall had been. She sucked in a freezing breath of night air and ran along the short drive to the quiet emptiness of Millbank Lane – empty, save for a white Range Rover that was cruising towards her.

The young driver braked as the pale figure of a stark-naked man stepped out into the headlights. "What on earth are you doing?" he demanded, clearly shocked as he jumped from his car. "Hey, are you all right, mate? Do you need help?"

Cyra smiled at the bespectacled young man and then peered at his vehicle. Its bulky size, coupled with the darkly tinted windows and chrome bull bars bolted to the grille, suggested that this diminutive human worked in computing and enjoyed gaming. She stepped forward, smacking him hard with the back of her hand and watching with satisfaction as he rolled unconscious beneath a nearby conifer hedgerow.

"Yes, this body has such strength and power," grinned the Djinn, flexing Quist's fingers. "Even in its normal human form."

Climbing into the car, she spotted the open gymnasium holdall on the passenger seat containing a track suit and a towel. The driver was clearly returning from an evening workout at his local fitness centre. Cyra rummaged through the bag, then checked the glove compartment, before pulling a sour face.

"No cigarettes," she tutted, driving away up the lane. "Damn these fucking fitness fanatics."

* * * *

Chapter 30

Speeding east along the rural A59, Watson reached the ring road that encircles York and crossed the brightly lit roundabout to enter the outskirts of Acomb. The A59 becomes Boroughbridge Road at this point and the surrounding landscape begins to change from open countryside to clusters of semi-detached houses. The traffic was light; it was that early evening period between commuters heading home from work and people driving out for the night.

"This is insane," said Katie, in the rear of the Audi. "Yes, I recognised Anastasia Slaney, even though she looked really old. I accept I was in her home without any idea of how I got there, but the rest of this story you're telling me..." She shook her head. "I'm sorry, but this is straight from a book of fairy stories."

"Which is exactly what I thought," confessed Watson, heading through the suburb towards central York. "But believe me, it didn't take long before I found out that it was all bloody well real."

"But you're *you*," snapped Katie. "I'm a detective inspector in the police. Rather than just accepting the crazy shit that people tell me, I have to work with these things called *evidence* and *proof*."

"Oh, there's plenty of evidence," said Watson. "And if you want proof..." He turned to Kymina. "Um, those wishes of yours – pardon the inuendo, but I'd like you to give me one."

"Of course," said the Djinn, realising his intensions. "Go ahead."

"By the way," frowned Katie, "I seem to remember Bernie telling me that you don't have a driver's license."

"Seriously?" Watson gaped at her in the mirror. "We have a psychopathic Djinn chasing us for a lethal bracelet. We have to keep her away from it, but you're more concerned with a driving license?" He rummaged in his jacket pocket, pulled out a half-eaten chocolate bar and passed it over his shoulder.

"What am I supposed to do with this?" demanded the inspector.

"Well, you could eat it and take away the taste of cigarettes," sighed Watson. "But instead, could you just hold it tight for me? Okay, I wish it was a bunch of red roses."

The car headlights dimmed momentarily.

"What the *hell*..." Katie suppressed a yelp of shock and threw the flowers onto the seat beside her. "That's... *impossible*. How did you do that?"

"You know how," said Kymina. "It clearly *isn't* impossible and you heard him wish for them. Once again, everything we've just told you is the truth."

"*Magic?*" stammered Katie, timidly lifting one of the roses to sniff it. "You're telling me that you're a genie? I had another genie inside me and now it's using Bernie's body? Yes, I've come across real magic before, but you must know that I can't accept genies."

"They prefer Djinn," said Watson. "And come on, this shouldn't be so hard to get your head around. As you say, you've seen weird supernatural shit before."

"I have," admitted the inspector, laughing dryly. "But genies and wishes..."

"Yes, Djinn that possess people," confirmed the youth. "You know about people being possessed by supernatural entities – remember how we were once chased and nearly killed by a pretty fuckin' scary one. And what about that magical dagger from back then? Well, now we have a magic bracelet and we can't let Cyra get her hands on it."

"I know all that, but this..." sighed Katie. "Magic tricks with flowers..."

"What on earth was I thinking with the roses?" muttered Watson. "Kymina, can you give me one more wish?"

Smiling tightly, the Djinn nodded.

"I wish you believed us," said Watson, turning to Katie.

Once again the car lights dimmed slightly and Katie gave him a confused look. "I *do* believe you," she said.

"Thank heavens for that," said Kymina, looking around the leafy suburban road. Pubs and small rows of shops were beginning to appear on either side as they approached the city. "You both know York. Where can we go where we might be safe?"

"We need to go straight to the police headquarters on Fulford Road," said Katie. "Now that I know this is real, I can lock your bracelet in the vault of our secure evidence room."

Watson smiled to himself. *Yeah, the second wish had obviously been much better than the flowery first one.*

"That's no good," said Kymina, bitterly. "Cyra is so close to obtaining her amulet now and she won't care anymore about stealth. With that supernatural body she's currently using, she'll kill anyone who gets in her way. Trust me, she'll tear apart everyone in your headquarters to get to it."

"Supernatural body?" frowned Katie. "What are you talking about? Just get us to my police station."

Watson glanced uneasily at Kymina. *They'd told Katie everything, apart from the small fact that her boyfriend was a werewolf.*

"Look, what about if we chuck it in the river?" he suggested. "The Ouse is deep in the middle of town and, even though divers could eventually get to it, we'd buy some time to plan a better…"

The Audi lurched and swerved sickeningly as a Range Rover slammed into them from behind. Watson regained control and glanced in the mirror to see the driver of the large white vehicle – a furious-looking Quist. His shoulders were naked, as if he were stripped to the waist.

"*Jesus*, she's found us," yelled Watson. "The Guv's phone is in his trenchcoat here, so how did…"

207

"She doesn't need that tracker app," hissed Kymina. "She's following the amulet's song."

"It's Bernie." Katie turned in the rear seat to see the car. "He's right behind us."

"Believe me, it *isn't* him," said Watson. "Everything we told you is true and Cyra is using the Guv's body."

The inspector turned again. Yes, she *did* believe him. The driver's features were twisted into a hideous demonic grin and, to be honest, this didn't look *much* like the genial Bernie Quist.

Water End, a smaller side road, turned off to their left, the two lanes separated by a central traffic island. Seeing the Range Rover accelerating to ram them again, the youth jerked the steering wheel and took the junction down the wrong side of the island, speeding away along Water End as Cyra missed the turn and continued on the main road.

"Damn!" muttered Katie, thrown about in the rear of the Audi. "I honestly can't believe you don't have a driver's license."

"Yeah, well I lost her," said Watson, stamping on the accelerator. "She'll soon turn around and follow us, but I know this area and there are lots of little streets down here to hide in."

"I don't think we'll be *able* to hide," moaned Kymina. "Now that both segments of the amulet are together, its song is far too strong and Cyra can easily sense it calling. That's how she just located us and she'll definitely find us again."

"So what can we do?" croaked the frightened youth.

"I don't know," admitted Kymina. "The first thing we need to do is separate the two halves. If we can keep them apart, that should quieten the song."

"Wait a minute…" Watson spotted the junction with Leeman Road and took it. "I have an idea."

"Where are you going?" asked Katie.

"The *Railway Museum* is down here," said Watson. "They're

having some electrical work done and the back doors will be unlocked. Lendal Bridge isn't far from there, so why don't we separate the two halves by hiding one in the museum and then…"

"Throw the other into the river?" Kymina grimaced. "It isn't ideal, but yes, right now it's certainly better than nothing. The amulet is calling louder. It somehow knows that we're attempting to prevent Cyra from reaching it."

Watson raced along Leeman Road to the collection of huge museum buildings that loomed in the darkness ahead. Driving past the closed entrance lobby and down the side of the main building, he reached the private area at the rear. Quist had parked here on Sunday night when they called to meet with Calista Dawson. Several of her company vehicles stood on the tarmac beside the Audi.

"This is it," he said, pulling up in front of the large loading doors that opened into the *Great Hall*. "They leave these doors unlocked so the electricians can go in and out to their vans of equipment." Leaping out, he grabbed Quist's coat. "We can't separate the bracelet yet. If we left one half in the car, Cyra will probably find it. Until we can get to the river, we'll have to take both bits with us."

The two women jumped out and Kymina tried the closest door. "You're right," she said, as it rolled sideways. "It's open."

"Damn it," hissed Katie, nodding to a CCTV unit on the wall. "Our faces are on camera. How will we explain…"

"Don't worry," said Watson, darting inside. "They're all switched off."

They ran into the vast exhibition area and Watson looked about nervously. "Where are the workmen?" he whispered, hurrying through the silent fleet of gigantic locomotives. "The woman who owns the firm told us there were eight people working here."

"There they are," said Katie, as a large green steam engine came into view. "It seems they're on a break."

Like all British workers, the unsupervised electricians were indeed enjoying one of their many tea breaks, eating sandwiches on a pile of tarpaulins beside the *Flying Scotsman*. The eight men looked confused as the trio of strangers hurried towards them.

"Excuse me," called out the foreman. "Who are you? I'm sorry, but you people can't be in here."

"You have to get rid of them," pleaded Kymina, turning to the inspector. "They could be hurt if Cyra arrives."

"*Shit*," hissed Katie, reaching a snap decision. "Listen to me," she shouted. "I'm a police officer and you all need to leave for your own safety." Running up to the group, she held out her ID with a finger strategically placed over her name. "A crazed individual with a knife is at large in this area. He's already killed three people and he's heading this way."

"Wouldn't we be safer inside?" asked the foreman, nervously.

"No." Katie thought fast. "He um, blames the museum for his mental problems and we know he's coming here right now. Backup officers are on their way, but you need to get out and drive some distance away from this place. Get away… *now*."

Realising this was an officially sanctioned extension to their tea break, the men jumped up without further questions and bolted for the rear doors.

"Very good," said Kymina. "Now we have to do this as quickly as possible. I can't touch the amulet. It's calling to me right now and it's so powerful. It wants me to snatch it from you and run to my sister."

"Give it to me," snapped Katie. "Let's get this over with."

Watson handed her one of the serpent spirals from Quist's pocket and the inspector raced away, her raincoat flapping behind her. She ran behind the nearest locomotive, the *Duchess of Hamilton*, to arrive at the bright blue *Mallard* with the public inspection gantry constructed beside its cab.

"What am I doing?" she muttered, hurrying up the steps and

climbing inside to secrete the bracelet segment behind a cluster of pipework and pressure dials. "I believe their story. I believe everything about the Djinn and this magical amulet, but this still feels absolutely crazy."

The confused electricians waited outside in two of the company vans with the doors locked, the engines ticking over and the heaters blasting warm air. Keeping a lookout for any signs of a knife-wielding lunatic or the police backup, they watched as a white Range Rover skidded to a halt on the tarmac. A huge black wolf burst from the vehicle and bounded on all fours between their vans and into the museum through the open loading door. The shocked men glanced at one another momentarily before both drivers drove away at high speed down Leeman Road.

The wolf sprang onto the high roof of a locomotive and used the vantage point to scan the vast exhibition space for any signs of movement. Somewhere ahead and perceptible only to the ears of the Djinn, the bracelet began to sing louder and the grinning creature homed in, pouncing from train roof to train roof as it moved further into the hall.

"Where do you think she's hiding it?" said Watson, waiting nervously at the front of the *Flying Scotsman*.

"Perhaps it's best if we don't know," suggested Kymina. "That way we wouldn't be able to tell Cyra if she got here before we could leave and…"

Catching movement in his peripheral vision, Watson glanced to his right. He was just in time to see something large and black leap silently from a neighbouring locomotive and onto the *Scotsman's* coal tender.

"Leave?" he moaned. "Something tells me we might have missed our chance to leave."

The wolf jumped the gap between the tender and the engine cab and, crouching low, began to creep along the length of the apple green boiler towards them.

"Oh, no, she's here already," whispered Kymina. "So this is how Bernie looks in his *other* form."

Moving slowly on all fours like this, the furry creature reminded her of a black tarantula. Watson looked around, but knew exactly how fast his boss was in lupine form and realised there was little point in attempting to run. The youth clutched Quist's trenchcoat tightly to himself, his spine icing over as he saw the creature's eyes were bright red. Various tools had been left by the workmen on the pile of tarpaulins and he grabbed a small crowbar as Katie arrived back to join them.

"Okay, it's time to go," she panted. "I've hidden it back there and we can…"

The words choked in her throat as the enormous wolf leapt down from the locomotive funnel above to land in a crouch in front of them. It rose slowly to its full height on two legs, eyes gleaming and tendrils of saliva dangling from a wide grin.

"*What is this…*" croaked Katie, frozen to the spot. "Oh, my God, what the fuck *is* this thing?"

"This?" echoed Watson, trembling. "I'm afraid this is Cyra and she's using the supernatural body that we mentioned."

"Hello, Kymina," growled the wolf, through a mouthful of glistening fangs. "All that time working with little Toni Nelson and I never once guessed it was my beloved sister. How sneaky of you."

"Don't touch her," stuttered Watson, his teeth chattering. He wasn't the most courageous of young men, but he suddenly found himself stepping in front of Kymina and shakily holding out the crowbar.

"What good do you think *that* will do?" chuckled Cyra. "Oh, don't tell me you've developed feelings for my sister and you're hoping to protect her? You need to drop that ludicrous thing… *now*, before I force you to eat it."

Not feeling particularly hungry, the youth tossed it down and backed away slightly.

Whimpering with fright, Katie also began to shuffle backwards.

"No, you stay right there," snarled the wolf. It turned to Kymina. "No more running. I want my amulet." It held out a paw. "Oh, and I'll take that bottle too."

"Bottle?" she asked.

"Don't be so stupid," snapped Cyra. "You know I have access to all of this scabbard's memories. You had Quist steal a Dugdana bottle from a museum, obviously with the intention of imprisoning me once again."

The crystal bottle was in Kymina's pocket, but she didn't answer.

"You know what?" laughed Cyra. "Why should I care? Keep your bottle and the best of luck in getting me inside it. As soon as I wear the bracelet, I'll wish *all* Dugdana prison bottles out of existence." The wolf turned to Watson and pointed to Quist's coat. "Didn't you hear me, boy? I *want* my amulet. I can feel that one segment is extremely close. I presume it's still in the pocket there."

"No, you can't let her have it," moaned Kymina. "Please let go of this obsession, Cyra. Even now, you can stop all this. No Djinn should be allowed to wield such awesome power and…"

Forming its right paw into a large furry hand, the wolf snatched Kymina by her neck, lifting her body several inches from the ground. Cyra smiled evilly at Watson, her red eyes glinting.

"It's up to you," she snarled. "You can either give it to me now, or I'll tear out the throat from my sister's pretty scabbard and then take the amulet from your gutted corpse. Your choice."

It wasn't *much* of a choice.

"It's here," said Watson, instantly tugging the segment of bracelet from Quist's coat pocket and holding it out. "Please don't hurt her. *Please*."

"Why thank you." Dropping the choking Kymina, Cyra took the glittering spiral and moaned with ecstatic pleasure, her lupine legs buckling slightly. "Oh, yes, this is truly amazing. This is the first time I've ever held the amulet and the magical power feels so sensual. It has finally found its owner and it's singing to me with happiness." She glared at her sister. "And now the other half; where *is* it?"

"Katie, don't tell her," gasped Kymina, massaging her throat and coughing. "You really can't imagine how dangerous she will be with the whole amulet."

"I see." The wolf turned to Katie. "So *you* know where it is, do you? In that case, there's no need to waste time threatening anyone." Squeezing her paw into a fist, Cyra punched the inspector hard on the jaw.

"Shit," yelped Watson, watching her collapse onto the tarpaulin pile. "You've no idea of the Guv's strength. You could have killed her."

"No," chuckled the wolf. "I need her again for this."

Cyra gripped the unconscious Katie's wrist and vacated the werewolf to enter her limp body. Slightly dizzy from the Djinn's departure, Quist tottered unsteadily, allowing Cyra the time to snatch Watson's crowbar and bring it down hard on his skull. The wolf collapsed face-down beside the tarpaulins and Cyra took the half-bracelet from his paw.

"Ah, very good," she smiled. "The police officer's recent memories tell me exactly what she did with the other segment. Yes, it's hidden in the cab of the blue engine." She slammed the crowbar down upon Quist's head again.

"No, stop it," moaned Watson. "Why would you do that?"

"To ensure he remains comatose," said Cyra. "I've decided to keep this lycanthrope scabbard. It's immortal, powerful and self-healing. It's exactly what I need until I master Koura's bracelet and

214

get around to constructing a new *more* powerful body of my own design."

"Guv?" Watson peered in horror at Quist's broken furry skull. He attempted to swallow, but his throat was too dry and tight. "Oh, shit, Guv."

"Be a good boy and keep my wolf scabbard safe for me, would you?" Cyra left to retrace Katie's steps. "I'll be back for him very shortly. If you're a *really* good boy, I might allow you to live."

"*Blue engine*," whispered Watson, watching the inspector walk out of sight behind the *Duchess of Hamilton* locomotive. "She means the *Mallard* and it's just around the back of that red engine there. It won't take her long." His mind spinning, he turned to Kymina. "A wish," he hissed. "Quick, I need you to give me one of your wishes."

"What do you intend to do?" she asked.

"We don't have time to talk about it," said Watson, trembling uncontrollably. "I honestly don't know if this shit will work, but I need a wish right now."

Cyra returned less than sixty seconds later, striding triumphantly back to the *Flying Scotsman*. "Finally," she said, grinning at her sister and holding the two bracelet spirals aloft, one in each hand. "Finally, the amulet is mine and the radiating power is intoxicating."

"Oh, well done, luv," muttered Watson. Sitting dejectedly on the pile of tarpaulins, he shook his head sadly. "We should throw a party."

"Ooh, sarcasm?" Cyra laughed. "You know, I was pretty furious after you robbed me in Harrogate. I fully intended to kill you, but I took my anger out on Slaney and her people and I've now changed my mind. Once I have the wish power, I think I'll transform you into a tapeworm instead."

"So you found the other segment," sighed Kymina. "I can't

believe you're not wearing it."

"What, on *this* pathetic scabbard?" Cyra shook her head. "Of course not; I'm leaving the police officer right now. Besides, I need *you* to witness the historic moment when I place Koura's bracelet upon my arm. You'll be pleased to know, I've decided to show you mercy."

"Mercy?" echoed Kymina.

"Yes," said Cyra. "You tricked me into that Dugdana prison all those years ago and left me there to rot. I had such plans for you after obtaining the amulet. I pictured so many hideous fates for you – wishing you into an eternity of torture – but now that I'm victorious, that has all changed. I now want you alive and with me to watch my rise to power as the supreme leader of Persia."

"Oh, Cyra..." Kymina shook her head. "Please remember that I'm your sister and I love you. I always did and I always will. So much power will destroy you and everyone around you."

"We'll soon see." Cyra grinned at her. "Despite your futile opposition, you'll soon realise that this is the greatest triumph for our kind. For the first time ever, a Djinn will have the power of the wishes – I'll be able to wish for things *myself*. Who knows? In time and despite everything, I may choose to grace you, my dear sister, with that same power."

Kneeling beside the unconscious Quist, Cyra entwined the silver spirals together to form the complete bracelet and placed it in readiness by the werewolf's left wrist. "In just a few seconds, you will watch as I slide it upon the arm of my favourite scabbard and, at long last, I will experience Koura's wish power. Yes, Kymina, this is my victory."

Cyra gripped the wolf's paw and entwined him, as Watson immediately lunged forward with the crystal bottle stopper.

"Yeah, *victory*," he mumbled. "Fuck you, luv."

* * * *

Chapter 31

"Good Lord, my head…" mumbled Quist. The werewolf crawled out from beneath the heap of tarpaulins where Watson and Kymina had hurriedly bundled him. "What happened to me and where am I…"

"Where are you?" Watson pointed to the *Flying Scotsman* looming above them. "Take a wild guess, Guv."

"Intriguing," growled the wolf, frowning. "Well, I'm sure there's a perfectly good reason for us being in the *National Railway Museum*, but I can't imagine what it might…" He noticed Katie sitting trembling on the floor, her terrified features bleached whiter than chalk. "Ah," he murmured. "Well, this is going to be a little awkward, isn't it?"

"You were beaten unconscious," said Kymina. "We hid you beneath those electrician's sheets and Watson wished for the open Dugdana to exactly resemble your comatose body. Cyra was ecstatic and so engrossed in her victory that her guard was down. She entered it, believing she was possessing you."

"Impressive," said the wolf. "And then you immediately twisted in the stopper to trap her?" Quist staggered up onto his two hind legs and saw Katie recoil in fear. He massaged his healing scalp, the powdered blood showering down and his pain swiftly receding. "Yes, that was rather clever."

"It was Watson who thought of it," admitted the Djinn, studying the sealed crystal bottle with her imprisoned sister. "By the way, he's put the bracelet back in your coat pocket. I'm unable to touch it."

"It looks exactly the same," said Quist, also peering closely at the bottle in her hand. "It's strange to think that a Djinn is now imprisoned inside that tiny object. Just a moment…" Frowning, he looked around the hall. "If I'm in lupine form, then it's obviously nighttime. Where are the electrical contractors who should be working here?"

"Your girlfriend managed to get rid of them," said Watson, nodding to Katie. "She fed them a story about a nutter with a knife, so I don't know how long it'll be before someone comes to see what's going on."

"Bernie, is that really *you*?" whispered the inspector, shaking violently and clamping a hand over her mouth. "I don't believe this. Oh, my God, what's happened to you?"

Quist gave the girl a warm smile of reassurance. With a mouthful of three-inch fangs and an inherent inability to look either warm *or* reassuring, this wasn't the best idea.

"What's happened to him is obvious," said Watson. "He's a werewolf, but you needn't worry; he can control all that savage killing and evil monster shit. Most werewolves are pretty nasty, but the Guv is a good one. He never chases cats, he sits when you say *sit* and, best of all, he never craps in the house." He peered into Quist's eyes, carefully checking the colour. "Er, you *are* okay, aren't you, Guv? Your eyes are the usual deep yellow again, but they were bright red when she was using you to…"

"No, fortunately they weren't *my* eyes," corrected the wolf. "Whatever Cyra did whilst possessing my body, that was *her*, not *me*. She was in total control and my psyche, for lack of better words, wasn't present. Don't worry. Her actions won't affect my ability to hold back my dark lupine side."

"I hope you're right," said Watson.

Quist glanced again at the trembling inspector and wagged his tail. "There's no need to be afraid," he growled. "Yes, I know I look a little different, but I can assure you, it's still the same old me. Wait a moment and I'll, um, make myself more presentable."

Turning his back to the onlookers, the wolf bent over double and began to shapeshift. Fur and fangs fell to the floor as the creature shrank and swiftly vanished, leaving in its place the smaller, and much less intimidating, form of the naked Bernie Quist. Clearing his throat, Watson averted his eyes and presented his boss with the trenchcoat.

"Thank you." The detective gave Katie an apologetic smile as he tugged on the leather coat and buttoned it up to conceal his nudity. He took the signet ring and wristwatch from the pocket where he'd zipped them away outside Slaney's house and slipped them both back on. "I know this must have been quite distressing for you, but I'm sure we can…"

"Quite *distressing*?" croaked the girl, incapable of speaking properly. "Yeah, you could say that this has been fucking *distressing*. All this time you've been some supernatural monster and I never knew? You couldn't tell me about your secret?"

"Er, *okay*." Watson grinned uneasily. "You've found out there's a *third person* in your relationship – a really big, furry guy – but maybe you could talk about it later? We might not be alone for much longer and we need to get out of here."

"You're right," said Quist, reaching to help Katie up from the floor. "We should leave right now."

She jerked away from his touch and Kymina stooped to assist her instead. Slipping a supporting arm around the dizzy inspector, she helped her to hurry across the hall to the rear loading bays. Watson saw the white Range Rover parked outside with its door left wide open.

"Did you come in this, Guv?" he asked.

"A somewhat silly question," sighed Quist. "Obviously, I have no idea; you could say I wasn't myself at the time." He nodded to the black Audi and held out a hand. "I'll drive. I presume this is Kymina's lease car?"

"You'll drive in bare feet?" Watson passed him the key fob and jumped into the passenger seat. "Is this a good idea? They reckon one pint of lager can affect your driving skills, and you've just had a psycho Djinn inside your brain. Not to mention your skull's recently been cracked open by a friggin' crowbar."

"My head has never felt better," smiled Quist, climbing in behind the wheel. "And there are no after-effects from the possession. Luckily, it would appear that lycanthropes only experience those feelings of disorientation for a few seconds."

"A lycanthrope?" rasped Katie. Still shivering from the mild shock, she sat in the back of the car with Kymina, staring with wide eyes at his reflection in the rearview mirror. "Were you like this when we first began seeing each other? I mean, how long have you…"

"It was quite a while before we met," confessed Quist. "I was bitten by a werewolf in the year 1790."

Shaking her head, Katie returned to her silent trembling.

The detective drove through the lengthy tunnel that connected York's *Railway Museum* and railyard area to the city centre. The imposing bulk of the *Milner* stood on their right. Built in 1878 next door to the newly opened train station, this was one of the great railway hotels that appeared in every city during the Victorian era to accommodate the wealthy travellers.

"Could you pull into here, please?" said Kymina, gesturing to the hotel car park. "I can feel the power of the amulet radiating from your coat. I'm trying to resist it, but it *really* wants me to open the Dugdana and release its owner."

"Mmh, I see," nodded Quist. "I believe it would be best if you gave me the bottle for safekeeping, don't you?" Turning onto the *Milner* parking area, he pulled up in an empty section well away from the building. "Why do you want to stop here?"

"Because I need to do something," sighed Kymina. She closed her eyes. "Despite the power being almost irresistible, I need to wear the amulet very briefly. Just long enough to enable me to make one wish for myself."

"Wow, really?" Watson turned to her, frowning. "You keep

saying how you can't look at this thing or touch it, so isn't that going to be dangerous for you? For *us* too?"

"*Really* dangerous," she admitted. "But I'm afraid this is something I have to do."

"What do you need to wish for?" he asked, puzzled. "For the prison bottle to be on the moon or something? Some place where no one can ever find it and open it?"

"No." Kymina passed the Dugdana to Quist. "Like before, it *does* need to be secreted away from mankind, but I intend to leave that in Bernie's trustworthy hands."

"So what then?" asked Watson.

"I'm sorry." She smiled sadly. "I'm going to wish for myself to be inside the bottle with Cyra."

* * * *

Chapter 32

"*What*?" Watson's lower jaw fell. "You want to be inside the prison bottle with your psycho sister. What the hell are you talking about?"

"I trapped Cyra once before." Kymina gazed forlornly at the crystal bottle as Quist held it. "As you know, I locked her inside a Dugdana where she spent centuries of raging anger and resentment all by herself. It had to be done, of course, but I can't possibly do that to her again."

"Er, *yeah*, you definitely *can*," snapped Watson. "Remember all those people she killed and all those batshit-crazy things she was intending to do with the bracelet. Did you know she was intending to take over Iran and…"

"I agree, she's far too dangerous to be loose amongst humanity." Kymina nodded. "She deserves her imprisonment, but not alone. This time I want to be with her."

"Are you out of your mind?" demanded the youth.

"The two of you confined together?" Quist shook his head. "No, Watson is right; this is an insane idea. You'll spend the entire time fighting."

"Well…" She laughed quietly. "Perhaps for the first century or so, but then who knows?"

Katie sat beside the Djinn, still trembling with shock. She listened to the bizarre conversation with an open mouth, but her reeling mind was still attempting to come to terms with everything that she'd just been through. Especially the revelation that she'd been sleeping with a centuries-old werewolf.

"It's a bit small for the both of you, isn't it?" Watson gestured to the bottle. "There's not even a bathroom in there." He grinned uneasily. "What I'm trying to say is: you really don't have to do this, Kymina. Please don't do it."

"Try to understand…" The Djinn reached forward to take the youth's hand. "I've been a kind of prisoner myself. All those centuries, as I watched over the site where Cyra was entombed, I had no free life of my own. I may as well have been inside the bottle with her. If I *had* been, then maybe she would have turned out to be very different."

"I doubt it," scoffed Watson. "From what you told us, she was bad enough to start with. I mean, come on – that's why you had to get rid of her all those years ago."

"Yes, I couldn't allow her to have that amulet," admitted Kymina. "But she's my sister and I can't escape these feelings of guilt. The construct that you call *time* isn't the same for the Djinn, but three-thousand years is still so very long. If I'd been with her, been a true sister and friend to Cyra, then perhaps I could have changed her nature. Maybe I could have stopped her lusting for power, and taught her compassion and the human concepts of right and wrong."

"Kymina," murmured Watson, squeezing her hand, "I really don't want you to do it."

"I know you don't," she smiled. "But I've been thinking about this for quite a while, ever since Cyra escaped." Leaning forwards to hug him, she kissed the young man softly on his mouth. "Thank you for attempting to talk me out of it. If I'd known you for a little longer, I honestly believe you may have weakened my resolve, but this is something I really have to try. I have to try and help my sister."

Watson shook his head. "Listen to me…"

"No, *you* have to listen," she said. "I'm giving you three more wishes for when I'm no longer here. I know you'll have the sense to use them correctly when Toni Nelson returns."

"Correctly?" echoed Watson. "So I'm guessing you want me to wish for the bracelet to vanish in a puff of smoke or something?"

"Like I explained to you before," said Kymina, "that wouldn't be possible. The amulet and the Dugdana are both infused with ancient Persian magic and the wishes won't work on either of them. No, these last three wishes will help you to overcome more *human* complications." She glanced at Katie and then peered at Quist to ascertain if he understood. "I'm sure you'll be fine."

"What was that look?" quizzed Katie, frowning. "What do you mean?"

"Yeah, I'll be fine." Watson blinked back a tear. "So I don't imagine we'll be having that night out in York after all? We won't be strolling along the city walls and sipping Djinn and tonics together at sunset? I'm guessing you've known that all along, haven't you?"

Squeezing his hand again, Kymina smiled unhappily and nodded.

Quist cleared his throat. "Well, you're clearly committed to this," he said, quietly. "When are you intending to do it?"

"Right now," sighed Kymina. "I've been inside this poor human for long enough. I'm sure you recall me telling you about my personal code? I possessed Toni Nelson's body to get close to Cyra and prevent her from obtaining the amulet. Thankfully, we managed to succeed, so I no longer have any right to be here. I'm now intruding and Toni needs to have her life returned to her."

"Don't feel guilty about overstaying your welcome in there," said Watson, stroking her hair. "You brought Toni back to life after her overdose, remember. She'd be dead if not for you possessing her, so that's something you should be happy about."

Quist peered at the sealed bottle. "So if you really *are* absolutely sure about this?" he said, nodding slowly. "How will you go about it?"

"Watson can hold the Dugdana," she said, quietly. "I'll touch it as you slide the bracelet onto my other wrist. Only for a couple of seconds, remember, then quickly remove it before the magic has a chance to overpower me. Remember, Bernie, when this is done, the prison bottle needs to be hidden in a place where no one will ever find and open it. Watson mentioned the moon, but I'm sure you can come up with somewhere more terrestrial."

The youth took the bottle and watched uneasily as his boss produced the sparkling amulet from his pocket, the two serpentine segments now interlocked together. Kymina averted her eyes, reaching out her left arm to Quist and fondly stroking Watson's hand as she placed her fingers upon the crystal.

She kissed his cheek again. "Goodbye," she whispered in his ear, smiling warmly at him. "Do it now, Bernie."

Quist forced the bracelet over Kymina's wrist, heard her mumble a wish and swiftly tugged it back off. Watson gasped as the Dugdana vibrated momentarily in his grip, the crystal pulsing with bright red light. The mystical glow faded just as quickly, leaving the little bottle looking normal and innocuous once again.

"Did it work?" whispered Katie.

"I don't know," stammered Watson, wiping his moist eyes and peering closely at the crystal. "Is she actually inside this thing?" He turned hopefully to Toni Nelson. "Or are you still here, Kymina?"

"Where the fuck am I?" croaked Toni, snatching her hand away from the youth and dazedly looking around the car. "Who *are* you people?"

"Evidently it *did* work," nodded the detective.

"Who *are* you?" repeated Toni, scrabbling in fear for the door handle. She drew in a lungful of air to begin screaming in panic. "What's happening here…"

"I wish you'd fall asleep for eight hours," said Watson, quickly, "and when you wake, you won't remember anything after Egypt." He paused and thought for a moment. "Also, I wish you didn't have any feelings or emotions for your arsehole fiancé."

"Well done," said Quist, smiling grimly as the girl's eyes closed. "Well, that was two of those three wishes." He nodded to Katie. "I believe that equates to one wish remaining."

"No, wait…" shouted the inspector, realising what he meant. "No, you can't just..."

"Katie Bradstreet," said Watson. "I wish you'd fall asleep for eight hours and, when you wake, you'll remember nothing from the moment you arrived at Beningbrough Hall today."

"Thank you for that," said Quist, watching as the girl slumped back in her seat beside Toni. "I hate that we had to do it, but I could see no real alternative. Quite apart from my secret being exposed, I don't believe Katie would have been able to cope mentally with everything she witnessed tonight."

"I'm not so sure I can cope," muttered the youth, grinning weakly. He peered at the two sleeping girls. "But what the hell are we going to do with them?"

"We need to drive Katie home," said Quist, pocketing the bracelet and the bottle containing the two Djinn. "We'll leave her asleep in her bed. Then you can follow in my car as I get this Audi back to Beningbrough with Toni."

"Sounds like a plan," sighed Watson, still thinking about Kymina. "Pity I had to use that last wish on your lady cop. I was hoping to save it for a Rolex watch."

* * * *

Chapter 33

Standing at the end of Brett Street on the northern outskirts of York, *Oakshott's Iron Foundry* has been in business since 1822. They manufactured bridges, large railway components, lampposts and even roof trussing for inside the Minster. After downsizing two decades ago, however, the company sold off most of its buildings and Quist knew that Oakshott's now produced gates, fencing and garden sculptures for the domestic market. Compared to the original thriving industry, the single redbrick building, now closed for the night, looked strangely sad.

Two days had passed since the Tuesday night events in the *Railway Museum* and Quist had used the time to contact an old client and request a favour. Carrying a sports holdall, the detective checked that the quiet street was empty, before crossing over to the foundry with Watson. Light traffic could be heard on the main road away to their left and somewhere nearby an unseen fox let out a screeching cry.

The main gates were locked, but a smaller gate next to them had been left unsecured. The youth pushed it open and the pair walked into the cobbled yard beyond. A chubby man in a security guard uniform appeared from a cabin, brushing chocolate biscuit crumbs from his pullover and furtively waving them over.

"I assume you're Tim?" said Quist, checking his watch. "It's midnight, as we agreed."

"Yes, keep your voice down, mate." Tim unlocked the door to the foundry building and hurried them both inside. "Come on, quick, before anyone sees you. We won't be turning on any lights, but I've got a couple of torches."

"Thank you for doing this," said Quist, looking around as the guard's torchlight flickered over the dormant furnaces and machinery.

"Whooo!" muttered Watson. "Spooky."

"It's no problem," said Tim, handing the detective his spare torch. "I owe our mutual friend Vince a favour. Besides, you're paying me, aren't you?

"Of course," confirmed Quist. "Obviously, I would have taken her to the pet crematorium in Heslington, but they have quite a waiting list. I really didn't want to wait until they could accommodate me with a free time slot."

"Yeah, a waiting list for dead pets," scoffed Watson. "Can you believe that? Dad loved his cat far too much to stick her in the freezer until they could fit him in."

"*Dad?*" Tim shone his torch, peering quizzically at their complexions.

"I'm adopted," said Watson.

"By the way, as we discussed..." Quist passed the security guard an envelope of money. "A little something for your trouble, and also for your compassion."

"Cheers." Tim checked inside and stowed the envelope in his pocket. "A hundred quid is a lot of cash to incinerate a moggy, but believe me, I'm not complaining. I have to say, it would have been a lot cheaper if you'd just buried it in the garden."

"We live in an upstairs apartment," shrugged Watson. "Dad tried digging, but the window box just wasn't big enough."

"Right," said Tim. "When Vince rang me saying you wanted to call here after hours and throw something in the furnace..." He began to chuckle. "I naturally assumed it'd be your wife's body."

"Er, yes." Quist laughed too. "Naturally."

"What was her name?" asked Tim.

"His *wife?*" Watson frowned, slightly confused. "Ah, you mean the cat. Um... Purr-incess Leia. She really used to liven up whenever she heard the *Star Wars* music." He gestured sadly to Quist's holdall. "Not any more, of course. She's now gone to a galaxy far, far away."

"Sorry to hear that," said Tim, leading them to a bulky machine and running his torch beam over the control panel. "Anyway, you won't be needing the main furnaces back there. I'll turn on this smaller one for you. I know the guys who work here and I've watched them do it often enough."

"I notice this is gas-fired," said Quist, watching him throw the various switches. "What temperature does it operate at?"

"Oh, it goes pretty high," explained the security guard. "But I'll set it to 800 degrees; that's about the temperature of a cremation oven. Was she a big cat?" He nodded to the holdall. "What breed was she?"

"Persian," said the two men in unison.

"Right." Tim swung open the door and the intense heat blasted out. "That's it all ready to go."

"Cheers, mate," said Watson.

"I'll leave you both alone for a bit of privacy at this sad time." Tim glanced at his watch. "I'm sorry for your loss, but you won't take *too* long, will you? I have a sports channel on my cabin TV and they're showing a boxing match soon."

"We'll be all done in a few minutes," confirmed the detective. "And, once again, thank you for your compassion."

They waited for the security guard to leave before Quist twisted the temperature dial around to its highest setting. He opened his holdall to gaze at the gleaming bracelet one final time, before tossing the bag into the middle of the raging flames.

"Do you reckon that'll destroy it?" asked Watson, as he slammed the door shut. "I mean, it *is* magic, after all."

"Iron melts at 1500 degrees." Quist squinted through the small inspection window that was built into the door. "I don't know what this thing is made of – supposedly the metal from some meteorite – but I've turned the temperature up full, so we'll soon find out."

"So you say you visited Beningbrough today?" asked the

youth, as they waited. "The film production is closing down and Toni Nelson didn't recognise you?"

"I chatted with her for quite a while and she had no idea who I was," confirmed Quist. "Shortly after we left her sleeping in that lease car, Miss Nelson was awoken by the security people in some distress and they rang for an ambulance. The hospital put her amnesia down to some bizarre attack of anxiety. She can't remember anything at all from the past week or so and, fortunately, she has no feelings for her ex-fiancé."

"Good to hear," smiled Watson. "So that worked out okay then. How about your lady cop?"

"Katie is the same," said Quist, smiling tautly. "I'm pleased to say she remembers absolutely nothing from the moment she visited Beningbrough Hall with her sergeant until the moment she woke at home in bed. She doesn't understand what could have happened and she's naturally concerned, but I'm sure she'll be fine."

"The main thing is, are *you* fine, Guv?" Watson peered at him uneasily. "How have you been feeling over these past couple of days? Any unexpected cravings for a midnight snack of human flesh? I mean, I saw your bright red eyes and…"

"But they weren't *my* eyes, remember," corrected Quist. "I read all about the slaughter at Harrogate in the news, but my body was being used by Cyra. Bizarre as it sounds, my consciousness wasn't present when she killed those humans and tasted their blood. That should have been evident the moment she left me and my eyes reverted to amber."

Watson leapt back as the furnace inspection hatch suddenly blazed brightly with a shimmer of vivid colours, transforming the small window into a kaleidoscope.

"Bloody hell, check out this weird shit," he stammered, stepping further away. "Remember it's a *magic* bracelet, Guv. This thing could explode or something."

230

"Don't worry," said the detective, peering inside as the brief light show ended. "I believe we were successful. Those serpentine spirals have disintegrated into a bubbling molten mess and I would surmise that strange burst of colour was the release of the bracelet's power."

"So we did it?" Watson smiled hopefully. "We actually destroyed it?"

"We did indeed," said Quist. "Kymina told us how the Djinn are a small race. I don't know how many of them are out there, but none of them will ever be able to find and use that amulet." Quist rotated the temperature dial and, throwing the switches in reverse, closed down the furnace. "Come along. It's time for us to go."

"Of course, there's still one *more* thing," said Watson, walking beside him. "The thing that I just can't stop thinking about. The bottle, Guv. What are we going to do with it?"

"I've been giving that some serious thought," said Quist, heading back to the foundry entrance. "I've already secured it within a protective metal cylinder. Next, I intend to mix a little cement and encase the cylinder within a small block." He took a deep breath and lowered his voice. "And then, I thought perhaps we could take a ferry from Hull to Rotterdam."

"Ah, I see." Watson nodded sadly. "And drop it over the side, you mean?"

"In one of the deeper areas," confirmed Quist. "The North Sea is relatively shallow, but some parts are more than 150 feet deep and they don't allow any diving or dredging on those ferry routes. Um, are you okay with this?"

Sighing heavily, the youth nodded. "Poor old Kymina," he murmured. "I can't sleep for thinking about her trapped inside that prison. Do you reckon she'll be okay in there with that nutter?"

"Remember that Kymina had clearly been planning it for some time," pointed out Quist. "What she did was a truly courageous act of love and not some spur of the moment decision. Besides, the Djinn are creatures of ethereal light. Reality and time work differently for them and being trapped inside that Dugdana bottle won't be the same for her as it would be for you or I."

"Probably not," said Watson, hesitating for a moment. "Um, I suppose you know that I liked her?"

"Yes, I'm fully aware." The detective threw a comforting arm around his back. "Although, had she not made the decision to be with her sister, I believe any relationship with Kymina would have been somewhat, er… *complicated* for you. At any rate, because of your feelings, I assumed you'd want to be with me on the ferry when I commit her prison bottle to the depths."

"Yeah, of course," he murmured. "When I say I liked her, I mean I *really* liked her. Kymina said it was probably a magic thing. Apparently some guys are drawn to the supernatural light that the Djinn are made from, but I'm not so sure." He wiped a tear from his eye. "I wish…"

"Ah, Watson," broke in Quist, smiling warmly and squeezing his shoulders. "There's a sound piece of advice contained within *Aesop's Fables* and I feel it could be relevant here. *Be careful what you wish for.*"

The End